Utah
State Facts

Nickname: The Beehive State

Date Entered Union: January 4, 1896
(the 45th state)

Motto: Industry

Utah men: Butch Cassidy, *outlaw*
Donny Osmond, *entertainer*
James Woods, *actor*

State Flower: Sego lily

State Tree: Blue spruce

State Bird: Seagull

State Song: "Utah, We Love Thee"

State Name's Origin: Taken from the name of the
Ute Indians, whose name
means "people of the
mountains".

Fun Fact: The people of Utah consume
more ice cream and green
Jell-O than any other state.

Marina, my dearest friend,

I had almost forgotten.

After I came to Moab, I pushed the attack, my scar, all of it to the back of my mind. But when I gazed into the still pool of water, I was overwhelmed. How could I ever learn to live with the way I look now?

Mike spoke my name. "Caro," he said. All at once I realized that he must have seen the horror on my face when I saw my reflection.

If only I could have acted normal! But all I could do was kneel frozen in the same spot, covering my face, my ruined face, with my hands.

Mike lifted me firmly by the shoulders and pulled my hands away. He looked at me with an expression of utmost tenderness.

"So it does bother you," he said. "Caro, you've got to come to terms with it."

But Marina, I just don't think I can.

My modeling career is over. I won't be coming back to New York for a long time—maybe never. Please, please don't ask me.

Love,

Caro

American
HEROES
AGAINST ALL ODDS

Pamela
BROWNING
Feathers in the Wind

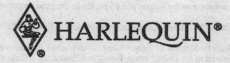

HARLEQUIN®

TORONTO • NEW YORK • LONDON
AMSTERDAM • PARIS • SYDNEY • HAMBURG
STOCKHOLM • ATHENS • TOKYO • MILAN • MADRID
PRAGUE • WARSAW • BUDAPEST • AUCKLAND

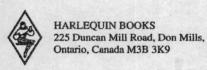

HARLEQUIN BOOKS
225 Duncan Mill Road, Don Mills,
Ontario, Canada M3B 3K9

ISBN 0-373-82242-1

FEATHERS IN THE WIND

Copyright © 1989 by Pamela Browning

This edition published by arrangement with Harlequin Books S.A.

® and TM are trademarks of the publisher. Trademarks indicated with ® are registered in the United States Patent and Trademark Office, the Canadian Trade Marks Office and in other countries.

Visit us at www.eHarlequin.com

Printed in U.S.A.

About the Author

Pamela Browning is the award-winning author of thirty romance novels—many of which appeared on numerous bestseller lists. Her books consistently win high ratings from reviewers and readers alike. She makes her home in North Carolina.

Books by Pamela Browning

Harlequin American Romance

Cherished Beginnings #101
Handyman Special #116
Through Eyes Of Love #123
Interior Designs #131
Ever Since Eve #140
Forever Is A Long Time #150
To Touch The Stars #170
The Flutterby Princess #181
Ice Crystals #194
Kisses In The Rain #227
Simple Gifts #237
Fly Away #241
Harvest Home #245
Feathers in the Wind #287
Until Spring #297
Humble Pie #354
A Man Worth Loving #384
For Auld Lang Syne #420
Sunshine And Shadows #439
Morgan's Child #451
Merry Christmas, Baby #516
The World's Last Bachelor #565
Angel's Baby #600
Lover's Leap #632
RSVP...Baby #786
That's Our Baby #818

Dear Reader,

A hero can be different things to different people.

When you're exhausted from chasing after three toddlers, your husband is a hero when he gets up at night to care for the one with an earache. When it's a bad hair day and you discover that you met two important clients with a run in your pantyhose, your boss is a hero when she compliments you on a job well done in spite of it all.

Caro Nicholson found her hero in Moab, Utah. After a vicious knife attack, her face was scarred from ear to chin. But Mike Herrick loved her for who she was inside, a person who would always be beautiful to him no matter what. Because of his support, she learned who she really was and who she wanted to be.

This book is for you and the heroes in your life. Enjoy!

Pamela Browning

Please address questions and book requests to:
Harlequin Reader Service
U.S.: 3010 Walden Ave., P.O. Box 1325, Buffalo, NY 14269
Canadian: P.O. Box 609, Fort Erie, Ont. L2A 5X3

Prologue

1

If you happened to pick up a magazine that spring, you couldn't have missed Caro Nicholson in page after page of ads for the Gaillardo Cosmetic Corporation. Her dark blond hair, long, sleek and shiny with bangs cut to follow the curve of her eyebrows, was her trademark. Caro was famous; people recognized her on the street.

Caro was the Naiad, the glamorous spokesperson for the fragrance of the same name. Caro's Naiad costume consisted mostly of mist and water droplets, and she was usually photographed emerging from some photogenic body of water—a pond at dawn, a waterfall at sunset, the sea silvered by a full moon.

Only incidental to Caro's new fame was the fact that the Naiad fragrance had, since its introduction the preceding autumn, become a phenomenal success in the perfume industry, earning enormous profits for the Gaillardo Corporation. By April, Naiad was the number one fragrance sold in the United States.

Hardly a woman alive didn't want to look like Caro Nicholson.

Until that fateful afternoon when Caro walked home alone through Central Park.

2

April

CARO ROUNDED the curve in the path through Central Park and increased her walking speed. She had misjudged the time; she wasn't accustomed to attending a late-afternoon aerobics class. She usually caught the morning class instead. But today there had been no avoiding an early appointment with Marina at the agency, and she'd had to miss her regular session.

The air was turning so chilly that she pulled down the sleeves of her gray fleece warm-up suit. The setting sun had dipped below the outline of the buildings on Central Park West, casting cool shadows across the path.

Caro shivered and cast an apprehensive glance at the sloping grassy bank ahead. She'd meant to reach home before dusk but hadn't wanted to take a cab. After a day of meetings and conferences about her public persona as the Gaillardo Company's Naiad, she welcomed the chance for extra exercise.

Suddenly Caro became aware that there was no one ahead of her on the path, and a glance over her shoulder told her that no one was behind her, either. It had been, she realized belatedly, foolish to walk home alone.

She never saw the razor. She only saw a furtive-looking male shape as it swiftly detached itself from the shelter of the bushes ahead, and her heart gave a lurch when she understood his intent. She screamed and turned to run, not comprehending, not knowing why she was the quarry.

Her assailant had thin lips, a prominent square jaw and

strange lightless eyes. She felt a quick stinging sensa-tion down the side of her face, and then everything went black.

3

CARO AWOKE to a glare of overhead fluorescent light in her eyes. She realized immediately that she was in an un-familiar place. Somewhere beyond her, wheels rolled on a hard surface, stopped, then resumed their journey. Con-fused, Caro blinked. Her vision was blurred. Where was she?

A panicky feeling rose in her throat. She felt weak. She tried to lift the fingers on her left hand, but they wouldn't move. Belatedly she realized that her hand was attached to a board and that a tube ran from the needle in her hand to a bag of fluid on a metal hook at the head of the bed. Her mind groped with wavering shapes. Eyes floated above her and the mouth below the eyes moved, but the resulting voice sounded garbled.

"Caro?" Her name echoed from a long way off and then her friend Marina's face, tense and worried, slipped into her field of vision.

Caro attempted a smile, but her mouth felt as though it were packed in cement. She felt no pain, only numbness.

"Caro," Marina said again, but Caro's eyes refused to focus.

"Don't try to talk," Marina urged.

Caro closed her eyes and opened them again. She had been planning to meet Marina for dinner after the aerobics class. Had they gone out afterward? *But no.* Wayne had said something about teaching her to play backgammon later.

As if reading her thoughts, Marina said, "Wayne just left. He was exhausted. He'll be back later, he said."

Caro licked her dry lips. "Dinner?"

"We never made it to dinner," Marina answered. "I know you didn't care to eat sushi again, but this is a ridiculous way to get out of it." A fond grin relaxed the worried lines at the corners of her mouth.

Caro realized that she had no idea how much time had elapsed since she'd last seen Marina.

"What—what happened?" Caro asked. She lifted her right arm and bent it at the elbow. Her hand moved tentatively toward her face. She touched gauze and adhesive tape. *Good Lord!* Her whole face was bandaged! Shocked and speechless, she let her hand fall away.

Marina's gaze faltered for the first time. She looked away and, unable to control her expression, rose and walked briskly to the window.

"You don't know?" she said finally, turning back toward Caro when she had regained her composure. Unbelievably, tears welled in Marina's eyes.

In the eight years that Caro had known her both as head of the modeling agency that represented her and as a close personal friend, Caro had never seen Marina cry. Also, Marina seemed determined not to look at her. Instead she kept her gaze firmly fastened on the wall behind the bed.

Marina dabbed at her tears with a tissue. She inhaled a deep breath. "You were attacked in Central Park, Caro," she said finally. "A man with a razor—he ran away when a passerby spotted what was happening, and you were rushed to the hospital. You were in surgery for hours. It's three o'clock in the morning now."

Caro stared at her friend's distraught face. A wave of exhaustion swept over her. Part of her refused to admit the reality of any of this, and her head began to throb.

She only vaguely remembered walking home through the park after aerobics class. She couldn't remember the man or the attack at all. *Funny, you'd think I would,* she reflected.

A nurse entered the room and offered a sip of water through a straw. Swallowing was an effort that brought tears to her eyes.

After the nurse set the glass of water on the bedside table, Caro managed to ask a question.

"Am I going to be all right?" she whispered.

The nurse exchanged looks with Marina. They both hovered over her, smoothing the coverlet, offering meaningless reassurances with words about "cosmetic surgery" and "just like new" and "lucky you weren't killed." There was no mistaking the pity in their eyes.

Slowly and painfully, Caro turned her head away, feigning sleep, assessing this new state of affairs as the sedative that the nurse piggybacked to the IV took effect.

Her last conscious thought was, *My face was my fortune and my future. What am I going to do now?*

Chapter One

June

The highway into Moab, Utah, wound between natural out-croppings of rock that Caro, minus a map or guidebook, had decided were buttes and mesas. Ahead of them, the town nestled in a green-rimmed valley, a visual relief from the harsh red and yellow of the sandstone outcroppings towering around them.

Sandstone is, let's see, sedimentary rock, isn't it? Caro thought uncertainly. She didn't remember much of the geography she'd learned in school, where all she seemed to have absorbed from the boring social studies books was a blurry picture of reindeer galloping across the tundra. Art had been her passion then.

"It's hard to imagine people living up on them mesas, isn't it?" asked the truck driver who had picked her up when her rental car broke down on a deserted stretch of highway about ten miles up the road.

"Pardon me?" Caro said. Her attention had been with reindeer on the tundra.

"Primitive people used to live in this desert," the truck driver told her, proud of his knowledge. "They built houses under the cliffs. I took the wife and kids to see one of 'em last summer. Mesa Verde was the name of it.''

Caro gazed at the great sweep of surrounding rock. It appeared unfit for human habitation. "I should think that survival would be difficult out there," she said.

"Yeah, well, they were pretty smart cookies. The Anasazi, they were called. They're supposed to be ancestors of the Hopi Indians. They planted crops up on the mesas, they worked out a system of irrigation and everything, and all before Columbus discovered America, too. Then the Anasazi disappeared.''

"Disappeared?" Caro entertained only a mild interest in this subject; she'd prefer to ride in silence, but the truck driver seemed glad of her company and had talked nonstop since she climbed into the cab of his truck. She supposed that a bit of conversation was a small price to pay for her rescue from the rental car whose engine had coughed, spat and died alongside a particularly dreary stretch of road.

"Yup, they disappeared, all right. You should visit some of the national parks around Moab while you're there. They'll know something about the Anasazi story.''

"I'm not planning to stay in Moab long," she informed him. "Just until I can get another rental car.''

"Oh, well, it was only a suggestion," the truck driver said.

Presently they reached the outskirts of Moab. After passing a few houses and gas stations, they rolled down a wide main street swarming with tourists, who were readily identified by the cameras slung on straps around their necks and by the fact that they congregated around one or two rock shops.

"You may have trouble getting a motel room tonight," the truck driver cautioned her.

"I'm sure I'll find a place," Caro told him.

He shrugged. "Maybe you won't. This is the high season for tourists around here, what with Dead Horse Point and Arches and Canyonlands National Parks in the area and the kids out of school. Tell you what, if you can't get a room, walk over to Kettle Street. I heard there's a nice lady there who runs a bed-and-breakfast place in her home. There's only one room, but maybe she'd put you up for the night."

"Thanks," Caro said as the truck driver pulled his rig to a stop in the parking lot of a big motel.

He climbed from the cab and courteously heaved her suitcase down for her. "No need to thank me, it's been no trouble," he said.

Caro smiled but hardened herself to the expression of pity that she knew would flicker across his features when he looked her full in the face.

Sure enough, it did. She was getting used to pity by this time. Still, two short months after the attack, Caro had decided that she much preferred the people who showed pity over the ones who found it altogether too painful to look at her marred countenance.

As the tractor-trailer truck disappeared in a cloud of dust on the highway south toward Arizona, she hitched the strap of her pocketbook higher on her shoulder and wheeled her suitcase into the lobby of the motel.

"Sorry, we have no rooms," the busy desk clerk told her. "We've got two bus loads of tourists for Dead Horse Point and Arches and Canyonlands coming in tonight. You might try the motel across the street."

Caro was glad that their conversation lasted no longer than it did. The clerk was one of those who, after the first shocked glance at the scar stretching in a dark jagged line from her right ear to her lower left jaw, would not look her full in the face.

A prompt inquiry revealed the information that the motel across the street had no vacancy either, and so Caro, exhausted by this time, asked for directions to Kettle Street.

"Two streets over," she was told.

"Do you know the lady who runs the bed-and-breakfast place there?" Caro asked hopefully.

The clerk considered. "That would be Annie Stendahl. She's got one room she rents out when she can. Don't know if it's already rented or not. Still, you better try. There won't be any rooms anywhere in town tonight," he said. He turned away, effectively shutting her from his sight.

Caro trudged down the street, trailing her suitcase. Moab was a small town, and she hadn't seen anything remotely resembling a city bus or taxi. She could only hope that the bed-and-breakfast place wasn't far and that when she got there Annie Stendahl would take her in.

When she reached Kettle Street, she paused to brush her long bangs to one side; they had grown out of their distinctive Naiad style and were becoming a nuisance. She stood indecisively for a moment, trying to figure out whether to turn left or right.

As she stood there, a boy rode up on a bicycle and screeched to a halt in the shade of one of the tall trees lining the street.

"What happened to your face?" he asked. Caro judged his age to be about ten, which was certainly old enough to know better than to ask impolite questions. But she sensed that he didn't consider the question rude. He was only curious.

"I—had an accident," she improvised. It was easier with children, she had discovered. After the first few minutes, they seemed to overlook the scar.

"Will it always look like that?"

She bit her lip, willing herself not to give in to the feeling of helplessness that always overcame her whenever she thought about the attack.

"I'm not sure," she said truthfully. "Do you know where the bed-and-breakfast place is? They told me at the motel that it's on this street."

"Oh, yeah. My friend Franklin's mom takes in guests. Want me to show you?"

"If you would," she said, trying to get a better grip on the suitcase strap.

"Want me to pull that for you?" the boy asked her. He eyed the wheels on the suitcase with interest.

"You can't help me with my suitcase and ride your bike at the same time," Caro pointed out.

The boy leaned his bike on its kickstand. "I'll come back for my bike later," he said. He eased the suitcase strap out of her hand.

Caro shot a look back at the bicycle. "Won't someone steal it?" He'd never be able to leave a bike parked unattended on a sidewalk in New York. It would disappear within minutes.

"Nah," the boy said. He glanced up at her curiously. "My name's Tony. What's yours?"

"Caro," she said.

"Caro," he repeated. He favored her with a gap-toothed smile. "I like the sound of it. I've never known anyone named Caro before."

"Actually, it's Caroline. Caroline Nicholson. It's such a mouthful that my friends shortened it."

"Neat," Tony said. He trundled the suitcase past a row of well-kept houses until it rumbled to a halt. "Here's the place," Tony told her.

They had stopped in front of a picket fence enclosing a white frame house whose paint was flaking off in chunks.

A crayoned sign declaring Bed and Breakfast hung lop-sided in the window. On the porch stood a planter over-whelmed with a profusion of flowers, and lace curtains curved away from the windowpanes. The house sent a mixed message. On one hand, the peeling paint suggested that the owner didn't care how the place looked. On the other, the starched lace at the windows bespoke pride in appearances.

Apparently she had no choice but to stay here for the night, no matter what the accommodations were like. Resolutely Caro pushed at the gate.

"See you later," Tony said.

"Uh, wait," Caro said, fumbling in the depths of her pocketbook. She handed the boy a dollar bill, and his face lighted up with a smile.

"Gee, thanks," he said.

"You were a big help," she told him.

The door to the house opened, and she turned quickly to see a man come out. He was tall and rangy with dark unruly hair, and he wore jeans and a faded blue chambray shirt.

Caro steeled herself for the eyes widened in shock at the sight of her extensive scar, but he only stopped and regarded her with an inquisitive expression.

"I'm here about the bed-and-breakfast," she said.

The man paused. He had an interesting face, craggy but not particularly handsome with its aquiline nose, heavy brows and generous mouth. His clothes hung on his lanky frame like an afterthought.

"You'll want to see Annie," he told her. "Franklin will show you."

He had looked her full in the face, but his reaction wasn't the common one. He completed a frank appraisal of her scar, but the expression in his eyes conveyed a de-

cided appreciation of her looks. She, who had once been
informally listed one of the ten most beautiful women in
New York City by one of Marina's sophisticated friends,
felt absurdly grateful to this man for his admiration.

"Thanks," she said, looking after him as he slammed
the gate behind him and got into a dusty Jeep parked at
the curb. He only waved and roared off down the street,
leaving her to find Franklin by herself.

A boy appeared at the door. He seemed to be around
Tony's age. "Are you a friend of Mike's?" he asked her.
He was eating a nectarine, and rather noisily at that. A thin
runnel of juice dripped down his chin.

"Mike is the man who just left?"

The boy nodded.

"No, I don't know Mike, but I've met Tony. He said
this was a bed-and-breakfast place. Are you Franklin?"

"Yeah," he said, staring at her scar.

"Well, I want to talk to someone about the bed-and-
breakfast. Is your mother here?"

"Yeah," Franklin replied.

Caro was about to lose patience. She was tired, and she
longed to lie down somewhere and close her eyes. She
wasn't over the ordeal of the attack yet, and if Marina
could have talked to her right now, she would have said
that Caro had been foolish to leave New York where there
were people to look after her, although Caro wasn't so sure
that there actually *had* been anyone to look after her.
Wayne, the man in her life, had decamped. Marina was so
busy. Caro had no one else.

Franklin evidently decided that, scar or no scar, Caro
posed no threat to him or to his family. "Come in," he
said. "Mom's in her studio."

Caro followed Franklin through a living room littered
with a couple of wadded-up potato-chip bags and several

empty glasses. A boy of about six sat engrossed in a rerun of *I Love Lucy*. Franklin led the way through an even messier kitchen to a small outbuilding behind the house.

"Mom," he called, pushing the door open. "Someone's here about the bed-and—and—well, I never can say that right."

The inside of the building was cool and dark after the bright sunlight outside.

"Bed-and-breakfast? Today?" A small dark figure straightened, peered at Caro over a tray of clay pots, and rushed forward.

"I'm Annie Stendahl," she said, holding out her hand. With her other hand she brushed short spiky black bangs away from her forehead. Overall she gave the impression of a harried elf.

"Caro Nicholson," Caro said.

"I *do* offer a bed and breakfast, but usually it's by prior arrangement," Annie said. "I'm not sure I can promise you a place to stay right now. I'm in the middle of getting a big order of pottery ready to ship."

Caro swallowed. She was so tired that she thought her legs might not hold her up any longer.

"Please," she said desperately. "There isn't a motel room left in town tonight. My car broke down ten miles out of Moab, and I don't have anyplace to go. I don't mind if you're too busy to make my breakfast in the morning. I can do that myself."

Annie lifted her shoulders helplessly and let them fall. "I don't know," she said. "I'm embarrassed for anyone to see my house in such a mess."

Caro sensed that Annie was somehow vulnerable; she looked as overwhelmed by the circumstances of her life as Caro felt about her own at present.

She was suddenly aware that something passed between

the two of them then. Maybe it was understanding, or perhaps it was empathy. In that moment, Caro experienced a flash of insight. *Everything will be all right, if only she lets me stay,* were the unbidden words that flashed into her head.

"I've already seen the house," Caro said. "Franklin walked me through."

Annie's eyes rolled heavenward. "And you still asked about a bed and breakfast? You're brave."

"I'm desperate," Caro said.

Clearly feeling sorry for her, Annie asked abruptly, "Caro, would you like a cup of coffee?"

Caro smiled in relief. "Yes," she said.

"Come into the house," Annie said, and Caro started to follow her.

Then Annie stopped and wheeled around. "I don't know what I'm thinking of," she said distractedly. "I'm firing some things in the kiln, and they're almost ready to take out. Do you know how to make coffee?" she asked, focusing dismayed eyes on Caro.

"Well, yes," Caro admitted.

Annie grinned. "Good! The coffee's in a canister on the counter, and the pot is on the stove. I should be there in about ten minutes, and oh, by the way, I guess it's okay if you stay tonight. Get Franklin to show you your room after you put the pot on." And with that, Annie disappeared into the back room of the small cottage.

It was a relief to know that her search was over. Slowly Caro made her way through the big backyard to the main house. In the kitchen, she found the coffee where Annie had told her it would be, and she put the coffee and water in the percolator and set it on the stove burner.

"It looks like you're staying," Franklin said when he wandered into the kitchen.

"That's right. By the way, your mother said that you'd show me my room," Caro told him, drying her hands on a dish towel looped through the handle of the refrigerator.

"Come with me, it's right this way," Franklin said, trying to look important.

Caro repressed a smile and followed Franklin through the living room where the six-year-old jumped up from the couch and tagged along.

Franklin led them into a large bedroom off the dining room. "This is your room," he said. "It used to be Mom and Dad's, but Mom sleeps in Holly's room since Dad left us."

"Oh," Caro said. Franklin's offhand remark had provided her with more information than she wanted to have, but at least it shed some light on the family situation in this house. She suddenly perceived that Annie, with her husband gone, a struggling pottery business to run and three children to bring up, might have even more problems than she, Caro, did.

The younger boy bounced on the bed until Franklin tossed him off, and while he was picking himself up from the floor, Franklin wheeled her suitcase into the bedroom.

"Come on, Peter," Franklin ordered, and they ran away, whooping like Indians. Caro closed the door and locked it after them. *Whatever you could say about this household, it certainly isn't dull,* she thought to herself.

Caro twitched the hand-quilted bedspread smooth again, and after pausing for a moment to admire the pottery figurines on the dresser, she spent a few minutes freshening up in the immaculate adjoining bathroom.

Catching sight of her reflection in the mirror, she saw that her scar was a dark purplish color and that her cheeks looked pinched and white. She reparted her hair on one side and fastened her bangs out of her eyes with a clip. As she applied a fresh coat of lipstick, she felt a quick stab of despair.

She who had once been so beautiful—would anyone ever think of her as beautiful again? And if no one did, how important was it? She lifted a finger and touched her scar lightly, almost in disbelief. How could the stranger in the mirror be Caro Nicholson? She didn't look the same, she didn't feel the same, and people didn't respond to her in the same way they had for all of the rest of the twenty-six years of her life; that is, with a sudden appreciation of the way she looked. And here she was in a small town in Utah, far away from everyone and everything that she knew.

The small voice inside her head said, *It will be all right.* If only Caro could believe that.

Stoically she told herself that there wasn't time for self-pity. She heard Annie setting out the coffee cups in the kitchen, decided to unpack later and cast one last appreciative look at the white lace curtains lapping in the air in front of the window before rejoining the household.

"Oh, there you are," Annie greeted her when Caro appeared hesitantly in the kitchen doorway. "I hope your room is all right."

Caro took the proffered chair. "It's lovely," she said. "Did you make the pottery figures on the dresser yourself?"

"Oh, yes. That used to be the master bedroom, but I decided to try to get a bed-and-breakfast guest occasionally after my husband moved to Salt Lake City. I like to sleep in the extra twin bed in my daughter's room, where I'm not so lonely. Oh, I didn't tell you how much I charge. It's twenty-five dollars a night. Is that okay?"

"It's fine," Caro assured her. She wondered what Annie would think if she knew that when Caro went on location for a Naiad shoot, the Gaillardo company customarily paid more than eight times that amount for her hotel room.

Annie poured two cups of coffee and slid one over to Caro. "I hope you'll forgive me for being so disorganized. It's been six months to the day since Tom, my husband, left me. I've been upset all day, and then after Mike came over—did you meet Mike? He must have been on his way out as you came in."

"Is he tall? With dark eyes and skin? And drives a Jeep?"

"That's Mike. He's my cousin. He's tried to help me out occasionally since my husband left, and today he stopped by to mow the grass."

Caro nibbled on a cinnamon bun that Annie had set on the edge of her saucer. It was good; she was hungry.

"But you don't want to hear about our family problems. How long will you be here?" Annie asked.

The question took Caro by surprise. She hadn't thought about staying more than one night. Then she remembered the car that she'd left sitting alongside the highway.

"I'm not sure how long I'll stay, but there's one thing I have to do right away. I need to let the car rental company know that one of its fleet conked out with only eight hundred fifty-eight miles on the odometer. Would you mind if I use the phone?"

Annie showed her the phone on a table in the hallway, and Caro made the necessary call.

"But how soon can you deliver another car to me?" Caro asked the car rental agent impatiently over the din from the living room, where Franklin was threatening his younger brother and Annie's voice rose as she tried to restore order.

The reply was indistinguishable.

"What?" Caro said loudly, plugging up her free ear with one finger.

"Maybe the day after tomorrow," the agent shouted back. "Let me have your phone number."

Giving up on the conversation, Caro recited the number printed on Annie's phone. When she arrived in the kitchen, Annie was leaning against the refrigerator with an expression of exhaustion on her face.

"I don't know when I'll be able to get another rental car," Caro told her with a shrug. "I suppose I'll be staying until they deliver one. If you don't mind, that is." Somehow the idea of staying in the pretty guest room of this boisterous but friendly household was comforting.

Annie brightened and joined Caro at the table. "That's good news. I can't tell you how much I miss having someone to talk to."

Caro was pleased to know that her presence was welcome. For weeks she had felt like nothing but a problem and a liability to everyone.

Annie drained her cup. "Well," she said, "I've got to get back to my workshop. You can rest, if you like, and then you might enjoy a walk around town. There are a couple of restaurants on Main Street where you can pick up a quick supper later. I'm afraid we'll be eating leftovers."

"Oh, I didn't expect dinner," Caro assured her quickly.

Annie looked relieved. "Franklin, Peter," she called to the two boys curled up among the cracker crumbs on the living-room couch. "You two behave yourselves and don't make a lot of noise."

"Okay, Mom," the boys chorused.

"See you later," Annie said, and with that, she was out the door.

Caro glanced at her watch. It was almost four o'clock.

She calculated the time in New York. Taking the change in time zones into account, it would be nearly six o'clock there; if she called right away, she might be able to catch Marina in her office before she went home for the evening.

She squared her shoulders and steeled herself to hear Marina's strident voice. Then she picked up the phone, punched in her credit card number and prepared herself for the ordeal of confronting her mentor.

Marina sounded even more harried than usual when she answered her phone. "Caro? Caro, love, where the hell are you? I can't tell you how upset I was to get the message that you'd left. Are you out of your mind?"

"Marina, don't get hyper. I'm in Moab, Utah. Yes, you heard me correctly, *Utah. U-T-A-H.* It's one of the forty-eight contiguous United States. And I'm not out of my mind. At least not yet," Caro said with a worried glance toward the living room where, silhouetted against the flickering TV screen, Peter seemed to be practicing a wrestling hold on Franklin to the accompaniment of a great deal of grunting and heavy breathing.

"What kind of stunt is it to place a message on my telephone answering machine that you're leaving the city and don't know when you'll be back? I've been frantic, *frantic*, I tell you! I mean, I was expecting you to show up yesterday at the agency. The Naiad people—"

"I don't want to hear anything about the Naiad people," Caro said stonily.

"You're *the* Naiad, they've built their whole advertising concept around you, that means they've invested a lot of money. They're not going to dump you off this ad campaign. Think how bad it would make the Gaillardo company look if they dropped you, after you've been through such an ordeal. Why, since the attack you've been on the national news programs and in all the papers, not to mention that *Women's Weekly* article,'' Marina said.

''The magazine article is something I'd prefer to forget. I didn't know that Nadine Zimmerman was a reporter for *Women's Weekly* when she appeared in my hospital room three days after the attack. She let me think she was there to water the flowers.''

''I know it made you sick afterward to realize that your remarks had been blown up into an unflattering article insinuating that you welcomed the publicity stemming from the attack, but at least it kept you in the forefront of the news,'' Marina pointed out.

''It wasn't a time in my life when I wanted publicity. I'd have preferred to be left alone to heal in peace. Do you have any idea how it feels to be a media curiosity? People I don't even know sneaked past the doorman and banged on my door until I opened it, and then they would say, 'I just wanted to see if you really look as bad as you looked on TV.' Can you imagine how demoralizing that is?''

''I know, darling. We should have taken measures to protect you better. When you come back and resume the Naiad campaign, we should look into some sort of security for you.''

Caro was silent for such a long time that Marina said, ''Caro? Are you there?''

Caro sighed. The wrestling match in the living room had accelerated into a series of loud thuds. New York seemed very far away.

''Marina, I don't *want* to resume the Naiad campaign,'' she said, her voice breaking.

''*What?* Caro, what are you saying?''

Caro slid a hand over her eyes, her fingers recoiling from the smooth surface of her scar.

''The publicity after the attack was awful, and the Naiad

campaign isn't important to me right now. I had to get away, Marina, don't you see? I couldn't live in the city knowing that every man I saw could be the one who attacked me. I couldn't walk down the street, I couldn't bear to be in crowds, I couldn't leave my apartment without being terrified.'' She willed Marina to understand, but her friend's next words revealed that she did not.

"Caro, dear, I think you need to see a good psychiatrist, a *counselor*, so you can better withstand the healing *process*,'' Marina said.

"I don't think the way I feel is at all abnormal,'' Caro objected. "In fact, it seems to me that if I weren't frightened, there'd be something wrong with me. My fear is normal under the circumstances, Marina, don't you see?''

Maybe she was babbling, but she had to make Marina comprehend how broken she really was, and what a long way she had to go before she could even begin to come to grips with the trauma of the attack.

"Now Caro,'' Marina said in her most understanding voice. "There's a lot of money riding on the Naiad account, and of course you must remember that you have a contract, and I've been talking with the Gaillardo company's lawyers—''

All this talk about money and contracts and lawyers proved to Caro that Marina was operating on a different wavelength.

"I'll call you soon, Marina,'' Caro said, and with great finality, she set the receiver carefully in its cradle, ignoring Marina's outraged shout.

Chapter Two

At the moment Caro didn't have time to be concerned about the psychiatrists and contracts and lawyers that Marina had mentioned. The wrestling match in the living room commanded her full attention, and, since Annie was nowhere around, she rushed to see if either boy was in truly dire straits.

"He kicked me," Franklin accused when Caro, unable to tell if anyone was bleeding, forcibly pulled the two boys apart.

"Did not," Peter said placidly. "Who are you, anyway?" He gazed up at Caro with wide blue eyes.

Caro turned down the volume on the television set. "I'm Caro," she said.

"She's the bread-and-beckfast. I mean, bed-and-breadfast. I never can say it right," Franklin said.

"Yes, and I'd like to lie down on that bed for a while. If you guys are going to fight, I won't be able to rest."

"Why do you need to sleep? Only babies take naps," was Peter's sage comment.

"Grown-ups take naps when they're tired," she said.

"Why do you have a line across your face?" Peter wanted to know. He was peering up at her with his mouth open.

"I had—an accident," Caro said.

"You dummy, it's not polite to ask questions about people's infinities," Franklin said to Peter.

"I think you mean infirmities," Caro corrected him. "And you're right. It isn't polite." She hadn't meant to be drawn into a conversation nor did she consider herself responsible for Peter's manners. Yet there was something appealing about him, and Franklin, with his seriousness and ingenuous humor, was a funny little fellow.

"Sorry," Peter said, crestfallen.

"Well, if you're really sorry, maybe you could be quiet while I lie down," Caro suggested in a reasoning tone.

"Maybe," Franklin and Peter said in unison.

"I'll see that they behave," said a voice at the door.

"Mike!" the boys exclaimed gleefully, jumping up and running to greet him.

"This is Mike," Franklin explained as Mike sauntered into the living room and surveyed the debris.

Caro self-consciously touched her scar. Then she realized that she was only drawing attention to it, and she dropped her hand. Hesitantly she stepped forward. Mike was the same man who had brushed past her on the porch, the one that Annie had identified as the cousin who tried to help her.

"I'm Caro Nicholson," she told him. "I'm the bed-and-breakfast."

"I'm Mike Herrick," he said. He studied her face, a strong, sympathetic look in his eyes. Caro had come to understand that the scar was a barrier and a distraction and that people wanted to be reassured when they saw it. But she could think of no way to reassure him, and she found that she was holding her breath.

"Can you stay for dinner, Mike? Please?" Franklin asked. Caro let her breath out slowly, wondering if anyone would notice if she just disappeared into her room.

"Well…" Mike hesitated.

"Please?" repeated Franklin.

Mike shot a glance toward Caro, clearly trying to figure out if she was included in the family dinner plans. She said nothing, and he turned back to the boys.

"Well, boys," he said, "I guess I might as well stay, since I'll probably be here until dinnertime, anyway."

"Hot damn," said Peter.

Mike pierced him with a look. "Where'd you learn to say that?" he asked.

"From TV," said Peter.

"Well, don't say it anymore. Your mother wouldn't like it."

"She doesn't like a lot of things I say. You want to hear some of them?"

"Uh, not right now," Mike said with a surreptitious glance at Caro to see how she was taking all this. She raised her eyebrows.

"Anyway," he said, "I'm headed for the utility shed to fix the lawn mower. I went over to the hardware store and bought parts for it, and maybe I'll even get it to work."

"I want to help! I want to help!" cried Peter, jumping up and down.

"That's a good idea," Mike said with a wink at Caro. "Especially since it gets the boys out of the house."

Caro smiled gratefully. Her face had almost forgotten how to smile in the past painful weeks.

"Thanks," she called after him as he shepherded the boys out the door. He waved in silent acknowledgment as he followed them.

Caro heard Franklin and Peter bellowing to each other as they passed the window. She watched them, finding humor in the way Franklin tried to swagger in imitation of Mike's manly gait.

In her room she removed the quilt from the bed and draped it over a nearby chair. She lay down on the double bed that was to be hers and closed her eyes, willing herself to relax. She could hear the children's shouts from the backyard, and at first it was hard to let herself go; it felt strange to find herself in a place so unlike her usual surroundings.

Maybe Marina was right. Perhaps Caro should have stayed in New York, where Marina could supervise her care and where Wayne would have—but Wayne, she reminded herself, had gradually stopped calling after the attack. When she called him, she more often than not got his answering machine. His explanations that he had been increasingly busy at work hadn't rung true, especially after her friend Donna mentioned on the phone one day that she'd spotted Wayne at a play on a night when Wayne had told Caro he was working late.

Once or twice Caro had even caught Wayne looking at her scar with what she could have sworn was a glimmer of revulsion in his eyes. *No.* There wasn't anything steady about Wayne anymore. In her heart of hearts, she knew she couldn't have depended on him.

At this point, the pain of Wayne's rejection was all mixed up with the anguish she felt over her disfigurement. Sometimes the two sadnesses ran together and seemed like one and the same. At other times, she mourned Wayne more than she did her ruined face. Now and then she'd bring herself up short by telling herself that of the two tragedies, her face was the worse. She couldn't replace a face, but there was sure to be another man in her life. Then she would despair; what man would want a woman whose face looked like hers?

After the attack, she had cooperated with Detective Garwood from the police department, telling him that the man who had attacked her was unknown to her. Although she remembered her assailant's strange eyes and prominent jaw well enough to describe him, she could contribute no motive. The investigation stalled. There were no suspects, the detective said. Which meant that the man was still out there somewhere, perhaps biding his time. Or maybe he was just some crackpot, but that made him no less dangerous.

Caro had gone home from the hospital after the doctors had done all they could for the extensive wound that stretched from her temple on one side to her jawbone on the other. She had expected to pick up the pieces of her life and put them back together again, much the way the doctors had fitted together the pieces of her face. After all, she wanted to put behind her the consequences of that horrible episode in the park.

She hadn't expected her memory of the incident to return in the form of terrifying nightmares about a man with oddly pale eyes, thin lips and a prominent jaw. And when the nights were over, she greeted each day with sheer mental agony, knowing that the perpetrator of the horrible crime against her still roamed free somewhere in the city.

She had told her doctor of her fears, but all he had done was scribble out a prescription for tranquilizers. Afraid of becoming dependent on them, Caro had picked up the prescription at the pharmacy but left the bottle in her purse. From time to time she contemplated taking one, but somehow never did.

She did, however, think about smoking, a habit she'd only recently abandoned with a great deal of agony. It was the agony that kept her from it. It seemed to her that she was undergoing quite enough agony, as it was.

Wayne had called less and less often and then began to limit his visits to one uncomfortable night per week. No one was there when Caro, crying and distraught, huddled in a corner of her bedroom all night, feeling emotionally as well as physically broken after another horrible nightmare in which the unforgettable face of her assailant paralyzed her with fright. At that point, she faced the prospect of becoming a prisoner of her own fears.

She had fled, knowing that for her own mental health she had no other choice. The next morning she jumped into a taxi, and, as an afterthought, tossed the bottle of tranquilizers into the storm drain in front of her apartment building. She rushed to the airport and bought a ticket on a plane, any plane that would take her west, where she had a vague idea that there were wide open spaces and few people.

In Denver she rented a car and struck out on her own, not caring where she went as long as she didn't have to brush elbows with anyone who could very well be the person who had attacked her. She'd ended up in Moab, Utah, a town she'd never heard of before in her life.

But from what she could fathom, the people here had never heard of her, either. So far no one had recognized her as the Naiad, and the name Caro Nicholson meant nothing to people who were caught up in their own day-to-day dramas.

Which was a good thing. She was far away from her own world, a world that had become impossible for her, and maybe getting away from it was the only way to make any sense of her life. Because whoever she was, she certainly was no longer the person she had been before the attack.

MIKE HERRICK SAT on the floor of the Stendahls' utility shed and reflected morosely that if Annie had the money—*heck,* if *he* had the money—he'd insist on taking the lawn mower to a repairman who knew how to fix it. But both he and Annie were barely managing to stay solvent at this point.

Annie stuck her head out the door of her workshop. "Mike? You staying for dinner?" she wanted to know.

"Yeah," he said with a grin. "The kids invited me. But it's the bed-and-breakfast I'm really interested in."

"The bed-and—? Oh, you mean Caro. Sorry, but she won't be joining us for dinner."

Mike hid his disappointment by picking up a wrench he didn't know how to use.

"How do you suppose she came by that scar?" Annie asked.

Mike studied the wrench for a moment before raising his eyes to hers. "I figure it's none of our business," he said slowly.

"You're right, as usual. You're the only one in this whole big family of ours with any sense, you know that?"

"Some would argue that point, but I'm not one of them," he said with a grin.

Annie only shook her head at him in exasperation and pulled her head back into the workshop, shutting herself off from the rest of them like a turtle.

Mike peered at the lawn mower's innards, reluctantly picturing that scar of Caro's in his mind. He'd wanted to wince when he first saw it. He had deliberately controlled his facial expression, and he had to hand it to her. She had held her head high, not trying to avoid his gaze. It couldn't be easy, going out into the world with a scar like that. He wondered, too, what had happened to her. One thing for sure—he wouldn't ask.

Caro Nicholson was one of the classiest women he had ever seen. He might be having trouble figuring out the workings of the lawn mower, but that was nothing compared to figuring out what somebody like Caro was doing refereeing a fight between two small boys in his cousin Annie's living room.

He was used to Annie's bed-and-breakfast guests by this time, although Caro was a far cry from any of the others. At first he'd thought that taking in lodgers was just another one of Annie's cockamamy ideas that would come to no good, but he had to admit that her bed-and-breakfast guests had been good for Annie. She needed the money, and they provided her with occasional adult company.

Mike had tried to fill in for Annie's husband in all sorts of ways after Tom picked up and moved to Salt Lake City, but Mike would be the first to admit that taking the boys under his wing, joshing Holly, and shoring up Annie's emotions wasn't enough. They needed their husband and father, and he'd had no experience along either of those lines. As many things as he did for the Stendahl family, he often felt that he was failing abysmally.

The kids liked him a lot, he knew that. Like today, when Franklin and Peter had fallen all over themselves racing him to the shed to help him repair the lawn mower. Their enthusiasm hadn't lasted long, however. Right now they were climbing the big tree that shaded Annie's pottery workshop.

He finished with the lawn mower and cleaned his hands on a piece of one of Peter's old shirts. He pulled the cord to start the engine, and nothing happened. He pulled it again. *Nothing.* He leaned back and admitted to himself that he hadn't accomplished a thing all afternoon.

He wiped his forehead with a clean scrap of the shirt. If he hadn't been wasting his time on this tomfool piece of machinery, he could have been doing something worthwhile. He was primarily of a scholarly bent, and had never been much good at working with engines of any kind. He certainly wasn't accomplished at repairing the things that broke around Annie's house, and trying to take Tom's place in this household seemed nigh unto impossible.

While Mike was staring at the stubborn lawn mower engine and trying to come to terms with his own inadequacies, Holly appeared at the back door, calling that supper was ready.

He turned to put the wrench back into the tool kit, and that was when Peter, uttering one surprised squeak, fell out of the tree.

MINUTES LATER Caro, Holly and Franklin stood at the curb, watching as Annie and Mike bundled the squalling Peter into Mike's Jeep, preparatory to a mad dash to the hospital.

"You'll look after Holly and Franklin, won't you?" the harried Annie thought to ask Caro before the Jeep roared away. Caro assured her that she would.

"Is Peter going to be all right?" Holly asked after the Jeep disappeared up the street.

"I hope so," Caro said doubtfully. Peter's arm had hung at a peculiar angle when Mike picked him up off the ground.

"I'm sorry Peter had to fall when you'd just got here," Holly said sympathetically as they went back into the house.

"I'm sorry Peter had to fall, period," was Caro's heartfelt reply.

"Oh, Peter's always falling," Holly assured her. "It's just that this time, he's really done it." She let her eyes fall curiously on Caro's scar. As if she realized that this was rude, she quickly blinked her eyes and looked elsewhere.

"It's all right," Caro said.

"How did it happen?" Holly asked with frank inquisitiveness.

"It was kind of an accident," Caro said.

"It's getting better, though, isn't it?"

"Yes, it's much better."

"Maybe it will heal so well that it will get invisible. See this little white line on my leg? That's where I hurt it when I jumped off a swing on the school playground. I had to have four stitches, and now you can hardly see it."

Realizing that Holly was only trying to make her feel comfortable, Caro smiled gently and said, "You're right. I can hardly see your scar. Now, didn't I hear you say that you were heating up a casserole? And shouldn't we do something about it?"

Holly showed her the casserole, which would stay warm in the microwave.

"I guess we'd better wait until someone comes back from the hospital and tells us whether to go ahead and eat it or not," Holly said.

Caro offered to help in the kitchen, and she and Holly dodged each other the best they could as they wrapped the French bread in aluminum foil to keep it warm and put the salad into the refrigerator to await the return of the absent family members.

"Did you make the salad by yourself?" Caro wanted to know.

"Mmm-hmm," Holly said proudly. "I fixed the French bread, too."

"A lot of girls wouldn't know how to do those things," Caro said.

Holly glanced down at the floor. "I've had to learn how to do all sorts of chores around the house since Daddy left," she said quietly. "Mom needs my help."

The telephone rang. Holly ran to answer it, but she returned almost immediately. "That was Aunt Nola. She heard that Peter had to go to the hospital," Holly said. The phone rang again. When Holly came back this time, she was grinning.

"Boy, it sure doesn't take long for news to spread. That was Aunt Lou, Mom's other sister. She heard about Peter, too. She wanted to know if she should come over and stay with us, but I told her no, you're here."

"I guess it's a good thing I was," Caro said with a little half laugh.

"Yes, but there's always somebody to take care of us if Mom can't. Besides my two aunts, there's Gert, Mom's cousin. And Connie, and Diane, and my grandma. And Mike, of course. We have a big family."

Just then they heard Mike's Jeep pull up to the front curb.

Holly rushed into the living room to look out the window. "Oh, good," she called, dancing with excitement. "Mike's back from the hospital. He can tell us how Peter is." She ran to the front door with Caro right behind her.

Mike hurried up the path. "Peter's having a cast put on his arm at this very moment," Mike said in answer to Holly's anxious questions. "It's a broken arm, all right. Dr. Harris says he'll be as good as new in six weeks or so."

Franklin appeared just in time to hear Mike's announcement about Peter. "I broke my toe once," he said in a classic attention-getting gambit.

Holly ignored him. "When will Peter and Mom be home?" she wanted to know.

"After the doctor finishes putting the cast on Peter's arm," Mike said. "Annie told me to make sure that you two eat dinner. Dr. Harris will drop her and Peter off here after he leaves the hospital. Dr. Harris is a relative of ours," he explained to Caro.

"I'm inviting Caro to eat dinner with us," Holly informed him. "You will, won't you, Caro?"

"But—"

"Mom always says I can invite anyone I want, as long as there's enough food. Don't you want to?"

"Well—"

"Sure you do," Franklin said.

She never did agree to eat dinner with the family, but agreement was apparently not deemed necessary. Holly tugged on one arm and Franklin pulled her by the hand until they had propelled her into the kitchen.

"You sit at the foot of the table where Mom is supposed to sit, and Mike can sit at the head of the table where Dad used to be."

Caro shot an embarrassed glance at Mike, who seemed to be taking all this in stride. They bowed their heads for a short blessing, then started to eat.

Caro was astonished as she got to know them around the dinner table that the children were so talkative. Holly at eleven was surprisingly mature, a pretty golden-haired child on the threshold of adolescence. Franklin, a freckle-faced nine-year-old, exhibited a lively intelligence. Caro found herself fascinated by both of them.

"They're really something, aren't they?" Mike said with a chuckle, after Holly and Franklin had excused themselves and raced each other outside to update their friend Tony on the condition of Peter's arm.

"The kids, you mean?"

"Yes. You seemed to enjoy them."

"I did. I've never been around many children."

"They've certainly taken a liking to you," Mike observed.

The way he was looking at her made her nervous, so nervous that she could feel herself starting to break out in a cold sweat. She wanted to run and hide. Quickly, her heart hammering, she stood and eyed the clean dishes in the dishwasher, wondering if she could figure out where they went. She opened a cabinet door, picked up one of the plates and tentatively slid it onto a shelf.

Mike was close behind her. "No," he said, reaching out and easing the plate from between her fingertips. "That goes over here." He opened another door and put the plate on a stack of several similar ones. "And these bowls go up here," he said, picking them up and putting them away. "The glasses belong over there," he told her, indicating another cabinet.

Together they unloaded the dishwasher, and when it was empty, they began to stack the dirty dishes in it. It felt good to Caro to be useful, for a change.

She couldn't recall the last time she'd done something as

purposeful as housework. Home was a luxury apartment on Central Park West, and a housekeeper took care of it. To her recollection, she'd never cleaned up after anything more complicated than a grilled cheese sandwich. Yet here she was, wearing Annie's faded apron over her silk slacks and shirt, and not really minding the work.

When they had finished, Mike glanced at his watch. "It's about time for Annie and Peter to come home. If you don't mind, I'll wait for them. I want to know how Peter is feeling before I leave."

"Do you live nearby?" Caro ventured as she wiped off the countertop.

"A few miles out of town. I live in a trailer on an old uranium prospector's claim in the desert." Mike was helping himself to another cup of coffee from the pot on the stove. "Want one?" he asked, looking at her over his shoulder.

Caro hesitated a moment. She could go to her room. But she didn't want to do that. When she was by herself, she couldn't avoid flashbacks to the face of her attacker or to some of the more unpleasant moments in the hospital.

"Yes, I'll have a cup," she said, deciding to take advantage of Mike's company; he would unwittingly help to keep her personal demons at bay. While she sat down at the kitchen table, Mike poured coffee for her and rummaged in a cupboard until he found an unopened box of fig newtons.

"Dessert," he explained, unceremoniously dumping several of them onto a plate and setting it in the middle of the table.

Caro reached for a cookie, thinking that she hadn't eaten with such abandon in years. Usually she had to watch her weight. Now it didn't seem important. *What if I never go back to modeling?* she thought. In the back of her mind, there had always been the knowledge that her flight from New York was only temporary, and that she could go back if she wanted to. What if she didn't want to?

But she had stayed here in the kitchen with Mike so that she wouldn't dwell on herself. She tried to think about something else.

"Have you lived in Moab all your life?" she asked Mike.

"I was born here, and I leave from time to time, but I always come back. I'm an archaeologist," he explained.

"What do you do here?" she asked with interest.

"I look," he said.

She stared, wondering if his answer was some kind of joke.

"What I mean," he said, his face softening at her perplexed expression, "is that I'm doing private fieldwork in the desert. I'm searching for something."

"You're looking for something archaeological?" Caro said, as puzzled as she had been a moment ago.

"I've pieced together an archaeological theory based on some findings of mine, and I'm hoping that I'll be the first to discover what I'm looking for. If you want to know the truth, I have a reputation around these parts as kind of an oddball."

Caro shook her head and smiled. "You look perfectly normal to me," she said, although he was certainly different from the urban types she knew.

Mike laughed. "I am, I suppose, except for this obsession of mine. People link me with some of the more unsuccessful local prospectors of yore, always searching, never finding. They'd like to tell me to give it up, only no one knows *what* to tell me to give up, so they're stymied." He laughed again, and she liked the way his dark eyes sparkled.

"What can you tell me about your work?" she asked.

"Not a whole lot, except that it has to do with Indian art, the drawings and carvings that appear so profusely on canyon walls and ledges and rocks in the Four Corners area."

"Is the Four Corners area around here somewhere?"

"It's a section of the country so called because it's where the states of Colorado, New Mexico, Arizona and Utah meet. Moab's in the heart of it. Anyway, when I was a kid I used to stare long and hard at those pictures on the rock, trying to determine their meaning. Their puzzle was one of the things that influenced me to study archaeology in college."

"The truck driver who gave me a lift into town was talking about the Anasazi. Are those the Indians who are responsible for the rock pictures?"

"They created many of them. If you've heard of the Anasazi, you must know that they lived in this area from sometime before Christ until around 1300 A.D., when their culture slid into a mysterious decline. We're still trying to figure out why the Anasazi disappeared."

"It sounds to me as though you've made prehistoric rock art your speciality," she said.

"You could say that," he said noncommittally.

"But *you* wouldn't say it," she said; he looked as though he thought he'd revealed too much.

Mike shifted uncomfortably in his chair. "Well, many other archaeologists refuse to take the subject seriously. In the past they've focused instead on the leavings of the Anasazi—their pottery, their personal effects, their housing. Those artifacts have been well preserved in the dry climate of southern Utah. It's my feeling that traditional archaeology has ignored the real story of the Anasazi, which is the record that they left on the rocks."

"And what does that record say?"

Mike smiled. "If I told you that," he said firmly, "then you'd be like everyone else. You'd tell me to give up."

Her interest flared, but he had folded his arms across his chest in a characteristic pose of noncommunication. If he insisted on being mysterious, this line of conversation was a dead end. Caro decided to switch topics.

"I've heard about the national parks around here. Are they really something to see?"

"You mean you haven't seen Canyonlands or Arches or Dead Horse Point? Well, you shouldn't miss them. It's some of the most spectacular scenery in the world."

"Maybe I'll go when the rental company delivers another car. I was just driving through this part of the country when my car broke down, you see."

"Driving through? Where were you going?"

Caro lowered her head. "I—I didn't really have a destination," she admitted.

He watched her carefully. Again he wondered about the scar. Now that she was blushing slightly, it was a dark, angry red. As if she were capable of reading his thoughts, she tilted her head forward so that her long straight hair fell across her cheek, partly concealing the scar. Her reticence intrigued him. What else was she hiding? A past? A misdeed? Herself?

The summer light was growing dim, and twilight cast deep shadows over the little kitchen. Outside the children were playing a loud game. Inside, no one spoke. Water dripped from the kitchen faucet, each drop seeming to echo in the stillness. Mike wanted to get up and turn on the kitchen light, but for some reason he didn't dare.

Caro struggled inwardly with herself, wanting to talk but hardly able to spill her feelings to someone who was nothing more than an acquaintance. After a minute or so, she lifted her head and looked at Mike, admitting to herself that it was only natural for her to want to confide in him.

He was a stranger. In a way, Mike was the perfect confidant, one to whom she could unburden herself for the sake of feeling better and then be on her way. He and the Stendahls would remember her, if at all, as the bed-and-breakfast guest who appeared on the day that Peter broke his arm, the lady with the scar. As far as she knew, none of them so far had identified her as the Naiad.

But it wasn't that simple to confide and run. The more she grappled with her emotions, the more she became tangled in their web. Was it going to be this way for the rest of her life? Was she going to be identified not by the person she really was but by the scar on her face? With a sickening jolt, she realized that her attacker had not only ruined her face but stolen her comfortable identity. The idea threatened to choke off her air, and she stood up abruptly.

"I think I'll go to my room," she said in a rush. "I—I have some postcards to write." She wheeled and fled, and Mike heard the bedroom door close softly but firmly after her.

Mike sat in the dim kitchen, staring glumly and thinking. He tried to name the emotions he'd seen flitting across her features. *Pain, sadness, confusion, a desire for secrecy—negative emotions every one,* and he had identified all of them in Caro.

Finally, as he drank the last drops of coffee from his cup, Mike decided that there was nothing he could have done to stop her running away. Furthermore, he had no obligation to help her. He hardly knew her, yet something about her hesitant smile, her downcast eyes and the way she had positioned her head, so that her long hair would cover her scar, made his heart go out to her.

She was a lady with a problem, that was for sure. And his life was already bent out of shape by one such lady—his cousin Annie. For six months now he had altered his usual ways of doing things to accommodate Annie, Peter, Franklin and Holly. He had postponed asking for permission to explore a particular canyon because he wanted to be around if Annie or the kids needed him. He had mowed their grass, taken the boys fishing, and rushed Peter to the hospital tonight. But enough was enough. He longed for his previous uncomplicated life-style.

One thing was certain. He didn't need to know any more ladies with problems.

Chapter Three

Mike had affectionately named the trailer where he lived the Tin Can. It was an aluminum box situated on an old mining claim off a rocky dirt road. The road wound around strange sandstone formations that put many people in mind of scenery they might expect to find on another planet. Mike, who had grown up on a steady diet of Flash Gordon movies on Saturday morning television, was used to the scenery, but on occasion he expected to see Flash's sidekick Dr. Zharkov and girlfriend Dale Arden dashing around one of the distant buttes, running from the bad guys.

Then the reality of the here and now would settle in on him, and Mike would realize that this was no Saturday morning fantasyland. He was not Flash Gordon, and Dale Arden did not exist. This was merely a portion of the Utah desert, and the only creatures nearby were perfectly ordinary jackrabbits, kangaroo mice and a mule deer or two.

He had lived in the trailer for several years now, preferring it to town for several reasons. For one thing, he liked his solitude. In the desert there were no automobile horns, no telephones, no door-to-door salesmen. There were no responsibilities other than those to himself.

It wasn't as though Mike had ever made a conscious decision to be alone. It had more or less just happened, and he was used to it. Once he had wanted a family, but that required a wife, and the right woman had never presented herself.

First of all, the woman would have to be intelligent. Despite his downplaying of his intellect, Mike was more than a mere wanderer of the desert. He was an archaeologist with a PhD after his name, and he was also an accomplished linguist, two accomplishments that served each other well.

He had discovered while still in high school that he had an affinity for languages, but the pull of archaeology had been greater, and so, as most people who wanted to be archaeologists did, he had declared anthropology as his college major. He had learned Spanish and French in school, later picking up Greek during a summer he'd spent working on a Greek freighter in the Mediterranean between his junior and senior years of college. His co-workers on a dig in the Middle East had been astounded when he easily acquired Arabic, and then as a hobby, he had expanded his knowledge to include ancient Arabic, as well. Nowadays he studied ancient Greek for fun.

All of this, he was well aware, made him seem eccentric to most women. No woman he had ever met wanted to participate with him in a dig, and none had ever cared to accompany him on his frequent treks into the Utah desert. He couldn't talk about some of the things he'd found there because he wanted to preserve their secrecy, and that had annoyed the women. So it was no wonder that the relationships had been unsatisfactory, he reflected.

In fact, as soon as a woman found out that he was an archaeologist, she'd associate him with persnickety old men poking around in dusty Egyptian tombs, never bothering to find out whether he was interesting or not. He gave such women short shrift. His life was busy and fulfilling. He was a member of several scholarly societies, including the Rosetta Society, to which he was scheduled in the fall to present a paper about his unparalleled discoveries in the Four Corners region of Utah. If a woman couldn't or wouldn't appreciate such a life, then he had no time for her.

Instead, he found pleasure in spending time with Annie's kids, who needed him. Mike was a member of a large extended family, mostly female, who provided companionship and occasional home-cooked meals. He was happy, he supposed. Only occasionally did he mourn the absence of one special woman who could be both lover and helpmate. Even so, he wasn't sure that he was mourning. Never having known such a person, her absence was tolerable.

Tonight he intended to develop some photographs he'd taken. He had rigged up the trailer's small bathroom to serve as a darkroom, and that was where he did his developing. It was important to him to be able to process his exposed film efficiently and to be able to decide quickly what darkroom techniques he would need to employ, in order to enhance the picture.

Once in a while he took film into Moab to be processed. Because of a talkative clerk in the camera shop, everyone knew that Mike Herrick shot roll after roll of nothing but Indian pictographs and petroglyphs.

"What do you intend to do with all those pictures of Indian rock art?" was a question he heard now and then. He was hard put to answer it.

He supposed that he could have told his well-meaning interrogators that the Anasazi's art was the only real communication between the ancient tribe and modern man. He could have told them, but he didn't. Not only did he not want to be laughed out of town, but he preferred to keep the importance of his discoveries to himself until this fall, after he had presented the paper on the subject.

He had no plans to participate in any other digs in the immediate future. He intended to concentrate on southeast Utah. He wanted to reserve his personal involvement for his own mission, deciphering the rock art of the Anasazi. He was not in the mood for serious emotional ties or strings. After all, he didn't want anything to interfere with his mission: to uncover the secrets of the Anasazi.

IN THE DAYS after Peter broke his arm, Caro settled into life at the Stendahls' house. It wasn't so much that she consciously decided to stay there; it was more that she still was in no condition to make a decision to leave. Decisions were beyond her for now.

The rental car never arrived, and on most days Caro felt so lethargic that she didn't call to find out why. Other days she ventured into the household, and more and more, as their lives began to spill over into one another, she felt like a fixture there.

Before long, the children were coming to her with concerns

with which they were reluctant to trouble their busy mother. Caro didn't mind. In a way, the children were giving her more attention than she was giving them, and that seemed beneficial. She began to think more clearly and to focus on something outside herself. Once in a while she phoned Marina, who was frantic with wanting to know where Caro was and when she would be back. Caro had a sure remedy for such questions. She merely hung up the phone.

One day as she sat on the porch staring into space, Franklin approached her timidly, which was unusual for Franklin. He perched on the top step next to her and fidgeted until she noticed him.

"Caro, will you listen to me read?" he asked unexpectedly.

With difficulty, Caro brought herself back to the present time and place.

"Of course, Franklin," she said without much interest. Then she noticed the book. "That looks like a school textbook. Isn't school dismissed for the summer?" she asked.

Franklin opened the book. "Sure, but I'm LD. I have to practice and do therapy all summer."

"LD? What's that?" She'd never heard of it before.

"Some people call it 'learning disabled.' At our house we call it 'learning different.' I'm dyslexic," Franklin told her matter-of-factly, pronouncing the difficult word very carefully.

"Dyslexic," repeated Caro. "Doesn't that mean that you get your letters mixed up?"

"That's part of it. Sometimes I write them backward, too. And I write 'was' for 'saw' and things like that. I learn differently from most people, that's all."

"Oh," Caro said, not sure how to respond.

"I go to this teacher twice a week for therapy and I'm supposed to work at home. That's why I thought you might listen to me read. Mom's awful busy, and Holly gets tired of it."

"I'll listen as long as you like," Caro assured him. Franklin beamed and settled his back against the stair railing. Then he read her a funny story about a boy and his pet bullfrog.

When he finished, Caro said, "That was very nice, Franklin."

He flushed with pleasure. "Maybe sometime I'll show you the games my teacher plays with me. Maybe you'd like to play one."

"I probably would," Caro said, and Franklin looked even more pleased.

That night after all the children were in bed, Caro made a point to ask Annie about Franklin.

Annie sighed. "We found out about Franklin's learning difficulty two years ago, when he was having trouble in school. Fortunately, it was diagnosed right away, and we found help for him."

"He's a smart kid. I was surprised to find out that he has a problem."

"Thanks for helping him, Caro. He needs someone to take an interest in him, and my mind is on so many other things."

"Don't worry about him. I enjoyed my time with Franklin today. I'll ask him about those games he wanted to play tomorrow."

Annie brightened. "Would you? They're part of his homework."

"I'll make a point of it," Caro said.

She went on working with Franklin and soon found herself doing anything else that needed to be done in the Stendahl household. She learned to make peanut butter sandwiches to Peter's specifications—"I want jelly on *both* slices of bread, Caro"—and found that she liked folding the children's sweet-scented clothes fresh from the dryer.

By the time two weeks had elapsed, Caro had stopped calling to inquire about the rental car. She didn't care whether it came or not. She was enjoying herself too much to leave.

"Why don't you borrow my station wagon and go see some of the local scenery?" Annie suggested one day as she dangled the keys tantalizingly in front of Caro's nose.

It was an offer Caro couldn't refuse, and to return the favor, she took the kids to Dead Horse Point, Canyonlands and Arches National Monument.

"We've been to all of these places before," Franklin complained, but even if they weren't overly impressed, Caro was in awe at the sight of huge arches and fantastic shapes carved by eons of rock and water.

And once I used to gawk at skyscrapers? Caro thought, wondering how she could have marveled at anything man-made, when these majestic stone formations were so much more artistic.

"Look at the pretty colors in the rock," she urged the children. "Can you name them?"

"Red," said Holly.

"Orange," said Franklin.

"Ugly brown," said Peter, scuffing at a pebble.

"That's rose, vermilion and umber," she told them, but they seemed uninterested in any colors that weren't in their crayon box at home.

On their daylong exploration of Arches National Monument, the gritty desert dust filled her nostrils, coated her clothing, and grated against her skin like sandpaper. Toward the end of the afternoon, the children patiently pleaded that it was time to go home *now*, but Caro was enchanted by the desert and was reluctant to leave.

Later, going alone to revisit the places where she'd taken the children, she saw many examples of Indian rock art, and found them all the more interesting because of the little she knew of Mike's work. Again she wondered what the petroglyphs and pictographs had taught him about the Anasazi people.

Someday perhaps she would find out, perhaps the next time she was alone with him. That never seemed to happen, however. Still, she saw him almost every day during his visits, which seemed to be lasting longer and longer each time.

She knew that Mike Herrick watched her the way that a man watches a woman when he's interested in her, and she wasn't sure how she felt about that. In one way she was flattered. In another she despaired. Why would an attractive man like Mike—and she'd decided that she did consider him attractive, although not precisely her type—why would he be interested in someone with a face like hers?

She tried not to think about Mike, carrying out her increasing duties in the household as though she hadn't noticed him. While she was deliberately not paying attention to him, he remained warm and friendly.

Caro didn't miss her well-appointed apartment, nor did she miss her work or the city. It began to irk her that on the increasingly rare occasions when she summoned the nerve to telephone New York, Marina acted as though nothing had changed.

"When are you coming back?" she asked every time Caro called.

"I can't," Caro would whisper into the telephone. She was terrified of blowing her cover. If Annie and the kids found out she was the Naiad, there would be questions to answer, and Caro still found the attack simply too painful to discuss.

"We need to look into scheduling those operations to minimize your scar," Marina reminded her, but Caro resisted going back to New York for any reason.

"Not yet," she would say, and then make an excuse to hang up.

Not yet, maybe not ever. That was what she was beginning to think more and more often these days.

IN NEW YORK, Marina was puzzled by the attitude of her star model. She spent a great deal of time worrying about Caro, wondering how she could shut herself off from the world for so long.

"Is Caro ever coming back?" asked Suki, one of Caro's best friends and a top model herself.

"Of course she is," Marina declared staunchly, wishing that she knew exactly where Caro was. All she knew was that Caro was somewhere in Moab, Utah. She didn't even have a phone number or address where Caro could be reached.

Marina would have gone to fetch Caro if she could have. It was time for Caro to stop wasting time. Caro had a career, one that they both had struggled to promote. Now Caro was a big money-maker, and she had encountered a piece of bad luck, but there was no reason that, working together, they couldn't overcome it.

"I keep telling her that she'll eventually look the same as she did before, but she doesn't believe it," Marina explained to Wayne, Caro's ex-boyfriend, when she ran into him at the Rainbow Lounge, where they had both gone for a drink after work with separate groups of friends.

"Will she?" Wayne asked skeptically.

Marina shrugged. "Her doctor says he can fix up the scar," she said. "After all, her face is her livelihood."

"Of course. Well, tell Caro I said hello next time you talk with her," he said, backing away with drink in hand.

Marina studied Wayne as he sat with his arm curved around a sloe-eyed beauty whom he seemed to find particularly fascinating. Perhaps Caro was well rid of him, although Marina wondered if Caro wasn't staying away because of a broken heart. When Caro came back, she'd make it easy for the two of them to get together, in case there was still a spark between them. You never knew.

Marina nursed her drink and wondered what Caro had meant when she'd said that repairing the scar wouldn't change her back into the person she'd been.

"It's much more complicated than that," Caro had said, but Marina wasn't so sure. She was always telling her new girls at the agency to act as though they were top models, even when they were just starting to cart their portfolios around, trying to get jobs.

"Appearance is everything in this business," she'd say as she twitched a hopeful newcomer's skirt to a more becoming length or wielded her own eyeliner pencil to apply a neater band of color on the eyelid. "Act like the person you want to become, and pretty soon you'll be that person."

It took some convincing sometimes, but time and again she'd watched this philosophy work. If she could just get Caro back to New York, see her through the necessary operations to minimize her scar, then get her to act like the person she had been before—well, Caro would still have a chance in this business.

Never mind that Caro didn't seem to want her career anymore. Often people didn't know what they wanted until she, Marina, told them.

AT THE STENDAHLS' Caro felt safe, and she felt wanted.

Not that Annie really lacked for companionship—she was blessed with a whole host of female relatives who trooped in and out with their children, husbands and friends. More than once Annie dropped everything to rush to Lou's or Nola's or Connie's rescue. Caro couldn't figure out if this was normal or not. Since her own mother's death several years ago, Caro had no family at all and didn't know if this was the way it was supposed to be.

Sometimes Caro thought that Annie's relatives took advantage of her, as on the evening several weeks after her arrival when Annie's cousin Diane called at the last minute and begged her to come sit with her sick mother-in-law, while she and her husband went to a party.

"I was going to mend the kids' torn blue jeans tonight," Annie said distractedly as she rushed around getting ready. "I guess they'll have to wait."

"I'd mend them if I knew how," Caro offered, causing Annie to stop in midflight.

"Oh, I wasn't hinting," Annie said, looking flustered.

"I know. It's just that I want to be useful."

"Caro Nicholson, you're the best thing that's happened to us in months. As for being useful, don't be silly. I—" They heard a noise on the front porch, and Annie stopped talking and went to the door. She opened it on a surprised Mike Herrick, who was standing there holding a pan of something in his hands.

"I brought you some blueberry cobbler that Gert made," he said in rapid explanation.

"Oh, Mike," Annie said, recovering and relieving him of the pan of cobbler. "Come in and visit with Caro. I've got to run over to Diane's tonight. Come in, come in," she insisted when he hesitated.

Mike stood in the doorway regarding Caro uncertainly. She bent her head so that she was looking at the book in her lap and wished that Annie hadn't been so insistent. Mike came in and looked around, appearing uncomfortable with the situation. Caro tilted her head forward even more.

Annie didn't notice this byplay but talked nonstop until she finally hurried out the door, admonishing Mike not to drink all the milk with the blueberry cobbler because if he did, there wouldn't be enough for breakfast.

When she had gone, Caro and Mike were left sitting in the living room and staring at each other through the vacuum left by Annie's departure.

"Annie," Mike said at last. "She puts herself out for her family too much." He was sitting on the couch, directly across from Caro where he could look her full in the face.

"She's a very kind, warm, loving person," Caro said in Annie's defense.

"Annie carries it too far." He watched Caro as though thinking something over carefully, then said, "You'll have to be careful not to get that way, too."

"What do you mean?" she replied, startled.

"I've been watching you around here, and I wonder, don't you get tired of being everything to everybody in this house? While I was here earlier today, you spent most of the morning reading with Franklin, you helped Holly wash and dry her hair after lunch, and you made fresh lemonade for Peter. Then you volunteered to make phone calls to Annie's customers, explaining why their most recent orders would be late. Now Annie's run off on a goodwill mission, leaving you to cope with the kids if they wake up."

Caro closed her book. "I like doing all of it," she said, bewildered by his concern. What she couldn't, wouldn't explain was that she found helping other people therapeutic.

"Look, I don't know where you came from, but you wear expensive clothes and you're a far cry from anyone else who lives in Moab. Don't let Annie's problems or the children persuade you to stay if you want to leave."

Caro's startled expression made him temper his words.

"I mean, if you want to stay, I think it's wonderful. But if you don't—" He interrupted himself in midsentence, wishing he hadn't made a mess of what he had been trying to say. He hadn't meant Caro to think that he *wanted* her to leave. He just thought it was such a waste. Caro, tall, cool and elegant, obviously wasn't used to this domestic kind of life.

"If you think it would be best, I'll go tomorrow," Caro said, becoming white-faced and still. She felt struck to the core. She'd never dreamed that anyone wanted her to leave.

"No, Caro, that's not what I meant. Obviously you're a source of great strength for Annie." Mike ran a hand through his hair so that it stood on end. "I guess I'm just fishing," he said unhappily, staring down at the toe of his boot.

"Fishing?"

"Trying to figure out what a nice girl like you is doing in a place like this," he said ruefully.

Caro faltered. "I like it here," she said. She paused to gather

her defenses and decided on the spur of the moment that she might as well be honest. "Also, I don't have anywhere else to go," she said.

"If that's true, I can't imagine why," he said in a quiet tone. He was more than a little curious about her. He wondered what it would take to persuade her to open up to him. Or to anyone, for that matter.

"I can't go home to New York City, and—oh, it's too difficult to explain," she said. The book she had been reading fell to the floor. She was so agitated that she seemed not to notice, and all hope that she might confide in him evaporated.

"Then you don't have to try," he told her, although he felt a certain triumph. It was the first time that she had mentioned anything about home.

Whatever it was that she didn't want to discuss, it must be a humdinger of a topic. In order to give her a moment of privacy during which she might pull herself together, he bent over and picked up her book from where it had fallen. He turned it over and read its title, pretending not to notice how she was trembling.

"I didn't realize that you were interested in Anasazi pottery," he said when she had composed herself.

"I found that book in Annie's workshop," she said.

"Have you ever tried your hand at pottery?" he asked.

"A few times. I—I studied art in college," she said.

"I didn't realize that," he replied. He knew so little about her, despite seeing her here almost every day.

Caro shrugged. "I can't decide if I'm more interested in the pottery designs or in the Anasazi people themselves," she ventured.

"If you're interested in the Anasazi, you should come with me into the desert. I know the way to some otherwise inaccessible places decorated with their pictographs and petroglyphs. Would you like to go sometime?"

"Well, I'm awfully busy here, and—"

He might have guessed that she'd have an excuse, but at least she seemed calmer now.

"You need to take time for yourself," he told her firmly. "Anyway, you should treat yourself to a trip into the desert—

the *real* desert, not just the parks where the tourists go. It would be a fascinating experience for you.''

''Well...'' she said, but the way she said it, he knew he was winning.

''Come on, Caro,'' Mike urged with an encouraging smile. ''Let me give you the fifty-dollar tour. We'll drive out to Tanglewood Canyon in my Jeep next Sunday. I heard Annie tell her sister Lou that she's going to bring the kids over for a long visit, and you won't want to stay in the house by yourself.''

''Fifty dollars?''

''I'm only kidding. It's not really a tour. It's merely a trip to one of the most beautiful places in the world.''

''You must have something you'd rather do. I don't want to take up your valuable time,'' Caro said.

''Tanglewood Canyon is one of my favorite places,'' he said lightly, rising to his feet and smiling down at her in that gentle, thoughtful way to which she had become accustomed during the past few weeks.

''All right,'' she heard herself say. ''I'd like to go.''

''See you Sunday,'' he said, closing the door quietly behind him.

After he left, Caro remembered that she was supposed to check in with Marina again on Sunday. And even allowing for the difference in time zones, she didn't dare call Marina before they left; Mike was going to pick her up at seven in the morning, and she knew for a fact that Marina would never forgive such an early interruption of her sleep.

In the end, her concern about calling Marina dimmed before the excitement of looking forward to something special.

She was going to Tanglewood Canyon, and Marina would just have to wait until Monday.

Chapter Four

Mike's Jeep lurched over ridges and gullies, and a jackrabbit hopped out of their way. Caro steadied the topographical map on her lap and tried to decipher its jumble of red section lines, brown contour lines and sparse green smudges indicating vegetation.

"Is the map beginning to make any sense?" Mike asked as he maneuvered the vehicle around a rock carved by wind and water to look like nothing so much as a giant toadstool.

"Sort of," Caro replied. She glanced at him. "I suppose you know this desert like the back of your hand."

"I know it even better than that," he said with a grin.

It was Sunday, and Caro had been waiting eagerly on the porch when Mike picked her up at the house early in the morning. She had looked forward to this trip to Tanglewood Canyon with a mindless anticipation that she hadn't felt since she was a little girl.

"Oh, you'll have a great time," Annie had said when Caro told her she was going. "You and Mike." Annie slid a long speculative look in Caro's direction, but Caro pretended that she didn't know what it meant.

Now she leaned forward in her seat. "What kind of hawk is that?" she asked, shading her eyes against the sun.

Mike cast a practiced eye at the bird riding an invisible stream of air overhead. "A red-tailed hawk," he said. "Confounds me why they go out in the heat of the day like this. There's precious little for them to eat; their prey stays in the shade or underground.'' He pulled up the Jeep to the third in a series of closed gates and started to climb out.

''No, let me get this one,'' Caro said quickly, hopping down.

It was hot on this June day. The heat rose from the surrounding rock in waves, distorting the shapes of the formidable buttes and mesas in the distance. Caro swung the gate open, and the Jeep roared through. As she climbed back in, Caro felt the heat sucking the moisture from her pores. She uncapped the canteen Mike had provided and drank deeply.

They crossed a wide plateau covered with rolling red sand dunes sheltering clumps of scraggly sunflowers. From there they saw the junipers and pinyon pines bordering Tanglewood Canyon.

''This doesn't look like much of a road,'' Caro commented when Mike headed the Jeep down onto the steep trail that would lead them to the canyon floor.

''It was built for uranium prospectors a long time ago,'' Mike told her. ''I'm probably one of the few people who know about it.''

The Jeep tilted forward at a precarious angle as it began its descent, and Caro clung to the sides of her seat as a series of switchbacks led them to the bottom of the canyon. The strata in the rock, Mike explained, had been deposited three hundred million years ago when a sea ebbed and flowed here; later, the layers of limestone and sandstone were eroded by a fierce river that had since dried up and now reappeared only in times of heavy rain.

When they stopped beside a lone juniper on a reasonably level bit of ground, Caro gazed up at the scrap of blue sky that seemed to be caught on the sandstone precipice over a thousand feet above. Mike handed her a sandwich and a handful of pinyon nuts. They got out of the Jeep and ate leaning against it. A grasshopper, red like the soil underfoot, whirred out of a thicket of rabbitbrush, then whirred back into it.

''Come on,'' Mike said as soon as they had eaten. ''We'll walk in the dry gully down the middle of the canyon. It's sandy and will be easier walking.''

Caro followed him to the streambed, which was littered with large boulders broken off from the steep walls of the canyon.

The navigable part of the gully was so narrow that she had to walk behind Mike.

He looked over his shoulder once or twice. "How're you doing?" he wanted to know.

"Fine," Caro said.

She had borrowed a pair of sturdy hiking boots from Annie, and she was in good physical shape. She found the isolation of the canyon exhilarating. It was amazing how this distance from people made her feel free and unfettered, and there was a welcome reality to placing her feet one in front of the other, making progress toward a goal.

Suddenly she felt in control again, master of her environment. The attack had robbed her of the certainty of familiar surroundings. It had made her doubt everything, suspect everyone, because nothing was the way it had been before. This new place was pristine, unsullied by hapless circumstance.

Mike forged on ahead of her, swinging his shoulders slightly as he walked. His body was tight and fit, and he looked like a man in his element. The next time he glanced over his shoulder to make sure she was keeping up, she shot him a bright smile.

She wasn't sure how far they had walked when she found the piece of pottery.

Her foot bumped against what she thought was a curved gray rock, one side of it oddly corrugated. Curious, she bent to pick it up.

Mike noticed that she had stopped and hurried back to see what she'd found.

"What is it?" she asked.

He took it in his hands and ran a finger along the corrugated side. The other side was quite smooth.

"Anasazi pottery," he said. "Part of a small container from the looks of it."

When she was still in college, Caro had tried her hand at making pottery. She had been developing a feel for it when Marina, who was already head of her own modeling agency, met her at a student art show and suggested that Caro try a career as a model. Caro had always thought that she'd resume her art studies someday, if only as a hobby.

"The Antiquities Act of 1906 prohibits us from disturbing such artifacts, so I'm afraid you can't keep it as a souvenir,"

Mike told her as, clearly entranced, she turned the potsherd this way and that, studying its finely corrugated surface.

The fragment felt firm in Caro's hand; she thought of the joy its Anasazi creator must have felt when she formed this pot all those years ago. There was a certain fine contentment in making something useful, something that was also attractive to the eye.

It didn't matter that she couldn't keep it. She had already felt a closeness, a kind of communion with the pot's creator. Caro stooped and put the sherd back exactly where she had found it.

"It belongs here," she said. She gestured at the wild and rugged landscape. "To take it home and put it on a shelf inside a house someplace would seem—well, almost sacrilegious."

There was new respect in the way he looked at her. "I'm glad you feel that way," he said. "When I'm in a canyon like this one, I can almost feel the ancient ones—the Anasazi—walking alongside me, cautioning me not to disturb things too much."

Although this confidence surprised her, Caro understood.

They resumed their walk, and in a few minutes the dry riverbed widened until finally she was able to walk beside Mike.

"The gray color of that piece of pottery back there comes from a firing technique characteristic of this area," he told her. "First the pot was formed using a basic coil construction, and then it was smoothed and polished. After the pot dried, it was put in a kiln. It was fired in a reducing atmosphere, which is one in which the fuel uses up all the oxygen in the kiln and then takes oxygen from the minerals in the clay, turning it gray."

"What color was the clay originally?"

"It could have been red or yellow or ocher or brown or any mixture thereof, and it still would have turned gray from the firing. Annie could tell you more about it."

"I didn't think you'd know so much about pottery," she said.

"I have to know about it. Archaeologists learn about ancient peoples by the things they used in their daily lives, and, thank goodness, they used containers of all kinds." He laughed a little. "I often wonder what archaeologists are going to make of the millions of unbiodegradable Styrofoam hamburger containers they discover in their digs of our present civilization five hundred years from now," he said.

Caro smiled. "Archaeologists will probably uncover countless golden arches in towns all over the North American continent. Maybe they'll figure that the arches have some sort of ceremonial significance, and that the fragments of Styrofoam that they find in the vicinity are printed with mystic symbols," she said.

"Maybe," Mike said, but when he laughed again, she knew she had amused him.

After they had walked for another half hour or so, something made Caro glance upward, and there, huddled against the canyon wall between two ledges that seemed suspended from nowhere, was a small pueblo.

Mike followed her gaze. "That's a place where the Anasazi lived."

"I can't believe it's survived all these years," Caro commented, shading her eyes against the blue brilliance of the sky to look at the pueblo.

"It probably wouldn't have if this canyon weren't off the beaten track and if the dwelling itself weren't virtually inaccessible. We're going up there."

"How?" Caro asked, dumbfounded. The rock face below the small house was a sheer drop and offered no clues as to how anyone might climb it.

"Follow me," Mike said, striding up the canyon. At a notch in the cliff sheltered by fallen slabs of sandstone, a series of ledges provided hand- and footholds, leading away from the pueblo rather than toward it. The ingenuity of this approach was revealed when they came upon one ledge that sloped gradually downward until it rounded several natural rock formations and culminated in a cleverly engineered stairway cut into the rock. The stairway ended in a ladder leading directly onto the ledge where the pueblo was located. They paused to rest before tackling the stairs.

"What do you think of the scenery?" Mike asked, gesturing at the canyon below.

"Breathtaking," she said, her chest heaving after the strenuous climb.

"Literally," he said, laughing.

The wooden ladder leading up to the pueblo had obviously been made recently.

"Who put the ladder here?" Caro asked.

"I did," Mike said. "I come here sometimes. It's my favorite place to be alone."

They ascended the stairway and the ladder. Caro refused to look down into the canyon because she was sure that she'd be dizzy if she did.

"You can see that they constructed the approach so that their enemies couldn't mount a surprise attack," Mike told her when at last they stood inside the pueblo. "When the Anasazi family living here pulled up the ladder, they were isolated and unreachable."

Caro looked around her, marveling at the ingenuity with which the house was constructed of fitted sandstone blocks. Prodigious labor had evidently gone into the building of this dwelling. Some of the thatched roof remained, shored up by beams with carefully rounded edges.

"They sanded the ends of their roof beams with pieces of sandstone," Mike explained when he saw her studying them.

More juniper beams covered the rock floor, and the back wall was blackened by the smoke of ancient fires. Now that her eyes had adjusted to the dimness, she peered through the dust motes floating in the air and saw two modern Navajo blankets folded neatly in a corner.

"This has always seemed like a special place to me," Mike explained after he saw her looking at them. "When I'm struggling with a problem in my work, I come here. Sometimes I stay overnight, trying to think as the Anasazi thought. Lots of times I wake up in the morning and the answer is there, waiting for me to pluck it out of the air."

He seemed thoughtful, quiet, with an awareness as though all of life's experience registered on his emotions, and she realized that he had confided a bit of information that he probably didn't tell many other people. He was a loner, she'd known that, but she hadn't realized that the times when he was alone were productive times for him, perhaps even necessary to his work. Away from Annie and the kids, he was a different person. She had never suspected that.

"I wonder if you can actually think as the Anasazi thought unless you live as they lived," she mused, voicing her thoughts.

"I doubt it," Mike said. "I've tried it for several days at a time, but my underlying beliefs never match theirs, and that's the difference. For instance, I know that a full belly doesn't depend on some Great Spirit's sending enough rain to make the maize grow. In the end, I can always go back to the grocery store in Moab and buy enough to eat. I also know that hordes of invaders aren't going to sweep out of the plains and kill me. With the fear of starving and dying at the hands of savages removed, how can I ever know the existence of an Anasazi?''

"It puts my own life in perspective to see how they lived," Caro murmured, thinking of how streamlined modern life had become with its dishwashers, automobiles, electric toothbrushes, and other things now regarded as necessities.

"Yes, but I'm not sure their lives within their own framework were as difficult as we assume," Mike said, crossing the room to stand beside her. "Maybe we're the ones who have a hard life. They only worried about the essentials of survival. We concern ourselves with disagreements with the boss, whether we're toilet training the kids properly, and accumulating all the bright and glittering things that advertising convinces us we need."

Caro thought of the Naiad campaign and especially of her part in it. In her own case, she had not only convinced American women that they should buy the Naiad fragrance but that they should style their hair like the Naiad and wear their eye makeup like her, and Caro felt guilty about it because she didn't even like the Naiad scent.

Not that she had ever mentioned this fact to anyone. The Gaillardo Corporation would definitely take a dim view of a Naiad who confessed that she never wore their perfume. Even Marina didn't know that. But Caro's duplicity was something that she wasn't up to thinking about at the moment; it had to do with her life in New York and seemed like part of another world and time.

When they left the small pueblo, they followed the same series of ledges that they had used to reach it. At one particularly sharp switchback, Mike pushed aside the branches of a pinyon pine to reveal a small arch in the rock.

"Through here," he said, indicating that she should slip past the tree.

On the other side lay a hidden ravine, and above it spread a wide terrace bordered by boulders. The canyon wall here formed a flat panel and was virtually covered with pictographs and petroglyphs.

"You know the difference between pictographs and petroglyphs, don't you? Pictographs are painted to create an image on rock or some other surface, and petroglyphs are cut into the rock without use of pigment or coloring."

Caro nodded, taking it all in. *Surely this must be one of the finest displays of Anasazi rock art in the area,* she thought. She had seen many pictographs and petroglyphs, but never such a profusion of both. And the subject matter! It was diverse, to say the least.

There were outlines of human hands and feet; there were anthropomorphic figures, some crude and some more elaborate. Animals were represented—bison, fish, bears, snakes, and even a long-legged, long-necked bird that looked for all the world like an ostrich.

"An ostrich?" Caro murmured. "I didn't know ostriches were native to this area."

"They aren't," Mike said with a keen look. "And as far as I know, they never were."

Caro stared at the ostrich for several minutes, trying to figure out if perhaps the bird carved into the rock merely represented a flight of fancy on the part of the artist. Still, there was something undeniably realistic about it.

"How did the Anasazi know how to draw an ostrich? They would have had to have seen one, wouldn't they?" She was sure it was an ostrich. The artist had quite deliberately given it only two toes. Caro knew that ostriches were the only birds with two toes; it was probably the only thing she remembered from the social studies book other than reindeer on the tundra.

Mike only shrugged his shoulders, then wandered away a bit too deliberately to study a row of geometric patterns carved into the rock.

There were so many other things to look at that Caro filed the ostrich in the back of her mind to mull over later, and went to study a picture of a large cat with curling claws and a mouth wide open in a snarl.

"That's a cougar," Mike explained before they moved on.

"I wonder why Annie doesn't incorporate more figures like

these into her pottery," Caro said as she contemplated a group of archers chasing a bison.

"Annie's never been particularly interested in reproducing Anasazi art. She prefers modern things."

"I'd like to take pictures of this panel," Caro said suddenly.

"Pictures?"

"Sure. Maybe I can talk Annie into using some of these designs. They're great, really. Look at the emotion in this scene. Here are two adult figures, one more rounded than the other, therefore probably female. And there's a tiny figure being borne away by a great winged bird. It's reaching its arms out toward the adults, who could be the child's parents."

Mike studied the scene. He didn't know too many people who would immediately pick up on the human dynamics portrayed in that small scene, which was so tiny that it was almost obscured by the shape of a giant warrior sprawled nearby.

"If you want pictures, I can help you. I've spent years making my own record, and I have thousands of photos of Anasazi rock art. They're at my trailer."

"Do you have extra copies?"

"I can make copies of whatever you want, and I'll be glad to give them to you. I think they'll serve your purpose better than snapshots you'd take yourself, because getting the light exactly right when photographing rock art is tricky. Also, you have to use special darkroom techniques sometimes to make the figures stand out. You can't outline or enhance the rock art itself when you're taking the picture, because it's against the law."

Caro returned to the representation of the ostrich. "This is the one I can't help wondering about. Cougars and warriors and bison were part of the Anasazis' world. But an ostrich?"

Mike touched her arm. "We'd better be getting back. It's getting late."

It could have been her imagination, but Caro thought she saw him mask a flash of excitement in his eyes. As she followed him carefully down the intricate system of ledges and stairs to the canyon floor, she wondered why her speculation about the ostrich had lighted that brief spark in his eyes. Maybe he was just happy that she was so interested in the Anasazi art.

They walked along the gully until they reached the junction to a small side canyon. There Mike led her into a narrow chute

of rock no more than eight feet wide, scoured into the side of
the canyon by the river that had once flowed here. At the end
of the chute, greenery bloomed unexpectedly. Caro drew in her
breath. Like a jewel caught in the pale surrounding limestone,
a fern-fringed pool of water reflected the canyon walls.

Mike bent to refill his canteen, and she did, too. Their movements disturbed the tranquility of the pool, and they sat to watch
it resume its peace, Caro on a limestone slab, Mike sprawled at
her feet. Tiny columbines trailed from infinitesimal cracks in
the rock, their creamy rose-tinged flowers adding a bit of
whimsy to its hard face.

The sides of the canyon shaded them here, and a fresh breeze
trifled with Caro's hair. She turned her face so that the air would
cool it, closing her eyes and inhaling the scent of the water.
The silence lapped around them, waiting.

For a long time they didn't speak. A dried leaf twitched in
the wind, looking for all the world like a tiny playful animal.
And then Caro really did see an animal, an inquisitive lizard
that ran alongside her on the rock, dropped to the ground and
skittered away. It happened so fast that she didn't have time to
be startled.

She wished she could stay here forever, the wind on her face,
the pool at her feet, and a congenial companion with whom to
share what must be the most beautiful scenery on earth. She
wondered what Marina would think if she could see her now.

Marina, city person that she was, probably couldn't even
imagine a Caro who wore hiking boots, who found pleasure in
sitting motionless at the bottom of a canyon, and who had absolutely no desire to rise out of or swim across or dive into the
pool in front of her.

I hope the Naiad people never discover this place, Caro
thought. *They'd bring in camera crews and account executives
and makeup artists. And maybe me.*

"Why are you smiling?" Mike asked.

She hadn't realized that she was. "It was just a thought I
had," she said.

"You should smile more often," Mike said. "Your smile is
brilliant."

To have a man saying something that even remotely resembled flirting made her feel alive again. "I'll try to smile bril-

liantly as often as possible," she said—with just the right light touch, she thought to herself.

After that he didn't speak again, but she couldn't help uttering a small sigh of pleasure, one that he surely couldn't hear.

Finally he asked, "Do you want to rest a while longer?"

"It's so pleasant here that I don't want to leave. I'm not sure why I like it so much. The canyon walls should give me a hemmed-in feeling like I had in New York, but they don't seem like barriers. It's as if I look up at them and feel my mind expanding."

"The desert does that to people," Mike agreed.

"Explain it," she said.

"I can't. No one can. Few people understand the desert, and everyone admits that it's a demanding environment, but no one knows exactly what its appeal is. For me, it boils down to a challenge. There are secrets here to be unraveled."

"I'm not sure that's what it is for me. I think it's the—the nothingness that intrigues me. And the grand scale of everything, all created by nature. Nothing has been changed by man. Probably nothing ever will be." Her voice was low, almost expressionless.

With a look of regret, Mike glanced at his watch. "We'd better get going. It's late," he said.

Caro knelt beside the pool, intending to bathe her dusty face in the water. The pool was as still and as glassy as a mirror, and unexpectedly, like the brief flash of a strobe image, she caught a glimpse of her face in the moment before she dipped her hands into the water.

She had almost forgotten. Today her scar, the attack, all of it had been pushed to the back of her mind. Now, suddenly, it was all brought home to her again by something that used to be heartening rather than depressing—seeing her own reflection. Overwhelmed by the suddenness of it, she despaired of trying to learn to live with the way she looked now.

She pressed her wet hands to her face, letting the water drip, willing her heart to stop pounding.

"Caro," Mike said, and all at once she realized that he must have seen the look of horror that registered on her face when she saw her own reflection.

If only she could have acted normally! But she knelt frozen

in the same spot, covering her face, her ruined face, wondering how she could have forgotten about her scar for even a minute.

Then Mike was lifting her firmly by the shoulders and pulling her hands away from her face. And he was looking at her with an expression of utmost tenderness.

"It *does* bother you then," he said quietly, his hands still clasping hers. "You seemed so cool and calm about your scar that I thought you had come to terms with it."

She said nothing, only gulped deep gasping breaths, ashamed of herself for showing so much emotion.

"Do you want to sit down?" he said in concern.

Mutely she nodded. He led her to the limestone rock the way he might have led Peter or Franklin or Holly. He sat down beside her and slid an arm around her shoulders.

"If you'd like to talk about it," he began.

"No," Caro whispered.

He was silent for a while. "Does it have something to do with the reason you don't want to go back to New York?"

Caro nodded.

"I see," he said, although she knew he didn't. He pulled the bandanna from his back pocket and dried off her hands and arms. Then, gently and tenderly, he blotted at her face. She winced when he touched the scar.

"Does that hurt?" he asked anxiously.

"No," she murmured. She thought, *If he tells me I'm beautiful, I'll know he lies.* He said nothing of the kind. Instead he kept his arm around her and finally asked, "Are you ready to go?"

"Yes," she said. "I shouldn't have—"

"Shh," he said. "You don't need to apologize." He stood and pulled her up beside him. It was, he thought, extremely difficult to maintain his customary emotional distance from someone who was so very vulnerable.

She bit her lip. "Thanks," she said. She was beginning to feel better. She couldn't help the desolation she still felt at the sight of her maimed face, but at least he didn't tell her that she had no right to feel that way, as Wayne had once, nor did he pretend that her scar didn't exist, the way Marina was wont to do.

He released her hand, and Caro was surprised to find herself wishing that he hadn't. He didn't walk ahead of her but stayed close to her side. They left the cool oasis beside the pool and resumed their walk along the dry streambed. Once or twice he took her hand to help her over a rough spot, and when they had to walk in single file, he glanced back frequently and anxiously to make sure that she was keeping up.

Shadows were beginning to cast eerie shapes across the desert as Mike's Jeep climbed out of the canyon. They accomplished the drive back across the desert mostly in silence, working as a team to open the several gates and drive the Jeep through, closing them once they had passed.

At a fork in the trail where Mike should have turned toward the highway to Moab, he took the other route instead. Caro turned to him with questioning eyes.

"You don't mind, do you?" he said, looking down at her anxiously. "I'd like to stop at my trailer before I take you home."

She didn't mind. She was coming to understand that the day they had spent together was special. In Tanglewood Canyon they had shared a secret, silent world and a rare confidence that had drawn them closer together. She was aware that something warm and solid had been built between them.

There were a lot of uncertainties in Caro's life right now, but Mike had a knack of shining light into all the dark corners. In the back of her mind a kind of surprise was growing, and along with it she felt a certainty that Mike Herrick was beginning to be important to her.

He must have noticed that something had changed in her, because he slowed the Jeep and half turned toward her.

"Is anything wrong?" he asked. The glow of the dash lights illuminated his face; his eyes were bright with concern.

"No," Caro said, taking in the dark brows, the aquiline nose, the wide mouth. She was intensely aware of him physically. Not attracted, just aware, the way she had become aware of his thoughts back in the Anasazi pueblo.

"No, nothing is wrong," she said, and sat back in the seat to wonder if she could actually be falling for someone she probably wouldn't have given a second glance a few short months ago.

Chapter Five

Caro was curious about the trailer in the desert where Mike Herrick lived. The children's descriptions had colored the place with more than a little mystique.

"The water tastes awful there," Holly had said, making a face.

"Lizards mate on his doorstep," Franklin told her solemnly.

"A snake lives under his *bed*," Peter insisted, although Caro had questioned this.

"It really does, Caro. Right under his bed. And not in a box or *anything*."

Peter's words came easily to mind when Mike stopped the Jeep in front of a nondescript house trailer. Though it was almost dark, she could see that the front yard, if you could call it that, was infested with cactus plants.

"This is home. I call it the Tin Can," Mike said as he switched on the light inside, and Caro was pleased to see that he had fixed the place up as though he enjoyed living there.

The walls were hung with rugs in bright colors, and the furniture was of oak and leather. If it hadn't been for the low ceiling, she might have forgotten that it was a trailer at all. Caro was much relieved that there wasn't a snake in sight.

"I want to find some photos of Anasazi rock art for you to take home with you," Mike said, opening a closet and burrowing around until he found a box. He set it on the table and motioned for her to sit down. "I'm starved. Would you care for something to eat? I make a terrific meatball sandwich."

"If you're going to have one, I will too," Caro said.

"It'll take me a minute," he said. He started to putter around the kitchen.

Caro flipped through photograph after photograph of Anasazi rock art. When she exclaimed at the variety, Mike grinned.

"I've taken pictures of every scrap of Anasazi graffiti I've ever laid eyes on," he told her.

"You've been collecting these photos for how many years?" she asked.

Mike considered. "Maybe twenty, ever since I was about twelve and got my first camera." He inserted the meatballs into heated rolls and brought the sandwiches to the table. When he popped open a beer for himself, he offered Caro one, but she asked for a glass of iced tea instead.

"Aren't you hungry?" he asked, and Caro realized that she was looking at the pictures more than she was eating.

"Yes, but the art is so interesting," she said.

"Why is it?" he asked suddenly and abruptly.

The question was unexpected, and Caro sat back and stared at him, trying to frame her answer. She wanted to sound intelligent, as though she thought about things before she said them.

"Well?" he said, and she understood that in some way this was a challenge.

"I suppose it's the connection," she said, struggling to explain. "It's knowing that the Anasazi were real people living actual lives, and they had something to communicate. Now they're gone, but their communication—their scribbling on the rocks—is still there, and it's like a bridge from them to us. Am I expressing myself well?"

"Quite well," he said reassuringly.

"You must feel that link between the Anasazi and modern-day man," she said.

"That's why I'm studying them. But there's more to it than that. There's the promise of discovery, of knowing exactly who they were and what the Anasazi did and why they did it. And where they went when they disappeared so suddenly around the year 1300 A.D. That's puzzled archaeologists for years."

"Where do you suppose the Anasazi went, Mike?" she asked with interest.

"I think I know where some of them went," he said with a twinkle. "But I'm not telling."

"You sound like Peter, when Franklin wanted to know where Holly hid a package of Reese's Pieces the other day."

Mike smiled. "The difference is," he said, "that what I'm hypothesizing could change everyone's perception of American history."

She stared at him, unwilling to believe what she'd heard him say. "I can't imagine what you mean," she said slowly.

"What I mean is," he began, but then, his eyes searching her face, he stopped. He was clearly reluctant to take her into his confidence.

"Go on," she murmured, realizing that he was serious.

"I haven't talked about this to anyone around here," he said.

"If you don't want me to speak of it, I won't," she reassured him, her interest peaking.

Caro had shown more enthusiasm about Anasazi culture and art than any of Mike's family or friends. She was leaning forward in her chair, lips slightly parted and looking as though she would relish any new information about the Anasazi that he cared to impart.

Mike looked off into space for a moment, weighing the pros and cons of discussing his theories with her. At best, he would win a willing ear for his views. At worst, she would laugh.

Knowing Caro, he doubted that she would treat his information lightly. Even if she didn't believe him, she would only study him with her wide brown eyes, and then would press him to explain, trying to understand why he thought as he did.

"I'm pretty sure," he said slowly, watching her expression, "that the idea that America was unknown two thousand years ago is false."

Caro pressed her lips together and held her head slightly to one side. Her eyes darkened—in thought?

She seemed to be waiting for him to continue, but he took a deep breath before he spoke again. "There are signs that permanent colonies of Celts, Basques, Libyans and Egyptians existed on this continent as early as 500 B.C.," he said.

"Oh, Mike," Caro said. "What signs?"

Was she thinking that she might have been wrong to take him seriously? he wondered.

"Ancient writings in the rock. Like the petroglyphs we saw at Tanglewood Canyon today."

"You think they were created by—by Celts?"

"Not Celts."

"Who then? Basques? And who else did you say?"

"It's the Libyans I'm betting on, at least in this part of Utah."

"You really aren't joking, are you?" she said, plainly bewildered.

"I'm as serious as I can be. In fact, I'm driven to find the final proof."

"Which is?"

"A site in this part of Utah. It will provide new evidence, and I'll publish a scientific paper that I'm writing on the subject so that American history books will have to be revised. Goodbye, Columbus!" For the first time during this conversation, his expression relaxed into a smile.

"What makes you think you'll find this site?" Caro asked.

"I was told about it by Charlie Deer Walk, an old Navajo sheepherder who wandered some of the most remote areas. Charlie's the one who introduced me to rock hunting when I was a kid. Some of my happiest hours were spent exploring canyons and old ruins with him. Anyway, I became an archaeologist precisely because Charlie interested me in the profession, and then when I came back here we became close friends again. Charlie discovered an unexplored canyon, but he died before he could tell me exactly where the place was."

"How will you find it?"

"Charlie left me a map. Not a very good one, and all it showed was the canyon itself, not the canyon in relation to the surrounding area. He called it Yalabasi Canyon, saying that he had heard about it in legend and myth, but I couldn't tell from the map where the canyon was. Now I think I know."

"Where?"

"It must be located on a privately owned piece of land; the land was bought for uranium mining by a foreign company, the El Karak Mining Company, which presently has no use for it. For years the El Karak tract was closed to everyone. I've recently applied for permission to explore the land. It's going to be the experience of a lifetime, especially if I find what I expect."

"Mike, I'd like to believe your Libyan theory," Caro said.

Her head was spinning with all this farfetched information. She shrugged. "But I don't know. It all sounds so far out."

"It might help if you knew that in the ancient world, Libya was the Greek name for all of northern Africa, excluding Egypt."

"Mike, how in the world would Africans travel to the North American continent in 500 B.C.?"

"They were a seafaring nation, highly developed like the Greeks. In fact, the pharaohs of Egypt employed Libyan seamen for their ability to navigate the oceans."

"*What* oceans?"

"The Atlantic, the Indian and the Pacific," he said.

Caro groaned. "I think I need to look at a map," she said.

Mike pushed aside their half-eaten sandwiches and went to a desk, from which he removed a world map. He spread it out on the table.

"They started from here," he said, tracing a line on the north coast of Africa. "Libyan influence began to spread when Libyan chiefs seized Egypt and established Libyan dynasties. We know that under Libyan leadership, the Egyptians mined gold in faraway Sumatra, here in the Indo-Pacific region." He pointed to a large Indonesian island across the Indian Ocean from North Africa.

Caro nodded intently.

"After Alexander the Great conquered Egypt, Libyan seamen settled in the Pacific. This explains the early rock inscriptions in Polynesia that consist of Libyan language and alphabet with a little bit of Greek thrown in for good measure."

"Greek?"

"The Greek and Libyan cultures intermingled. For instance, it's known that there were Greek colonies in Libya," Mike said.

"This still doesn't explain how Libyans got to Utah," Caro said impatiently.

"Libyan writings have been found on the North American continent in places as disparate as Quebec, California, and along the Arkansas and Cimarron Rivers," Mike said, and he went on to explain that he had studied the language of Zuni Indians in New Mexico.

"Even though their language shows influences of the Aztecs and Mayans and Algonquian tribes, the Zunis' main vocabulary is North African. I believe that some of the Zunis' ancestors were most likely visitors from Libya who may have landed on the coast of California," he went on.

"And from there you leap to the conclusion that the Libyans traveled inland as far as Utah?" Caro was incredulous.

"I've found local inscriptions that resemble the Libyan writing system and are made up of the Libyan alphabet. There are pictures of elephants that we once thought were depictions of mastodons, but they've been dated to the third century before Christ. Mastodons were extinct on the North American continent by 6000 B.C., but a Libyan from the African continent no doubt would have been familiar with them. And by the way, don't forget that petroglyph of the ostrich that you saw today." He leaned back in his chair and let a tiny smile play across his face.

"The ostrich!" Caro exclaimed, half to herself. "It's an African bird, isn't it?"

"Its closest relative in this hemisphere is the South American rhea, and the rhea has three toes. You see?"

Caro stared at him long and hard. "It makes some sense, I suppose," she conceded.

"Trading was important to Libyans. So was exploration. A little bit of both brought them here."

"So the Libyans traded with the Anasazi, do you think?"

"Right. And intermarried, possibly. Certainly the Libyans passed along cultural elements. I've often thought that the motifs on certain kinds of pottery excavated in New Mexico are derived from figures in the Libyan alphabet."

Caro expressed surprise at this, but she let Mike go on talking.

"One thing is important—the Anasazi were never a nation or a real tribe or language group," he said. "The Anasazi were communities of people who grew crops the same way, built their houses the same way, and were united in their means of worship. They certainly traded among themselves as well as with others and traveled between their communities on well-engineered roads. But they never called themselves Anasazi. That name was given to them by Navajo and Apache interlopers who began to settle their land after the Anasazi were already gone."

"Why would they bother to name them if they weren't even here?" Caro asked skeptically.

"The newcomers saw evidence of the old civilization in the ruins and called the departed people 'Anasazi,' meaning 'alien ancient ones.' The present-day Navajo are the descendants of the invaders, and the Hopi Indians are descended from the Anasazi. Perhaps not surprisingly, the two tribes still have a strained relationship today."

"I thought the Anasazi disappeared around the year 1300," Caro said. "If that's the case, how can the Hopi be their descendants?"

"We know that there was a succession of droughts after 1150 A.D. The Anasazi abandoned their elaborate pueblo villages to go where conditions were more favorable. When their efforts to appease the gods failed, some moved south where the mountains were green. Some died. Some climbed the mesas to the north to join their relatives. These people were the ancestors of today's Hopis. And others—well, there were others," he said, trying to read Caro's expression.

"And the others—what happened to them?"

"They may have gone farther west than we've ever imagined," he said, still watching her. "They may have gone back to Africa with the traders who came here every year."

"There's no proof," she said.

"Don't be so sure. By piecing together the evidence written in the rocks, I'm slowly reconstructing the scenario of what happened to make the Anasazi disappear around 1300 A.D. The epigraphs I've found in the desert gave me fragments of the idea that the Libyan-Anasazi connection was a strong one, and that they had the knowledge to emigrate when they became desperate to survive."

"This is almost more than I can absorb," Caro said with a sigh.

"That's understandable. After a lifetime of believing that Christopher Columbus was the first one to reach America, it's hard to change your mind-set to encompass the idea that the New World was actually discovered two thousand years earlier than the history books tell us. And if you have a difficult time, imagine what professionals in my field think about it." He laughed.

"What *do* they say?"

"A lot of them prefer to ignore my work. Some are interested. Some are out-and-out derisive. I try not to pay any attention to my detractors. I wouldn't be devoting my life's work to this if I didn't believe in it with all my heart."

With that, Mike stretched, stood and pushed in his chair. "End of history lesson for tonight. It's late, and I'd better get you back to Annie's."

"I'd love to hear more, Mike."

"Oh, you will," he said, smiling.

"We only picked out a few pictures," Caro said, fingering the short stack of photos she meant to take to Annie.

"If you like, I'll go through this box tonight and bring you the ones I think will be most adaptable to Annie's pottery," Mike said.

He went into the bedroom for a minute. "The desert tends to be chilly at night," he said when he reappeared, and he settled his denim jacket over her shoulders.

Together they picked their way between the cactus plants in the front yard to the Jeep, and Mike cranked the engine to life. Caro's head still swam with the information imparted so matter-of-factly by Mike; it seemed so fantastic that Libyans could have been here, in Utah, thousands of years ago. And yet Mike, who was much more learned than she, seemed alight with the fire of conviction. If he believed so wholeheartedly, could she do less?

The ride home was longer than Caro had thought it would be, and she found as she watched the dotted white line on the highway disappear beneath them that she could barely keep her eyes open. Once her head started to droop, and she could feel herself falling asleep; quickly she jerked to attention. Mike noticed and glanced over at her, smiling slightly, and then he slid his arm around her shoulders and pulled her close. Her head rested on his shoulder until he parked the Jeep in front of Annie's house.

"Do you want to come in?" she whispered at the front door.

Mike shook his head. The house was quiet and dark. "I don't want to wake anyone," he said. "Sleep well, Caro."

"Thank you for today," she murmured. "It was wonderful." She smiled up at him and his own smile widened in response.

He squeezed her arm. "I'll bring the pictures tomorrow," he said.

Caro stood inside the door and watched as the Jeep disappeared down the street, then she turned and tripped painfully over a large metal dump truck that belonged to Peter. She stiffened at the noise, hoping that no one had awakened. When nobody stirred, she made her way to her bedroom and shut the door as quietly as she could.

It was then that she realized that she hadn't returned Mike's jacket. She tossed it onto the bed, rushed through a shower, slipped into her most comfortable nightgown and fell into bed.

After a few minutes of lying there, she realized that Mike's jean jacket was crumpled beneath her, and she pulled it out, meaning to set it to one side of the bed until morning. It smelled faintly but intriguingly of Mike's pungent after-shave, and she rubbed her cheek against it momentarily as she thought about those few minutes beside the pool in the canyon, when Mike had been so kind and tender after she nearly went to pieces.

He was a nice man, Mike Herrick, and he genuinely liked her. There was something to be said for not being beautiful, she supposed. She no longer had to worry about men being so bowled over by her beauty that they never bothered to explore what kind of person she was. Any man who took the trouble to spend time with her must see something besides a fabulous body and a pretty face; though her body was much the same as it had always been, her face could no longer be classified as pretty.

She didn't shove Mike's jacket to the other side of the bed, after all. Instead she folded it beneath her head and slept with her cheek cradled against the smooth, well-weathered denim.

The nightmare didn't overtake her until slightly before dawn. It started innocently, the way all her nightmares since the attack had started. She was standing in front of a motel on her first day in Moab, talking to the friendly truck driver who had given her a ride. He was as garrulous in her dream as he had been in real life, and she suspected nothing sinister about him.

He turned away for a moment, and she thought it was to lift her suitcase out of the truck. When he turned back toward her, she was horrified to see the strange lightless eyes, the thin lips and the prominent jaw of the man who had attacked her in

Central Park. She screamed, jolting bolt upright amid sweat-soaked sheets.

She must not have screamed out loud, because no one else in the house woke up. She sat clutching Mike's denim jacket, her heart racing, afraid to close her eyes again to try to go back to sleep.

Last night she had forgotten to pull the shade down, and soon the first rays of the sun slipped through the lace curtains, dotting the wall on the far side of the room. She lay back with her arm protecting her eyes from the too-bright light and despaired of ever being able to escape the nightmares. Worst of all was the form they took—the attacker always changed from someone known to her into the man in the park. It was a terrifying dream, reflecting her fear that anyone, anyone at all could be the man whose razor had ruined her face.

She managed to fall asleep for another twenty minutes or so, then Franklin, Peter and Holly presented themselves at her bedroom door in their pajamas, clamoring to know if she wanted pancakes or ZooRoni for breakfast.

"YOU MEAN you didn't even see the snake?" asked Peter.

"No, Peter, I didn't. Would you like another glass of milk?"

Peter sighed. "No thanks. And the snake is the best part of the trailer where Mike lives. You didn't even ask him about it!"

"We talked about other things," she said, picking up Peter's plate and dumping his uneaten sandwich crusts into the garbage.

"Like what?"

"Like—" Caro wasn't supposed to talk about the Libyan presence in Utah, so she tried to think of something else to tell Peter. Fortunately Annie chose that moment to swoop into the kitchen.

"Peter, let's go brush your teeth before we go to the dentist," she said. "Thanks for fixing the kids' lunch again, Caro. How can I ever thank you?"

Caro waved Annie away. "Just let me stay here a while longer," she said.

"Done! I couldn't manage if you—oh no, Peter's going to

get his cast wet again!'' and Annie hurried after her small son, who was running water into the bathroom sink.

Caro hummed as she put away the peanut butter and jelly.

"Bye, Caro!" Peter and Annie called as they rushed out the front door, and then all she could hear was the giggling of Holly and her friend as they picnicked beside the redbud tree in the backyard.

"Anybody home?"

Caro wheeled and saw Mike smiling at her through the back door screen.

"Mike, come in," she said, hurrying to open the door for him. His arms were piled high with boxes.

"I brought those pictures. In this box are photos of animals, and in this one, pictures of people and—" He stopped talking, and they looked at each other without speaking for a few moments. His eyes held her mesmerized until she broke the contact.

"Where's Annie?" he said, his voice shattering the stillness.

"She—she took Peter to the dentist," Caro said.

"Did she say anything about my keeping you out so late last night?"

"She was asleep when I got home. I don't think she knows."

"That's good. What I don't need is the meddling of my family in my life. I've seen enough of that with Annie and Tom."

"Oh, I hardly think that Annie—"

"Maybe not. But if she gets wind of the fact that you and I are staying out together late at night, she's liable to start matchmaking." The words sounded casual, but Caro could see that he was watching her. She looked down in confusion.

"Caro," he said, moving toward her, but she was momentarily distracted by a peal of laughter from outside near the redbud tree. Mike cast a brief glance out the window. "Kids," he said wryly. "Peter and Holly are accounted for. Where's Franklin?"

"He—he's at his teacher's house for his LD therapy," Caro said. "Did you want to see him?"

Mike laughed softly, and his eyes were bright.

"No, Caro. It's you I want to see," he said.

His meaning and intent were unmistakable. Caro looked

around wildly, backing up, but Mike captured her shoulders and held her while he looked at her.

"I've thought about you all night," he said. "I couldn't sleep for thinking of you."

Caro's heart began to beat harder. She thought that surely he could hear it.

"I've spent time with you here with Annie and the children, and I've grown to think of you as part of this household. In the last few weeks, I've found myself thinking about you more and more, and that's unusual. Sometimes I try to concentrate on my work and I can't." A note of bewilderment crept into his voice.

"Mike, don't," Caro whispered.

He paid no attention. "Yesterday when I took you to Tanglewood Canyon I tried to fool myself into thinking that I was merely taking you on a sightseeing trip, much as I would any other tourist that Annie befriended. When I got home, when I was lying there in my bed in the dark, I realized that it was more, much more than that."

He tipped a finger beneath her chin and she closed her eyes. It seemed excessively hot in the tiny kitchen, so hot that Caro found herself unable to breathe. When she opened her eyes again, they focused on a tiny pulse beating at Mike's right temple.

She remained very, very still, aware that her world was changing. She knew that if she moved, she chanced realigning her life from its previous pattern. It flashed through her mind that perhaps she had never seen all of the design; part of it had remained unrevealed to her. Was she now about to see it in its entirety? Then Mike's face was drifting inescapably toward hers, something leaped in his eyes like a small dark flame, their mouths met—and she found herself clinging to him as his arms went around her all at once.

Naturally that was when the phone rang.

Chapter Six

"Let it ring," Mike said against her lips.

She wrested herself away. "I can't," she said shakily. "It might be an order for Annie's pottery."

"It might not. It might be Gert or Nola or Lou or—" He went on naming cousins and aunts and sisters.

Caro whirled and headed for the telephone, her pulse pounding in her ears. She already felt guilty about kissing him. She shouldn't lead him on; she wasn't interested in a sexual dalliance to brighten up her brief stay in Utah. She had enough problems to work out, without taking on another one.

"Hello?" she said into the receiver. She didn't sound at all like herself.

"Annie?"

"No, this is Caro, Annie's houseguest," she said. The caller had a deep, unfamiliar male voice.

"Houseguest? Oh, one of the bed-and-breakfast people," he said, sounding impatient.

"Yes, Annie's out. May I help you?"

She heard nothing but silence on the other end. "I need to talk to Annie," he said at last. "This is her husband, Tom."

"Are you in town?"

"No, I'm calling from Salt Lake City. Look, Caro, will you please ask Annie to return my call?"

Caro was aware of Mike standing in the doorway. His lanky form outlined against the light from the kitchen window disturbed her with what she now realized was its effortless air of sexuality. How had she not noticed it before?

"I'll be glad to have her call you," Caro said. She wrote down the number Tom reeled off, the phone jammed between her shoulder and chin, trying to make it clear that she was ignoring Mike but failing abysmally to get this point across.

After she hung up, Mike inquired, "That was Tom?"

Caro nodded. "He's never called before," she said.

Mike sighed. "Annie hasn't heard from him in a while. I wonder what he wants."

"He didn't say," Caro said.

They heard the clatter of shoes on the back porch, and Mike ran his fingers through his hair.

"It sounds like the troops are back," he said. "Is there any chance that I could see you alone tonight? And stop turning away from me like that, please."

"I don't know, Mike," she said helplessly. "As for what happened a few minutes ago, there's no point in going on with it."

He moved closer in the narrow hallway. They were both conscious of Holly and her friend in the kitchen.

She inhaled deeply and went on. "I'll be leaving Moab soon, and I don't see any reason to start something that we can't finish. You've been a good friend to me, you and Annie, and I'm grateful for that. I'll be going back to New York, you know."

"When?" Mike asked under his breath.

"What?" She shot him a startled look. She had expected him to buy her excuses; maybe he hadn't.

"I said, when are you planning to go back?"

"In a few days," she said, pulling the words out of thin air.

"Oh? Is that why I overheard you on the phone talking to someone named Marina and telling her that you had no intention of returning to New York anytime in the near future? Is that why I've heard variations of that same conversation every time Marina calls?"

"You shouldn't have eavesdropped," Caro said with false dignity.

"The walls in this house are thin," he said. "And Marina has a loud voice."

"I might not go back to New York. I might—I might go somewhere and take an art course. I used to be an art major in college, did you know that? I was a promising young artist, everyone said so.'' Aware that she was beginning to babble, she slid past him into the living room and pushed aside a toy parking garage so that she could sit down on the couch.

He loomed above her, then leaned over her with one hand on the couch arm and one on its back, effectively imprisoning her.

''You could study art right here with Annie,'' he said quietly. ''With your interest in Anasazi rock art, why don't you try to recreate some of their designs on her pottery? It would help Annie with her business and give you an artistic outlet. *If* that's what you're really looking for.'' The look in his eyes flattened her already thin resistance, and abruptly he straightened and pulled an armchair closer to the couch. He sat down and leaned forward, resting his elbows on his knees, then waited for her to say something.

Caro pressed a hand to her mouth and stared out the window. ''I never thought of that,'' she said.

''There may be a lot of things you haven't thought of,'' he said.

She didn't reply to this, only clasped her hands in her lap. Part of her took in the way he sat in the chair so vigilantly. He seemed tightly coiled and alert, as though he were waiting for her to make a move. Another part of her wandered away in thought, wondering how Annie would feel if Caro suggested applying designs from Anasazi rock art to her pottery.

Then suddenly Mike stood up. She had to lift her head to look at him now, and inside she felt knotted up with a peculiar excitement.

''Don't forget your jacket,'' she had the presence of mind to say. ''It's on the back of a kitchen chair.''

He didn't reply to that. ''I'll be back tonight when you're alone,'' he said quietly, then he was gone.

Caro let her head fall back, so that all she saw was the ceiling as she heard him start up his Jeep and drive away. She felt like crying, but overlying that emotion was a ridiculous impulse to laugh.

Didn't Mike know that in this busy household it was almost impossible to be alone?

MIKE ROCKETED his Jeep toward his and Annie's cousin Gert's house. When he arrived, Gert, who lived by herself, was picking beans in her small garden behind the house.

"Mike!" she exclaimed when she saw him.

"Hi, Gert," he said. "Those beans look fat and sassy."

"They are. I'm going to get a couple of bushels of them in my freezer tonight, if it's the last thing I do."

"Gertie, Gertie, you really should have some help," he said.

"I know it. Want to come over and lend a hand? I'll be getting started right after supper."

"I can't, Gert. But maybe Annie could."

"I don't know, Mike. Annie's so busy these days."

"I wasn't asking so much for your sake as Annie's. Tom called today, and I have a feeling that Annie's going to need a strong shoulder tonight. You've got one of the strongest I know."

Gert stood and brushed dirt off her plump knees. "That's true, and perhaps you're right. Maybe I'll bribe Annie and the kids to come over and help me this evening. Do you think I should offer submarine sandwiches or fried chicken from the new take-out place?"

"Submarines, definitely," Mike said.

"That Holly, she's getting to be a big help around a kitchen. Franklin, too. It's a shame that Peter can't string beans with that broken arm of his. I guess we'll just have to let him play with the new puppy."

"This is just what Annie's going to need to get her mind off her troubles," Mike said with a wink.

"Thanks for letting me know she needed help," Gert called after him.

"Don't mention it," Mike said triumphantly, and figured on stopping over at Annie's house tonight around seven, when Annie and her children would be up to their elbows in beans at Gert's house.

ANNIE APPEARED in Caro's room with red and swollen eyes after she called Tom that evening. Caro was helping Franklin write a letter to his father, patiently pointing out his reversed

N's and *S*'s, but Franklin sensed a crisis and offered to come back later.

Annie sat on the edge of the bed and told Caro that Tom wanted her to come to Salt Lake City and bring the children for a visit.

"Are you going?" Caro asked.

Annie shook her head. "I have too many pottery orders right now to take even a few days off. Tom doesn't understand that if we don't reconcile, my pottery business is all I have to support myself. He thinks I should be able to drop everything at his whim."

"You want to get back together, though, don't you?"

"Yes," Annie said. "I love him. I think he loves me, too. He hates it that my aunts and sisters and cousins take up so much of the time that he says should be spent with him. That's what we always fought about. He never understood how important my family is to me."

"Your family does seem to come over a lot," Caro observed.

"It wasn't like that so much when Tom lived here. Oh, every once in a while there'd be a family emergency, and Tom could never understand how important it was for me to go to Diane when her baby was in the hospital, or run over to water Gert's plants when she was out of town. He always said we'd get along a lot better if I could get away from my family."

Annie sighed unhappily, then brightened. "Speaking of Gert, she invited the kids and me over to her house for submarine sandwiches tonight. Afterward I'm going to help her freeze beans from her garden."

"Don't worry about me," Caro hastened to say. "I'll forage around on my own and find some dinner."

Annie hugged her impulsively. "Caro, you're so good to have around," she said, then went away to change clothes and to round up the children for the trip to Gert's.

I'll be alone tonight, after all, was Caro's sudden thought, and she quickly decided to go for a walk after the Stendahls left. That way, if Mike stopped by the house as he so frequently did in the evening, she wouldn't be there.

CARO BORROWED Franklin's Walkman and settled the earphones over her ears as she started out on her walk at twilight.

She had eaten a bowl of soup with crackers, which was all she wanted. Thinking over the events of the day, she wasn't hungry.

She and Mike had moved past a companionship that had been beginning to feel comfortable and were involved in what was most certainly a strong sexual attraction. He was, she realized belatedly, one of the handsomest men she had ever met. The reason she hadn't realized it earlier was that the men in her life before this had never appeared in chambray shirts and worn blue jeans with bandannas hanging out of their pockets. She had to admit, however, that Mike did not belong in a business suit. A suit wouldn't do much to complement his dark rugged good looks.

With a conscious exertion of will, she tried to erase the memory of his kiss. It was impossible. She felt a nagging restlessness that wouldn't go away and found herself imagining the next kiss and the next, which was ridiculous, because she had firmly fixed the idea in her mind that there weren't going to be any more.

She walked past neat houses and yards containing plastic swimming pools, lost in her thoughts. She wasn't at all prepared to have someone walk up behind her and remove the Walkman's earphones from her ears.

For one sudden heart-stopping moment she was terrified. An unexpected touch from anyone would have done that to her; her legs started to collapse, and when she saw that it was only Mike, she grabbed him for support.

"I didn't mean to frighten you," Mike said, surprised and shaken at the way Caro had reacted. Her face was deathly pale.

"I'm all right," she stammered, recovering rapidly. "What do you want?" She pulled away from him and edged over to the far side of the sidewalk.

He couldn't imagine what had scared her so. "I said I'd see you when you were alone. I'm a man of my word," he said, folding the earphones and shoving them down into his breast pocket. He was relieved to see that Caro was beginning to regain her color.

"Maybe you'd better turn off that Walkman," he pointed out gently. "You'll run down the batteries if you don't."

Caro punched the proper button and, after a slight hesitation, resumed walking. Her scar itched furiously, which was supposed to be a sign of healing. Mostly it seemed to be a sign of emotional upset.

"I didn't think you'd find me," she said shakily.

"You've underestimated my persistence. We need to talk."

"I don't know about that." Resolutely she turned her face away.

"Is it a husband?" he asked quietly, so quietly that she almost didn't hear him.

"*What?*"

"A husband. If you're married, I'd like to know." He stared down at her with grim determination.

For some reason the idea tickled her sense of humor. She, Caro, with a husband? She had no family whatsoever, her closest friend was thousands of miles away and didn't even know where she was. And Mike thought she had a husband! She couldn't help laughing.

"I'm glad I've managed to amuse you, but I wish you'd explain why that's funny. A lot of men would want to be married to you."

She sobered quickly. "With *my* face? Don't be so sure of that." She spoke sharply and kept her eyes lowered.

He stopped walking. "Your face is beautiful," he said fiercely. "Don't ever let anyone tell you it isn't."

They started to walk again, but Caro was stunned by Mike's vehemence. She was humbled by it, too. If he could accept her scar, why couldn't she?

"You never answered my question. Are you married or aren't you?"

"I'm not married. I never have been," she said evenly, and she felt him relax his grip on her arm.

"That, at least, is good news. I thought that maybe you were running from someone."

"No. Only myself," she said, then realized what she was saying. She felt her face reddening and was struck with the strange truth of this. All this time she had thought she was fleeing the city and someone who could try to harm her again, but in reality that wasn't the truth at all. She herself was the enemy.

Mike's Jeep was parked at the curb in front of Annie's house. They had walked a full circle around several city blocks.

"Come for a ride with me," Mike said impulsively. "There's going to be a full moon tonight, and I'll bet you've never seen the desert by moonlight."

"Mike, I can't," she said, attempting to turn up the path to Annie's house.

"Why can't you?" he demanded, holding fast to her arm. She felt the full impact of his determination. She had woven her own fabric of resolution, however, and it disturbed her to see that little rips and tears were beginning to appear in it. A rip here, a tear there, and all at once seeing the moon shining on the mesas seemed to be the most important thing in the world.

Apparently sensing the disintegration of her resolve, Mike propelled her gently toward the Jeep, and she felt herself climbing into it. Mike got in beside her, and finally they were heading out of Moab. She saw, as if in a dream, that the moon was rising above the clouds that were scudding swiftly along the horizon.

Soon they were on a gravel road leading somewhere into the back of beyond; Caro didn't know where the road went and, to her surprise, she found that she didn't care.

Her thin dress felt inadequate against the desert's chill. "I should have brought a sweater," she said faintly.

"Here," Mike said, pulling the now-familiar denim jacket out of the space behind her seat and helping her to arrange it around her shoulders.

They headed in a different direction from the one they had gone yesterday to Tanglewood Canyon. Once Mike looked over at her and smiled reassuringly. He slid his hand over hers and squeezed it.

The Jeep started up an incline, and Caro realized that they had entered a landscape of surreal beauty. Ahead, a wide mesa gleamed in the moonlight, and the desert fell away as the road climbed higher.

"That's Sheriff's Mesa," Mike told her. "We're going around to the other side of it. There's something special I'd like you to see."

The rock formations here began to assume weird shapes.

"They call that one the Sphinx," he told her, pointing at one rock that strongly resembled the Egyptian monument. "That's the Devil's Nose," he said, nodding at one that featured a prominent sandstone nodule not yet worn away by wind and weather.

On the other side of the mesa, Mike urged the Jeep to the end of a sharp promontory and cut the engine. The vast silence of the desert night crowded in on them, and Caro shifted uncomfortably, drawing the jacket more tightly around her shoulders.

Then she saw it, straight ahead and shining extraordinarily brightly in the moonlight. The rock rose delicately from the desert floor into a great swooping arch, higher and narrower and more exquisitely wrought than any she had seen at Arches National Monument.

"It's called Fairyland Arch," he told her. "It must have been named that because of its ethereal grace by moonlight."

"Oh, Mike," she breathed, and a freshening breeze blew through the Jeep and almost wafted her words away. From here the view was overpowering. The cool blue light sharpened the outline of the arch against the velvety sky, and it seemed to Caro that the white rock must surely soar as high as the heavens. It was incredible that such an exquisite piece of sculpture had been formed only by wind and water over a period of millions of years.

"It's magnificent, isn't it?" he said with evident satisfaction.

"Yes," she agreed. "I'm glad you didn't try to describe it to me. I could never have imagined it."

"Let's walk along the road for a while," he said, pulling a blanket out of the Jeep and tossing it over his shoulder.

He held her hand as they left the Jeep behind. The blanket swung from his shoulder like a cape. Moonlight softened the rugged lines of his face; Caro hoped that it made her scar less noticeable, too. Once Mike stopped and pointed out a deer standing at attention not twenty feet away. It melted into the bushes, and when they bent to look, they found its heart-shaped footprints in the sand.

The mesa gleamed as though dipped in silver. Beside a boulder with a convenient sloped edge, Mike spread the blanket so that they could use the rock for a backrest. He put an arm around her shoulders and drew her close, so that his heart thudded against her ribs.

They heard a bird call, and Caro looked questioningly at Mike.

"An owl," he said, and she settled back against him, unwilling to think now of other creatures who might be near. He was the one who was the focus of her thoughts, and extraneous things, beautiful though they might be, seemed an intrusion.

When she lifted her head to look at him, she saw that he was watching her. He bent his head to kiss her lightly on the rise of her cheekbone, then dipped to seek her lips. She closed her eyes, giving in to the feelings that swept over her.

It had been so long since she had felt anything like this. She had almost forgotten how powerful were such urges. Her emotions were a fast current, swirling and sweeping everything and anything along its course. She was carried away, lost, reaching out for something to hold on to—Mike.

He shifted and wrapped his arms around her, and she laced her fingers behind his neck. She felt his mouth against her hair, tiny kisses like a strand of pearls on her neck. Finally his mouth captured hers.

She returned his kiss hungrily, clinging to him until he lowered her to the blanket. His face blotted out the sky, the mesa, the arch of stone vaulting toward the heavens. The moon was still there, huge and white, illuminating his features.

"You aren't going back to New York anytime soon," he murmured. "You know that, don't you?"

"Yes," she whispered, although she wondered if it wouldn't be better if she did. They were from different worlds, and what would happen after this? She already felt committed to him; she knew him, and he knew her, and they had established a bond based on mutual interest. That in itself was something new to her. Past loves had arisen solely from the man's attraction to her beauty, and her response had always been based on that. This was new and different.

At last all thought receded as he began to make love to her, drawing out the sensations that she had suppressed, reveling in her wonder and delight. Her mouth opened to his, the stubble of his beard rasped against her chin, his fingers sought and found the roundness of her breasts.

She gasped once in pleasure so that he rose on his hands above her to look at her face, but he barely had time to see the light in her eyes before she pulled him down to her. Getting out of their clothes was awkward. They didn't take off all of them. There was a mad rush, a mindless urge for completion. She heard herself murmuring his name over and over, and tears wet her face as the stars and moon overhead began to wheel and dip and finally exploded into splinters of gold and silver light.

Caro reluctantly let the world seep back into her consciousness. Mike lay with his head upon her breast, his breath teasing her skin. Gone was the sense of urgency. The night was luminous and quiet, and Caro felt a peace like none she had ever known. She could have stayed there forever, she thought, sheltered by Mike's body, warmed by his affection.

The wind picked up, and Mike wrapped them in the blanket. They didn't speak, only touched and smiled. Caro slept briefly, waking only when Mike said, "The wind's getting strong. We'd better go."

Caro resisted at first, but Mike insisted that they leave.

"A storm can hit suddenly in the desert. We don't want to be out in one if we can help it," he said.

They fumbled their way back into their clothes, leaving buttons unbuttoned and zippers unzipped in their haste. Mike skillfully backed and turned the Jeep until they were headed back the way they had come. In the distance, a fork of lightning rent the air.

Caro didn't object when Mike drew up the Jeep in front of his trailer.

"You don't mind?" he asked.

"No," she answered.

Inside, Mike kissed her and led her into his bedroom. His bed was narrow and covered by a simple but colorful Navajo blanket. Gently he unbuttoned her dress; she shrugged first one shoulder, then the other until it fell to the floor and lay around her feet.

"You are very beautiful, Caro," he said solemnly. He was looking at her body. She was sure that he wasn't referring to her face.

He saw the reticence in her eyes and realized that she was

embarrassed. He understood that, to her, being assessed here by the light of an electric bulb was different. Moonlight was mellower, kinder. Still, he didn't turn off the light. He wanted to see her.

He touched her scar, letting his finger trace it from the cheekbone on one side to the jawbone on the other, taking in all of its darkened length, studying the knitting of the skin here, exploring the way it was slightly puckered there.

"You are very beautiful," he repeated slowly and deliberately. As her eyes filled with tears he swept her into his arms and lowered her to the bed, and she wrapped her arms and legs around him, sobbing because she wanted to be beautiful for him and knew she wasn't.

He let her cry for a long time, and then, very sweetly and tenderly, he coaxed her body into a vibrating tension, letting her rise to a peak and then ease back again, and soon all she could think of was assuaging her passion. At the threshold she heard her own cry, then his, and finally she heard nothing but her own pulse in her ears.

Afterward she lay damp and peaceful in his arms, listening to the first pattering raindrops falling on the outside of the Tin Can. They both slept, and woke with a start as thunder reverberated in the distance.

"What if I can't get home?" Caro asked uncertainly, pushing herself to a sitting position and lifting the curtain over the window beside the bed so she could look out at the storm. Her scar ached. It always ached when it rained.

He traced teasing little circles on her back. "The rain will stop," he said. "I'd rather wait until the lightning has passed to take you home, though."

She leaned against him, letting him support her weight as they both watched the wind-driven rain dashing against the windowpane.

"Annie and the kids will think I've gone to sleep if my room is dark when they come home from Gert's," she said.

His hands cupped her breasts. "Then you can stay most of the night," he said, and she murmured her assent.

Finally there was no more talking, no more whispering, only the flash of lightning and the roll of thunder as the storm swept past, spending its fury.

Chapter Seven

After that night, things were different between them when Mike came to Annie's house.

Annie sensed right away that Caro and her cousin had become lovers. Her intuition told her that Caro's new glow came from more than a desert suntan.

Never one to mince words, Annie asked bluntly on Wednesday at breakfast, "Are you and Mike—um, you know?"

Caro glanced at Annie out of the corners of her eyes, a tiny smile turning up the corners of her mouth.

"Yes," she said.

"I thought so," Annie said with a delighted laugh.

"If it's a problem—"

"No, oh no." Annie covered Caro's hand with her own. "I can't tell you how happy it makes me that you and Mike have hit it off so well. I've always wished he'd find somebody, but not everyone understands him. He's brilliant, you know, with that PhD of his in anthropology. Mike downplays his scholarly side, at least around here. Why, one time one of his archaeologist friends called up and asked for Dr. Herrick, and for a minute I didn't know who he wanted."

"Mike seems to enjoy your family life so much. I can't figure out why he has never married."

"Mike's never met any woman who understood how involved he is in that work of his, and no woman wants to traipse around in the desert after him, and—"

"Oh, but I do!" Caro assured her.

"That's why you've managed to find something special in

each other," Annie said. "He's a loner who needs your warmth and interest in his work, and you need the intellectual stimulation."

"Maybe so," Caro admitted.

Annie chewed thoughtfully on a piece of toast. "For a long time I've thought there was more to those long, smoldering glances I've intercepted between you two than either of you let on," she said.

"I didn't know it was so obvious," Caro said, abashed.

"Maybe it's only noticeable to me," Annie hastened to say. "I'm in the frame of mind where I keep waxing nostalgic over Tom. Seeing you and Mike so happy together makes me wish I could go back to the beginning of my courtship with Tom and start all over. Did I tell you that instead of going to Salt Lake City, I'm trying to talk Tom into coming home for a week or two?"

"Do you think he will?"

Annie waved crossed fingers in the air.

"I hope so," she said fervently. "If he did, maybe we could make a go of it."

"I hope so, too," Caro answered.

Caro saw Mike every day. Sometimes he'd stop by early in the morning before heading out into the desert. Occasionally he'd take time off from the scientific paper he was writing to eat lunch with her and Annie and the children, if they happened to be around.

Afterward, sometimes he stayed for dinner. Later he and Caro would drive to his trailer, just the two of them, to spend long languorous evenings in bed. Mike was an unhurried lover, asking her what she liked and waiting for her response before he moved on. When it was over, they would lie side by side, their hands touching, and talk into the early hours of the morning.

She had never met a man who prodded and pulled at her the way Mike did, trying to get her to voice her thoughts. She had never talked so ceaselessly with anyone. The only thing she would not discuss was her scar or how she had happened to get it.

Whenever the conversation seemed to be leading in that direction, she would stumble all over herself, backtracking, changing conversational paths, throwing in verbal red herrings.

She was simply not ready to talk about it. He noticed, and she knew he noticed. Before long it was an unspoken agreement that the scar was a taboo topic. Her life in New York was equally to be avoided. If he minded, he never said so. And they found plenty of other things to talk about.

It wasn't until her third visit to the Tin Can that Caro actually saw the snake. She was coming out of the bathroom when it slithered in the door. She screamed.

Mike was there in an instant. When he saw the black gopher snake weaving around the perimeter of the bathroom, flickering its forked tongue, he slammed the door and hurried to Caro, who had jumped on top of his bed and was shaking like a leaf.

"Maybe I should have mentioned Drusilla," he said, looking unhappy.

Caro clenched her teeth to stop them from chattering.

"You're darned right you should have mentioned Drusilla," she said.

"She eats mice. I can't keep them out of this trailer no matter how hard I try, so I adopted Drusilla to police them for me. Come down off the bed, Caro. She's locked in the bathroom." He looked so contrite that Caro accepted his hand and stepped down beside him.

"Peter told me you had a snake. I didn't quite believe him," she said.

"Does she bother you? If she does, I could get some mouse-traps, but Drusilla is such an efficient way of controlling rodents that it seems a shame. She's quite clean, and she doesn't make any noise."

"Why haven't I seen her before?"

"She lives under the bed, and she only comes out when she's hungry. There's a new mouse hole behind the—"

"Never mind," Caro said. "I'd rather not hear it. Anyway, wouldn't a cat be better?"

"I'd have to worry about someone to take care of a cat when I'm away. Don't worry, Caro. I'll get rid of Drusilla," Mike promised.

"Don't," Caro said, thinking that she might be able to ac-custom herself to a snake. She had learned to think nothing of prickly pear cactus growing in the front yard and had grown to appreciate the beauty of the inhospitable desert; maybe she could get used to Drusilla, especially if she seldom saw her.

So Mike kept the snake, and Caro assumed that she rested comfortably under the bed. She saw her once or twice, and Caro even began to think that Drusilla was rather pretty with her shiny skin and her supple body.

WHEN CARO tentatively asked Annie if she would mind letting her paint some of the designs from the photos of Anasazi rock art on her pots, Annie grinned and said, "Sure! Over there's a couple of cracked pots to practice on," and she handed Caro some brushes and paints.

The brushes and paints that Annie provided proved to be insufficient for Caro, who was soon taken with the idea of making serviceable but decorative pottery exactly the way the Anasazi made it. In her browsing through Annie's extensive library on the subject of pottery making, Caro found a description of how the Anasazi made their paintbrushes. When she told Mike that she needed some yucca leaves, he wanted to know why.

"So I can make brushes the way the Anasazi did," she said.

Caro chewed the yucca leaves until they frayed, much to the amazement of the children.

"Yucca *yuck*," Franklin had said scornfully. "Is that the way the Indians really made their paintbrushes?"

"Of course," Caro replied.

"If it had been me, I would have invented crayons," Franklin said before trotting out the door.

Mike was pleased that Caro was showing such an interest in making pottery. Now there was something purposeful in the way she carried herself, and she never sat staring into space the way she had done so often before. She had something she loved to do.

Caro learned to shape her own pots of coiled clay, then to smooth them with a piece of gourd. After that, the pots were air dried and a slip, or thin wash of clay, was added. Finally it was time for polishing and painting.

She experimented with paints and learned to make her own from organic materials such as mustard or bee plant. She studied the photos Mike had given her before attempting to replicate the designs on her pots. Some were more successful than others. Her attempt at decorating a bowl with the picture of desert sheep was a failure, because the sheep was too large a design for such a small bowl; on the other hand, her design of birds on a plate was so successful that Annie persuaded her to let her sell it.

"This is really good, Caro," Annie said, holding up the plate and turning it this way and that in the light so that she could better admire the design.

"Do you honestly think that someone will buy it?" Caro asked anxiously.

"I have a customer in California who is always asking me to send something new and different. I'll enclose a note about how this is an authentic Anasazi design made in the old way by the new potter who works for me, and we'll see what happens."

"The new potter?"

"That's you, silly. With designs like this, I can't afford to let you work for my competitors. I want an exclusive on all Caro Nicholson designs," Annie said.

Annie's encouragement spurred Caro to try more new things. Before long there was a whole row of Caro Nicholson designs lined up on the windowsill in Annie's studio, and the California customer called to order more as soon as he received the bird plate.

She could almost have forgotten that New York existed, had it not been for Marina. As Caro formed new alliances and loyalties, as she learned to explore her artistic capabilities, Marina, who knew that something was up but not exactly what, became even more strident in her long-distance demands that Caro resume her modeling career.

"Caro, you're so exasperating," Marina said on the phone a couple of weeks after Caro accepted a big order from the California customer and was working hard to fill it.

"Mmm?" Caro said. As she listened to Marina's rantings and railings she flipped through some preliminary drawings she had made of new designs derived from Mike's photos.

"I wish you'd think about coming back to the city soon, if only for a weekend visit. Suki and Donna and some of the other models have been asking about you."

"I'm not ready yet," Caro said.

"I can't buy that, Caro. Why, lately you've been sounding like your old self. I've talked to Dr. Fleischer about your scar. He says it'll be nine months to a year before he can sand or resuture it. Just think, an operation could make you as good as new."

As good as new? Was *new* always synonymous with *good?* Lately Caro had begun to understand that she was the sum total of her experiences, including the terrible experience of being attacked and disfigured.

"I'm sure you'll want to get back to work before long," Marina said persuasively. "You made lots of money in the Naiad campaign, and you can do it again."

"Maybe I made too much money," Caro said darkly. When she thought of Annie struggling to support her family with her pottery earnings, the salary she had raked in as the Naiad seemed indecent.

Marina laughed. "It's impossible to make too much money, darling. Of course you'll want that scar off, and soon. Oh, by the way, I have news. I called Detective Garwood the other day, and he said he might have a suspect in your case. A hysterical woman ran into a police station last week claiming that a guy waved a razor at her in Central Park and yelled, 'I did this once and I can do it again,' as he grabbed her around the neck."

Caro's heart caught in her throat. "She's lucky she got away," she said.

"The odd thing is that the woman looked a lot like you. Same height, same hairdo."

"Did—did the attacker think that she *was* me?"

"Well, no one knows. The detective says that this time they have some clues, and the guy does sound a lot like the man who attacked you. I'll let you know as soon as I hear of an arrest."

Caro hung up the phone, dismayed by this development. For one thing, the man who had slashed her face was apparently still around. Part of her wanted him arrested and put behind bars; then maybe she could stop being afraid. But if he were arrested, she'd have to identify him, and for that she'd have to return to the city. There would be a trial and possibly more publicity.

Going to New York would mean that she could no longer hide the fact that she was the Naiad. Annie would know, the kids would know, and Mike would know. How would they react to such news?

Caro dreaded the loss of her anonymity. She was happy being liked for her personality and her talent. She didn't want to give up this newly earned identity to be known as the Naiad here in Moab. In fact, it was increasingly clear to her that she never wanted to be associated with the Naiad again, and that soon she'd have to break the news to an uncomprehending Marina.

All this was heavy thinking, and she didn't know what to hope for—the man's arrest, which would mean she'd have to reveal her identity, or his continued freedom, which meant that she'd always fear for her life.

When Mike arrived later that afternoon, Caro seemed uncharacteristically withdrawn. At dinner, he noticed that she wasn't doing justice to the excellent food at the restaurant where they had gone to get away from the chaos of the Stendahl household.

"What's wrong?" Mike asked.

Caro twisted the cellophane from a package of crackers between her fingers. "Nothing," she said, but Mike didn't believe her.

When they went to his trailer afterward, their lovemaking was subdued and lacking in spontaneity. *Something has upset her,* he thought to himself later as she lay in his arms staring at the ceiling, her mind seemingly miles away.

"Don't you want to talk about whatever is bothering you?" he asked, trying again.

For an answer she only turned and clutched him to her, holding him as though she would never let him go. He gazed into the darkness, hoping for a clue that would let him know what she was feeling, but she seemed to draw even further into herself.

Later they sat at the table eating a late snack, and he noticed that she kept dipping her head so that her long hair fell over her scar, the way she had done in the old days before they had become lovers. *The scar, then.* Whatever had upset her, it had to do with the scar and the past that she'd never mentioned. When would she ever open up enough to tell him about it?

He stood up and went around the back of her chair. He reached out and massaged her shoulder muscles, and she leaned her head against his arm.

"Do you want to go back to Annie's?" he asked quietly.

"Not yet," Caro replied. She sounded distracted, remote.

"I thought you wouldn't want to get in too late," he said.

"I really don't want to go back at all tonight," she said with a catch in her voice.

He held out his hand, and she placed her palm in his. He lifted her up so that she stood facing him. He, too, longed to be able to spend the whole night in her arms. He wanted to wake up beside her, slowly becoming conscious of her beside him in the morning twilight, and he wanted to eat breakfast with her before the sun rose over the mesas. He wanted more than they had now; a few hours together was no longer enough.

"Don't go," he said. "Stay here."

"I'm not willing to answer the questions that Annie's children would raise, if you were to bring me home in the morning after I've been out all night," Caro said, although the offer was tempting. She didn't want to be alone tonight.

"I guess Annie might not want her kids to know that we're sleeping together," Mike agreed reluctantly.

He stroked her cheek, amazed at how desire flared through him with this simple gesture.

"Maybe you should think about moving into the Tin Can with me," he said, hardly believing that he, who valued his privacy, could be saying it.

She glanced up at him in apparent surprise. "That's a major step," she replied.

"It's worth discussing, don't you think?"

"What about the children?"

"Annie could tell us how she'd like us to explain it. If you did actually move in here, I mean."

Caro sighed and kissed his neck. "For now, I guess you'd better take me home," was all she said, and the way she said it made him want to throw all their scruples out the window.

When she came out of the bedroom dressed to leave, his heart overflowed with feelings that were new to him.

I love her, he thought to himself in amazed certainty. *I don't know anything about the life she led before she came here. I have no idea when—or if—she'll go back to it. She's another enigma I can't solve. And yet I love her!*

The thought took his breath away.

TALKING ABOUT moving into the Tin Can with Mike was something that Caro, an independent woman with a considerable income of her own, could not have imagined a few months ago. The subject had never come up with Wayne; she wouldn't have relinquished her freedom, even if it had.

Would Mike mention the subject again? She waited for him to bring it up, but he didn't. Maybe he regretted having said anything about it. She knew how much he valued his privacy. And Mike had other things on his mind at present.

Caro had learned how worried Mike was that with the permission to explore Yalabasi Canyon pending, he was still unsure exactly where the canyon was located within the huge tract of land owned by the El Karak Mining Company. His concern was well-founded. He didn't want to waste valuable time searching for Yalabasi Canyon, once permission to explore it was granted; he could conceivably flounder about in the desert for weeks before locating the canyon that Charlie Deer Walk had discovered.

One night when Caro was at the Tin Can for dinner, Mike produced a crude map drawn on wrinkled brown wrapping paper and spread it out on his kitchen table.

"Is that the map Charlie Deer Walk gave you before he died?" asked Caro.

"Yes," he said. "As amazing as it may seem, there are many unexplored canyons out in the desert. They were never considered important enough to explore, or perhaps they were inaccessible."

"It's not a very sophisticated map, is it? It looks so haphazard."

"This map is a real puzzle. He's drawn this canyon, see, shaped like a dogleg. And he's put in the directions, north, south, east and west. But the configuration of this particular canyon doesn't jibe with what I know about the El Karak property. I'm afraid that when I get there, I won't be able to find it."

"Charlie wasn't imagining things, was he?"

Mike shook his head. "I doubt it. He was a shrewd, intelligent fellow. If he said he found Yalabasi Canyon and saw something important there, he did."

Mike continued to pore over the map, and Caro, ever interested in Mike's photos of Anasazi rock art, sat beside him and dug through a bunch of unfiled photos piled high in a box. A couple of them looked different from the others; they didn't appear to be photos of pictographs or petroglyphs at all.

"What are these, Mike?" she asked him.

Mike spared a quick look. "Oh, those are copies of some aerial photographs of the El Karak tract. Believe it or not, the originals were taken by Charles Lindbergh not long after his solo flight across the Atlantic in 1927."

"*The* Charles Lindbergh?"

"Exactly. He had an interest in exploring new frontiers, and no one had ever mapped the area when he flew over it. Look, the aerial photos show a network of depressions in the earth that are invisible when you're on the ground, and they converge on the rim of this canyon. The Anasazi built the roads, probably leading to a center of some sort. I've speculated that there's a ruin here."

Caro studied the photo. "What's this in the middle of the canyon?" she asked, pointing to what appeared to be a raised area at the place where the canyon curved sharply.

Mike glanced at it. "That's a mesa. We know that the Anasazi farmed the tops of fertile mesas and built their houses wedged onto cliffs below," he said before returning his attention to Charlie's map.

As she studied the photographs, something rang a bell in the back of Caro's mind. There were certain similarities in one of the photos and Charlie's map, but something about the configuration seemed out of whack.

She set the photos on the table next to the map and looked over Mike's shoulder at Charlie Deer Walk's crudely penciled canyon.

"Mike," she said with growing excitement. "Did Charlie often make his letters backward?" Across the top of the map was written Yalabasi Canyon. Both of the *N*'s in the word CANYON were reversed.

"Charlie was as smart as they come, but he wasn't very good at reading or writing," Mike said.

"Maybe he was dyslexic," Caro said softly, thinking of Franklin's struggles to read and write.

"Dyslexic? Charlie?" Mike said sharply.

Caro pointed at the reversed *N*'s. "This is what Franklin does when he writes his name," she said with growing excitement. "He reverses his *N*'s and a lot of other letters, too."

"I don't understand what that has to do with anything," Mike said.

"Don't you see? If Charlie was dyslexic, he might have drawn the canyon's mirror image. That's why you haven't been able to locate it on any maps of the El Karak property."

Mike's jaw dropped, and in his eyes dawned the light of understanding. "You mean that Charlie might have reversed the shape of this canyon on his map so that left became right and right became left?"

"It's possible," Caro said. "That's why you've been looking for a canyon that didn't seem to be there. Look," she said, and she took the map and raised it to the bright hanging lamp over the kitchen table with the penciled outline facing the light. The smudged image of the canyon shone through the brown paper.

Mike held up the Lindbergh photographs for a comparison. Seen this way, the canyon that Charlie had outlined on the map corresponded to one in the photographs—the one with the mesa in its curve.

"I think you're on to something!" Mike exclaimed. "Yalabasi Canyon curves to the west, not the east the way Charlie drew it on the map! Why didn't I see that?"

"You wouldn't have made the connection between Charlie Deer Walk and Franklin," Caro said. "I could, because I've worked with Franklin to help him overcome his learning problem."

"Caro, you are a wonder!" Mike jumped up and hugged her exuberantly.

She hugged him back, almost as excited as he was.

When he saw the expression on her face, he pulled her close again so that she couldn't read his. He had never met a woman who cared about his work. He had long ago despaired that he ever would.

Caro was a new experience entirely. Again he thought about asking her to move in with him. But something stopped him. It had never been mentioned since the first time they'd discussed it, and he was wary of being the one to bring up the subject. Unknowns abounded in their relationship, to his increasing unease.

Cautiously he allowed himself to imagine Caro as a permanent fixture in his life and found that the idea gave him pleasure. But he didn't know yet if a permanent relationship was what she really wanted, and at this point he had no idea how to find out.

IT WAS A QUIET AFTERNOON in the third week of July, and Caro was watering the geraniums on the front porch of Annie's house, while Mike sat in a chair reading an archaeological journal. Caro's fingernails were chipped and broken, a legacy of all the pots she had made. She didn't care; she had never heard anyone tell a woman that she had great fingernails, well maintained or not.

Annie came out of the house, dipped a hand into the mailbox and sat down on the top step to leaf through the mail.

"Bills, bills, bills," she said wearily, then held up one envelope and stared at it with a blank expression.

"That looks like Tom's handwriting," Mike said.

"It is," Annie said tersely, and ripped it open.

She scanned the lines of the brief note. "He's coming home! I don't believe it! He's coming home!" She jumped up and raced into the house in search of the children, scattering the rest of the mail all over the porch.

"Daddy's coming home," Caro and Mike heard her announce excitedly to Holly, Franklin and Peter. "He'll be here Friday night and he's going to stay at least two weeks."

A cheer went up, and Mike said to Caro, "Thank goodness. Maybe Tom will come to his senses and decide to stay." He stood and started to pick up the envelopes and magazines that Annie had dropped.

Holly burst from the house. "Did you hear what Mom said? Daddy's coming home!"

"That's wonderful," Caro said warmly.

Mike sat down on his chair and began to sort the mail. "Here's something for you, Holly. And a magazine for your mother," he said.

Holly sat cross-legged on the floor and began to flip through the pages of Annie's magazine. "I bet Daddy will bring us all presents," she said, her eyes shining. "Another thing is that Mom will move back into her old bedroom with Daddy. I'll have my room to myself again."

Mike zeroed in on the second part of Holly's statement. He was sure that Annie and Tom would want to sleep in their own bedroom, which meant that Caro needed a place to stay. It seemed like a perfect reason for Caro to move into the Tin Can with him.

But what if he wasn't capable of relinquishing his loner status and becoming one half of a couple?

And what if Caro didn't want to live with him? She hadn't mentioned it since the time he'd brought it up.

He was well aware that people who volunteer their emotions choose to put everything at risk. He had been handed a convenient opening. Did he dare to take it? His mouth grew dry just thinking about it.

"Holly? Hol-ly!" Annie called from the kitchen.

"Well, guess I'd better go," Holly said. She stood up and ran inside, leaving the magazine open on the porch floor.

Caro, who had finished watering the flowers, started to pick it up—and froze. There, staring up at her from the Stendahls' front porch, was her own image.

It was the Naiad, a new photo from the last session for which she had posed on behalf of the Naiad fragrance.

The picture had been taken on location at a waterfall in Jamaica. She wore a skintight swimsuit cut high on the hips. She was staring into the camera wearing a look of provocative invitation, her hair was plastered close to her head, and water droplets shimmered all over her body and on her face—her perfect face.

It was all she could do not to cry out. Instead, she merely picked up the magazine and closed it. She swallowed and tried to listen to what Mike was saying through the roaring in her ears.

She was peripherally aware that Mike's face was alight with earnestness; he must be saying something important.

She had missed his first words, but now he was saying, "...when Tom comes home, you could stay at my place. It would be perfectly logical and make a lot of sense, and he's supposed to be here for only two weeks, which would be a good trial period to see if we like living together."

She knew that in suggesting this he was offering something special, and at any other time she would have been overwhelmed with the meaning of it. To move in with him, to live with him twenty-four hours a day, never having to go back to her own lonely bed after so briefly sharing his? She had thought about it a lot, had willed him to bring up the topic again, and even been disappointed when he hadn't.

At this moment, with her own perfect image staring at her from the pages of the magazine, she couldn't respond, at least not in the way Mike expected.

"Fine, that's fine," she managed to say in a strangled voice, then jumped to her feet and rushed into the house, leaving Mike staring after her in complete surprise.

The door slammed behind her, leaving an echoing silence. Mike shook his head. Here was something he didn't understand. His invitation to stay at his trailer for the next two weeks had been tendered with the best of intentions, and the only reason he had made it was that he'd thought that there was a reasonable chance that it was what Caro wanted, too. He felt crushed to think that perhaps she didn't, that maybe she'd agreed only because she thought there was nowhere else for her to go.

He got up, marched into the house and stood outside Caro's door, listening for any sound. He heard nothing.

"Caro?" he called.

"I'll be out in a minute," was the muffled reply. She might have been crying; he couldn't tell.

"Caro, I want to talk to you," he said desperately.

There was no answer.

Surreptitiously he tried the doorknob, but it wouldn't turn. For a moment he thought about breaking down the door. He was upset enough, that was for sure. But then he remembered that if he broke anything, he'd have to fix it, and he was notoriously inadequate as a handyman.

Damn he thought. *What have I gotten myself into now?*

Embers of the Wind

that I'm more than happy to change so as to accommodate a few compromises for the sake of harmony.

Annie laughed. You can't expect perfection, though.

Chapter Eight

In her bedroom, Caro stared down at the magazine photo, feeling sick to her stomach. The person she saw was the Naiad. That person no longer had anything to do with her.

Trembling, she sank down on the edge of the bed and only got up to unlock the door for Annie.

Annie's cheeks were pink with excitement. "Caro, I'm so happy! Maybe Tom and I will get our marriage back on track again. I'm going to try my hardest to make everything perfect while he's here."

Caro shoved the magazine under a pillow. She forced a smile. "I'm glad he's coming, Annie," she said.

Annie's expression clouded. "There's only one thing that upsets me. Tom and I—well, we'll want to use this bedroom. It has the only double bed in the house, after all, and—"

"I understand," Caro said. "It's all right."

"Mike came into the kitchen to talk to me a minute ago. He said that you could stay at the trailer with him. For some reason, he seems to think that you don't want to. Do you, Caro?" Annie focused anxious eyes on her face.

Caro wasn't sure how she felt about anything at the moment. Tom's arrival was going to upset the Stendahl household, and she had come to rely on it as a stable place to stay, a nonthreatening environment.

A short time ago she had been wishing that she could stay with Mike all night, and now that he had suggested that she move in, she should be feeling as thrilled as Annie was right now. Yet that picture in the magazine had unleashed a host of emotions; paramount was the feeling that she had somehow cheated Mike by not telling him who she was in the first place.

She stood up and opened the closet door to get out her suitcase. "I've already told Mike that I would," she said evenly.

"Oh, Caro, is it really what you want to do? I'm not forcing you out? Why, you could probably go stay with Gert at her house—she lives all alone. Yes. Would you rather stay with Gert?"

"No, Annie. Mike and I—well, we've talked about living together before. It's a big decision, and I didn't want to leave you and the children. Now there's no reason not to try it. I want to."

"I hope you'll keep on making your pottery even while Tom is here. I was thinking that you could take my station wagon and commute back and forth from Mike's trailer to work here every day."

Caro forced herself to forget about the photo in the magazine. All of Annie's talk reminded her that she now had a life in Moab separate from her life in New York, and with more variety. Mike was part of it, and she wanted to explore the possibilities that he offered.

"Of course I'll come to work every day," she promised. "And I'll talk to Holly and work with Franklin and play with Peter just as much as ever. If you and Tom want time to yourself, I'm a willing baby-sitter." She tried to smile.

"Thanks, Caro. You're one of the best friends I've ever had."

"You'll have to let me know if I'm getting in the way too much," Caro warned. "I don't want to interfere with you and Tom in any way."

Annie laughed as she got up to leave. "Don't be silly—we're used to Gert and my sisters and my mother and a whole bunch of family. Nothing you could do could possibly aggravate Tom any more than they do! And by the way, I'm going to tell my family to cool it while Tom's here. Maybe then he'll see how independent I am and that I can get along without seeing one of them every half hour!"

Annie left, but privately Caro wondered how much hope she should hold for Annie's plan to downplay her family's role in her life, especially when she heard Annie pick up the phone and call her mother, sisters, aunts and cousins one after the other to tell them that Tom would soon be home.

WHEN SHE AND MIKE later found themselves alone in Annie's living room, Caro was able to express her enthusiasm for moving to the trailer.

"I thought I'd said something wrong when you jumped up and ran inside," he told her.

"No, I—I guess I was just overwhelmed at the idea of moving away from Annie and the kids," she improvised lamely.

This made some sense to him. He knew that they were her emotional prop and that she was theirs. Still, she was so agitated tonight, jumping up and down to get her sketch pad, running to answer the phone when one of the kids could have done it.

He was sure that there was more to the way Caro was acting than she had let on, but he didn't ask any more questions. It seemed pointless. He went home that night alone, wondering what sequence of events he had set in motion by his well-intentioned offer. At that point he regretted ever suggesting a live-in arrangement. He should have let Caro move in with Gert.

"EVERYTHING OKAY?" Annie inquired later that night, popping her head in the door of Caro's room as Caro was trying to read in bed.

"More or less," Caro told her.

"Want to talk about the 'less'?"

Caro made herself smile. Annie looked so happy that she couldn't ruin it with her own problems. Anyway, she couldn't confide in Annie without telling her that she, Caro, was the Naiad.

"I think it's just jitters about moving in with Mike," she said. She tried her best to sound convincing.

"That's understandable, Caro. You're so compatible, though. Still, there's always my cousin's house if you aren't happy at the Tin Can."

Caro thought of Gert's small bungalow with its shifting layer of old newspapers on the floor for training the new puppy.

"I'm sure it'll be all right," she said, finding it absurd that

Annie had ended up comforting her, instead of the other way around.

When Annie left, she tossed the book onto the floor and pillowed her cheek on her hands. Though Mike seemed satisfied with her explanation for her behavior, Caro despaired of ever explaining the truth. She had been fooling herself to think that she could go on living the charade, pretending to be something that she was not, withholding information about her past for her own selfish reasons. Unfortunately, it had gone on for so long that she could think of no simple way to tell Mike who she really was and about the life she had left behind.

She tried to stop worrying, and as scheduled, Caro packed on Thursday to move into the Tin Can. She told the children that she would be leaving the Stendahl house Friday afternoon.

"You mean you're going to be Mike's bread-and-beck—I mean, well, *you* know," Franklin said.

"Um, yes," Caro said.

"Don't let the snake get you," Peter warned.

"I'm sure it's a very tame snake," Caro replied.

"There is no such thing as a tame snake," Holly said.

"There is too!" Franklin said. "I saw this movie where a snake charmer trained a snake to dance out of a basket when he played a flute."

"Snakes can't dance, dummy," said Peter with a snort of derision.

"Can, too," Franklin insisted.

"Can*not*," and Caro had to pull them apart as they began to tussle on the rug. She washed their faces in her bathroom and sent them packing, realizing that tension ran high in this household as everyone eagerly awaited the arrival of Tom Stendahl.

On Friday, Caro drove to the trailer in Annie's station wagon before Mike came home. He customarily left the Tin Can's door unlocked, and she went inside, tugging her suitcase up the narrow metal steps.

Even though her words to Annie on the subject had been mostly a cover story, she did feel slightly apprehensive about the experience of living with Mike. It was one thing to engage in romantic trysts here; it was entirely another to be housemates. How would Mike, who admittedly enjoyed the solitude of the desert, take to having another person, even Caro, encroaching on his space, cluttering up his place with her possessions?

It was quiet. She looked around the trailer for something to do and saw that Mike had left her a note. "Make yourself comfortable," it said. "I'll be home around six." It was signed, "Love, Mike."

Love. He had signed it "Love." What did that word mean to him? Was it an indicator of his true feelings for her or merely the ritual closing of a message, signed with no more thought that he would give to writing the equally unfathomable phrase, "Dear Caro"?

She sighed and went to the doorway to take in the desert panorama. In the front yard, if you could call it that, optimistic runners of grass connected the cactus plants. A renegade beetle buzzed through the air and landed on her collar, its back gleaming brassy yellow in the sunlight. It rested for a moment, finally taking off and disappearing above her head.

She left the coolness of the doorway and walked, ever mindful of the ubiquitous prickly pear, to a knoll several hundred feet from the trailer. The day was hot and bright, and white clouds rolled across the horizon.

On one side loomed Preservation Mesa, its sandstone a garish layering of orange, vermilion and lilac. On the other side rose more fanciful formations. The horizon shimmered with the heat and she felt serenity settle over her like a protective cloak. Desolate it might be, but the purity of the desert never failed to refresh her.

On her deliberately circuitous route back to the Tin Can, Caro stumbled upon a plant bearing yellow pea-shaped flowers, which she picked and carried back with her. She tried their effect in a small blue vase that she found under the sink and put them on the table.

She noticed a brown paper bag full of fresh beans on the counter, probably a gift from Gert, who had sent a similar bag home with Annie and the kids after they had helped her with her freezing. Caro washed and strung the beans, then put them into a water-filled saucepan on the propane gas stove to cook. It felt homey to be doing it, and she wondered if maybe she was cut out to be a homemaker, after all. *How Marina would laugh at that,* she thought, amused at the notion.

But the idea of creating a comfortable home for someone she loved wasn't at all laughable to her. There was a knack to it, and she thought now that housewifery might be something she could do and do well. The thought pleased her, and she hummed as she began to slice greens for a salad.

MIKE APPROACHED the Tin Can with certain reservations about this whole experiment. *Sure,* he loved her, but he couldn't figure Caro out. She'd acted so moody since the day he'd asked her to move in with him.

He didn't think her attitude had anything to do with Tom Stendahl's return. Caro seemed genuinely happy about Annie's renewed hopes for a reconciliation. He'd watched carefully for any sign that Caro's work wasn't going well, but on the contrary, a store in Albuquerque had sent in a large order for her pottery, which seemed to delight her.

As for her excuse for running into the house when he'd first suggested the move, he wasn't sure he bought it. He was pretty sure by this time that Caro's moods must have to do with her former life, about which he was becoming more and more curious. Why wouldn't she confide in him? From whom was she running? How could they ever hope to construct a meaningful life together, if he didn't know more about her?

He'd been patient. He'd waited for her to open up in her own way and at a time she chose. It hadn't happened.

If she didn't tell him soon, he'd try a bit of prodding. He didn't think he could enter wholeheartedly into this living arrangement with her, if she was going to remain such an unknown quantity.

He pulled up the Jeep beside the Tin Can. When he saw her emerging from the trailer, he got out and watched her as she approached, radiant and smiling. He almost lost his resolve, but knew that if his curiosity kept gnawing at him, he'd become moody himself, and then where would they be? He would broach the subject of her past at the first opportunity.

She kissed him eagerly, then drew him inside.

"I've put beans on to cook," she said. He noticed the vase of wildflowers on the table. The beans cooking, the vase of flowers, Caro wearing a welcome-home smile—it all seemed overwhelmingly domestic, and since he wasn't by nature a domestic creature, all the fuss only increased his anxiety about this whole arrangement.

He hid his qualms successfully, he thought. He slid an arm around Caro's shoulders and said, "I'll help you unpack," as he escorted her into the bedroom.

"I've emptied out a couple of drawers in the dresser for you," he told her.

Caro opened them and saw that he had lined the drawers with fresh paper. It was a gesture that touched her heart.

"You wouldn't have had to do this," she said.

"I did it because I'm hoping you'll stay a while," he said as she opened her suitcase and began to unfold her underwear.

She busied herself arranging things in the drawer. "That depends on what happens between Annie and Tom, I suppose," she said evenly and noncommittally.

"We've already agreed that you're not going back to New York for a long time," he said. A nervous edge had crept into his voice, and she noticed it.

She spared him a long searching look before she fumbled with the lid to a can of hair spray. "Right," she said.

"Just how long is what I'm wondering," he said softly, watching her.

She didn't speak. She continued to put things in the drawer and pushed it shut. A lacy strap hung out; she opened the drawer again and tucked the strap inside, all the time aware of the way he was watching her.

"I've often wondered why you seem so reluctant to go home," he said.

"Please, Mike," she said wearily. He saw her shoulders tense.

"Caro, it has to be dealt with sometime," he said with extreme patience. "This topic had been on hold for much too long."

"But we don't have to talk about it now," she insisted. She pivoted to face him. "Can't we just enjoy our dinner, and make love, and—?" She lifted her shoulders and let them fall.

He moved closer. "I care about you very deeply, Caro. If we're happy living together here, I want you to stay, even if

Tom goes back to Salt Lake City. This might be an arrangement we'd want to continue for a long time.''

"You don't understand," she said, feeling her stomach muscles tense again.

"You make it awfully hard," he said. "First you show up in Moab with no place to go and nothing to do, and then you settle into my cousin's house. We start a relationship, and I think you like me a great deal. Oh, let's not mince words; I think you love me. But you won't tell me anything about that scar of yours or the phone calls you keep getting from Marina, whoever she is. Don't you think I'm a little bit curious?"

She was surprised to see blue veins standing out at his temples. She had never known quiet, gentle Mike to get upset over anything.

He had said he thought she loved him. Maybe she did. Oh, this was impossible. She would have packed and run back to the Stendahls', if they'd had room for her.

"Caro," he said, and now he seemed to have a handle on his emotions, which was more than she could say for herself. He brushed a hand across her face, and she couldn't help leaning into it, letting him cup the curve of her cheek. She felt the sting of tears high behind her eyelids.

"Isn't it strange how we retreat within ourselves, pretend, become defensive and aloof, anything to cut off the circuit?" he asked softly, sliding his arms around her.

He was right, of course. But all her defenses hadn't made her feel better; not talking about the attack or her former life hadn't made the bad feelings go away.

For a confused moment, she didn't know what she was going to do. She wavered, wondering if talking about the attack and its effect on her life would destroy the inner peace she had found here.

Then she realized that by shutting Mike out, she might destroy his love for her. Suddenly that seemed like too great a price to pay for a peace that was fast eroding under his critical questions.

Resolutely she twisted away from him and walked to her suitcase. He stood watching as she rummaged in its depths and pulled out Annie's magazine. She gripped it tightly before walking to him and thrusting it into his hands.

"Here," she said, "this should answer some of your questions. Look at page twenty-seven."

He blinked uncomprehendingly at the magazine he held, and then looked up at her for an explanation. She only shook her head and drew a deep breath. He thought she was going to say something, and he was stunned to see that her eyes glimmered with unshed tears. But she said nothing; she only turned abruptly on her heel and walked out of the room.

MIKE STARED at the picture in the magazine.

There was no doubt in his mind who the woman was. The shape of her face, the wide-set eyes, the exquisite line where her high cheekbone blended into her jawline—he knew right away that this was Caro.

But it was a Caro so different from the one who was familiar to him that this new knowledge didn't merely set him off balance, it nearly bowled him over.

This Caro in the magazine photo had a bold, aggressive look to her. His Caro had always been shy and reticent. This Caro's eyes were made up to look like blue reflecting pools. His Caro had brown eyes, and a scar bisected her lovely face.

When he had recovered somewhat from the shock, he walked slowly into the living room where Caro stood clinging to the back of a chair, her head bowed, her hair falling across her face.

"You're the Naiad," he said, his hands yearning to touch her. She looked so fragile that he didn't dare.

"Yes," she said. She didn't look at him.

"I recall hearing something about it at the time," he said, unable to stop looking at the photograph. "The model who posed for the Naiad ads was attacked in Central Park. There was a big to-do about it in the media. Then I didn't hear anything more." He still found it hard to believe that Caro was that model.

"She was in the hospital for a while before going home. And she fled New York because she was afraid that the man who slashed her face might hurt her again," Caro said. Somehow talking about herself in the third person made it seem as though it had all happened to someone else.

"She has blue eyes," he said. "Yours are brown."

"Contact lenses. I had blue ones and green ones and gray ones...." Her words trailed off into silence as she remembered. The contacts had been Marina's idea, so that she would have a chance at jobs that specified a model with eyes of a certain color.

"You came to Moab," he said. "Why Moab?"

She swiveled to face him, and he saw that she had been crying. Her scar was livid.

"I was only passing through. My car broke down and—" She shrugged. He'd already heard that story.

"Why didn't you tell any of us who you were?"

"It would have meant explanations. I couldn't bear to talk about it," she said, her voice an agonized whisper.

He put the magazine on the table, rife with conflicting emotions. The ad made him see that Caro was a different person from the one he had always thought she was; she really did have an important reason to go back to New York eventually. There was a whole other life to which she could return. At last all the long-distance phone conversations he'd overheard began to make sense. He passed a hand over his eyes, trying to think. He felt as though the bottom had dropped out of his world.

"Mike, I'm sorry. I know I should have told you who I am, but I was afraid."

"Afraid?"

"Afraid to shatter whatever peace I'd found. I—I was happy here. I couldn't bear to dredge up anything about the attack." She let her hands fall to her sides in a helpless gesture that tore at his heart.

He reached out to touch a fingertip to the tear that clung to her lashes. He couldn't help skimming his fingers across her scar, but she shied away from his touch.

"When will you ever learn?" he said softly.

Her startled gaze met his. She didn't understand.

"You're beautiful to me. The scar doesn't matter." He wrapped his arms around her and drew her closer. He could feel the thrum of her heart beneath the thin shirt she wore.

"I'm not what you thought I was," she answered.

"Yeah, for a while I thought you were married," he said. It

was an attempt to inject some ironic humor into the conversation, and he was rewarded when her forlorn expression eased.

"I guess I should tell you how it happened," she said.

"You don't have to tell me anything unless you want to," he told her firmly.

She rested her forehead against his chest, trying to summon the strength. Perhaps Marina had been right. Maybe she should have seen a psychiatrist to work out the problems within herself. The trouble was, and no one had seemed to understand this, when she had been in the throes of anguish over the attack, she hadn't had the strength to see anyone. Merely surviving from day to day had taken all the courage she could muster at the time.

"Come with me," Mike said, leading her into the bedroom. He tossed her suitcase onto the floor and pulled her down onto the bed beside him. The light was dim, its source the living room. The half-darkness conveyed a certain intimacy.

"I—I suppose what worried me most was that the man who attacked me was out there somewhere in the city, waiting. The detective on the case only had a couple of clues. There didn't seem to be a motive. I thought he might attack again and finish the job," she said, reaching for his hand and clinging tightly to it.

"So you left?"

"I ran away. Marina is the head of the modeling agency, and she's also my good friend. She couldn't, wouldn't understand how frightened I was. And the way people looked at me was awful. I felt like a freak. They'd take one look at my face and then glance away, embarrassed."

"Is that what made you decide to run away?"

"I did it to save my sanity. I thought I'd go crazy alone in my apartment. I could feel myself falling to pieces. I got on a plane one day and flew west. I had no destination and no plan."

"So that's how you ended up in Moab," he said.

"I'm so grateful that I did. Annie and her family were exactly what I needed at the time, and you—"

"What about me?" He cupped her chin in his hand and turned her face toward his.

"You were wonderful," she whispered, warmed by the fire in his eyes.

He kissed her then, slowly and surely, his lips searching and seeking and demanding. His hand covered one side of her scar; it tingled briefly, and then he was moving his lips across its entire length, his breath feathering against her skin. She closed her eyes and remained perfectly still.

"Caro, my sweet Caro, I love you. I've grown to care about you so deeply that I can't imagine being without you," and before she could frame an answer in her mind, his mouth closed over hers.

Her vulnerability, followed by the way she had confided in him had unleashed his most primitive, protective instincts, but they fell away as she turned toward him and adjusted her body to his in a fluid motion that he found extraordinarily arousing.

The blanket tangled around their legs. He ripped it away and tossed it over the side of the bed. Passion darkened her eyes, and he felt the bite of her fingernails on his back. Urgently she guided his hands to her blouse, and when he had slid the buttons through their holes, she sat up and gracefully slipped out of it.

She was so beautiful that he felt a deep insistent ache when he looked at her. She was lovelier now, in his small bed in this tiny trailer, than she had been in that magazine ad. He didn't even know the person in the ad, but this Caro, the one sitting in front of him, was real. She was real, she was touchable and she was his.

Reverently he slid his hands through her hair, weaving his fingers through the blond strands as he caressed her full mouth with his thumbs. Then she was on top of him and his senses were filled with her, with her scent, her taste, her touch. Now she was wild for him, desperate even, her body tormenting him.

Their meeting was swift and bold and insistent, and it followed no previous pattern. He needed to know that she, the Naiad, was truly his; she needed to know that he loved her despite her scar. They locked together, shutting out the world, shutting out everything but each other. When it was over they lay panting amid crumpled sheets, stunned by their own passion.

Mike felt dazed, not only by the urgency of their physical union but by the mental leaps that had been required of him as well. She was still his; the past half hour had proved that. But she wasn't who he had thought she was.

He had become accustomed to Caro as part of the Stendahl household, a kind of extension of his cousin Annie and her children. He'd learned her moods, how to respond to her. *And yes,* he'd learned to love her, all within the parameters of that tight little circle.

To know now how certainly she didn't belong there challenged his view of her and changed his attitude toward their future together. He had assumed that if their relationship grew and deepened, he would be able to persuade her to stay with him. After tonight's revelation he was not so sure.

"Tell me," he said as she sighed and nestled her head comfortably on his chest. "Was there someone in New York? A man?"

She answered without hesitation. "I had a friend. His name was Wayne. I cared about him, maybe too much. After the attack—" Here her voice faltered.

He tightened his embrace. "After the attack, what?" he demanded, trying to keep his voice level.

"Afterward, he couldn't look at me," she said in a small voice.

"My God, I don't believe it!" He sat up and focused his furious gaze on her. Under his intense scrutiny, she lifted her hands and covered her face.

He pulled her hands away, leaving her exposed and vulnerable.

"Don't hide from me!" he said. He couldn't bear the thought that by his neglect and subsequent defection from her life, this Wayne had made Caro feel unwanted, unadmired and unloved. The man must be a fool.

"I thought he loved me," she said, and tears welled in her eyes, overflowed and streamed down her cheeks. "When he made excuses not to see me, I was devastated. It was hard enough to lose my looks, but losing the man I thought I loved was worse."

Mike's heart went out to her. Slowly he folded his body around hers, as if to protect her from the pain and sorrow of the world. No wonder she had run away. Her life must have been unbearable.

When she had stopped trembling, he kissed her on the temple and said, "Don't ever go back, Caro. Stay here."

She heaved a great wracking sigh. "I'll have to go back someday, especially if they catch the man who did this to me. I'll have to identify him, and there'll be a trial. And even if they never arrest anyone, there's my apartment to see to."

"An apartment?" He was so accustomed to seeing Caro at Annie's house that he couldn't imagine her having any other home.

"A lovely apartment on Central Park West."

"Central Park West," he repeated thoughtfully. "It must be a pretty nice place." A bleak feeling began to descend over him. *Of course.* He should have known she came from that kind of background. It was obvious with her clothes, her bearing, even the way she talked. He had a vague idea that a Naiad must earn a lot of money.

"My apartment's very nice. Luxurious, even."

"I can't imagine what kept you here," he said, thinking of Annie's place with its perpetual array of discarded candy-bar wrappers and stray popcorn kernels in the pile of the carpet. Even more preposterous was the idea that he had so blithely invited her to share his quarters at the Tin Can, complete with cactus in the front yard and a gopher snake that lived under the bed.

She pulled herself up and rested on one elbow, winding her free hand through his hair.

"I found lots of important things in Moab, Mike. In Annie's house there was a feeling of normality, of security. Oh, there are plenty of ups and downs—in a household with three children there would have to be. But the love surrounded me, buoyed me up, made me forget about my problems. And then," she said slowly, leaning forward to kiss his cheek, "there was you."

"There still is me," he reminded her doggedly. "And I'm not going to let you go so easily."

For an answer Caro bent her head toward him, taking her time about it, not rushing, and kissed him as thoroughly as he had ever been kissed.

"You'd better not," she said, and he thought with a surge of hope, *Maybe there is a chance for us, after all.*

Chapter Nine

Caro and Mike settled into a routine in those first few days at the trailer. They rose early, breakfasted together, and then Caro left for the Stendahls' house, where she put in a day's work in the pottery workshop. Mike spent his days concentrating on the paper about the Anasazi that he was to present to the Rosetta Society in September.

Caro loved to see him sitting at the kitchen table typing on an old manual typewriter, his reading glasses sliding down his nose, his hair perpetually tousled. He worked hard, and he had utter confidence in his subject matter.

At night after dinner, Caro and Mike would go over Mike's work for the day. More and more Caro believed Mike's theory about the presence of ancient Libyans in the Four Corners area.

"It looks to me as though with all your evidence, these theories are worth a closer look from those so-called traditional archaeologists who are so quick to put down anything new," Caro observed one night.

Mike eyed her speculatively. "Does that mean you're a believer?" he asked.

"I'm not ready to rewrite the history books yet," she admitted. "But I sure am eager to see what you turn up at Yalabasi Canyon."

"So am I," Mike said.

"Is there any news about permission to explore the El Karak Company's tract?"

"Someone from the company's London office wrote to say that I should expect permission anytime."

"And then what?"

"I'll head out there immediately with Charlie's map in hand. He told me before he died that some of the writings on the rocks in Yalabasi Canyon looked like Arabic to him. My job will be to look for those epigraphs and determine if they're ancient Arabic."

"Ancient Arabic!"

"Don't look so shocked, Caro. Anasazi art can be bafflingly complex, but I've determined that some of it is Arabic written in a Libyan style that hasn't been used since a couple of centuries before Christ." He grinned at her.

"Mike, the implications of that are—are—well, words fail me!" she exclaimed.

"If I make a major find in Yalabasi Canyon, it could be the authentication that I need to land a meaningful research grant. That's what I hope to do after I've made public my findings about the Libyan-Anasazi connection in my Rosetta Society presentation."

"A research grant! That sounds like big-time archaeology."

Mike leaned back in his chair, his hands hooked behind his head. A dreamy expression came over his face. "A grant would be my dream come true. I'd be able to explore and possibly excavate whatever ruins I find in Yalabasi Canyon, thereby uncovering even more evidence. Public attention could mean a contract to write a book. With enough money, I could travel to California and investigate some epigraphs that have reportedly been found there, perhaps showing that California was the actual port of entry for Libyans. Oh, there's no end to what I could do with some real money."

"I hope all that happens," she said.

He bent over his papers again. "It won't if I don't get busy and have a paper to present," he said, smiling, and Caro, though excited by this new information, settled down to work beside him, sorting files that he had amassed on the subject of the Anasazi.

It was pleasant work, and she enjoyed doing it. In fact, they spent many evenings this way. Once in a while they would look up simultaneously and share a smile; sometimes one or the other of them would get up and put on the coffeepot. They passed the nights wrapped in each others' arms on Mike's narrow bed, glad that it was no wider because they didn't want to be too far apart.

Their joy in being together made Caro wish that everyone could be so happy, particularly Annie and Tom. However, the reconciliation was apparently not going well.

One morning Caro was working in the studio behind the house on Kettle Street when Annie came in, looking dejected.

"Go ahead with what you're doing," Annie said as she began to thumb through a new batch of orders.

"Is anything wrong?" Caro asked, noting the dark circles under Annie's eyes.

Annie shrugged and turned away.

"It's Tom, isn't it?" Caro probed gently.

Annie threw out her hands in frustration. "Yes, it's Tom. He keeps asking me and the kids to move to Salt Lake City. He wants to rent a house big enough for the five of us."

"It doesn't sound as though you want to go."

"How can I pick up and move? I have pottery orders to fill. Anyway, Nola is going to have her baby next month, and I promised I'd help take care of her other kids while she's in the hospital."

Caro set down the bowl she was painting on the workbench and turned around. "Annie, you worked so hard before Tom got here that you've actually made more pots than you can ship in the next couple of weeks. And why don't you ask Gert or Lou to help Nola with her kids? Why does it have to be you?"

Annie shrugged. "Nola helped me when Peter was born. I owe her the favor."

"Nola would probably understand if you told her that you want to move to be with Tom, and besides, somebody else could help her. Getting your family back together must be a priority with you. Isn't it?"

"Nola *is* family, Caro," Annie said.

"So is Tom," Caro reminded her. "You love him, don't you?"

Blinking rapidly, Annie nodded. "I had forgotten how much. It's so good to have him home, Caro. I've missed him terribly. I'd forgotten how his laugh echoes through the house and how it makes me smile just to hear it. And—oh, all sorts of things," she said.

Caro liked Tom. He had turned out to be a big bear of a man who had a knack with the children and also with lawn mowers. That meant the grass was now cut short and that Mike need not worry himself about it, which was a great help while he was putting so much energy into the paper he was writing.

"Go to Salt Lake City," Caro said firmly. "If you're worried about things around here, I'll look after them."

"I'll think about it," Annie said, and as Caro watched her hurry back to the house, she thought that Annie would be a fool not to follow her husband.

"So how are Tom and Annie getting along?" Mike asked Caro casually that night when they were sitting up on the rocky knoll that had become a favorite place to walk to after dinner.

"Not too well, I take it," Caro answered. She folded her arms around her knees and rested her chin on them.

"What's the problem?"

"He wants her to come live with him in Salt Lake City."

"She's still refusing, right?"

"She thinks she has an obligation to be here when Nola has her baby next month."

"Family ties, oh how they bind," said Mike musingly. He stared up at the sky for a moment.

"You don't seem especially bound by them," she observed.

"I broke away early. Both my parents died, and I went away to college. When I came back to Moab, I never got caught up in the family circus the way Annie did."

"You and Annie seem close."

"We are, for cousins. That's because our mothers were not only sisters but best friends, and Annie and I played together a lot when we were kids. I was the brother she never had. I still look out for her."

"What do you think about the situation between her and Tom?"

"Tom's a great guy. Sure, he makes demands on Annie's time, but maybe he should. Sometimes it seemed like Tom got the short end of the stick compared to Annie's female relatives. The women in this family take care of one another, which makes for a nice support group. But their tight little circle also closes other people out, and that's what Tom was fighting."

"Tom seems happy to be home. He loves his kids."

"That's the sad part. It's too bad that Tom felt that he had to walk out to get Annie's attention. Everybody suffered, not just Annie."

"Do you think you could talk to Annie? Make her see that she ought to go to Salt Lake City with the kids?"

Mike took Caro's hand and turned it palm upward, tracing the lines. "I've talked to Annie till I was blue in the face. Like all the women in this family, she can be stubborn. Seems like they all carry a common gene for pigheadedness." He laughed a little.

Around them, the mesas seemed to sink deeper into the darkness; they were cocooned in night, bound up in a starry blanket.

"I haven't told you my big news," Caro said.

"Mmm?"

"That man in California who likes my work—the one with the gift shop? He wants more of my designs. In fact, he's offering a contract. If I sign it, I'll be shipping a designated number of pieces to him every month."

"Caro! That's wonderful!"

"It is, isn't it?"

He held her hand between both of his now, obviously pleased for her.

"Are you going to do it?" He held his breath. He had been afraid to ask her about her commitment to her work, to this place, and especially to him.

"I think so," she said. "I love the work. I'm always trying new techniques or learning better ways to apply the old ones. There's a lot of freedom of expression in making this kind of pottery."

"More than in modeling?"

"I never found modeling particularly creative. For me it was merely a matter of reacting to the photographer. Doing nothing but reacting, never acting, becomes stultifying and old after a while."

"How long were you the Naiad?"

"I was the one they chose out of hundreds of models when they began their advertising campaign. The first ads came out last September."

"And what kind of modeling did you do before that?"

"I started out the way most models do, by showing my portfolio around. I got a few little jobs, then a few big jobs. Before I was chosen as the Naiad, I'd already done a number of covers for major magazines in the United States and Europe.''

"You must miss the excitement of traveling, wearing nice clothes, all of it."

She didn't speak, and when she finally did, he was surprised at her forceful tone.

"No," she said with great finality. "I don't."

He wondered why she was so vehement on the subject. "Would you care to explain?" he asked.

She bit her lip and stared toward Preservation Mesa. He sensed a struggle within her. He waited for her to speak again.

"The excitement fades after a while, and then it's not exciting anymore. It's merely false stimulation. You're led to believe that you're doing something special because of all the hype and hoopla, but you know in your heart that it's nothing more than that, so you feel empty inside. Does this make any sense?" She darted him an anxious look.

"Yeah," he said. "It sure does."

"After a while, you see that in order to preserve the status quo, you have to keep doing all of it, so you act like everything is wonderful, everything is fine. That was one of Marina's favorite axioms. 'Act like you're happy, and you will be.' Or, 'Act like a famous model, and you will be.' Now it's 'Act like you don't have a scar, and you won't.' Well, it doesn't work that way. I can't go on deceiving myself."

Mike said, "I can see that."

"Something happened to get me off the merry-go-round—the attack. I came here thinking that what had happened to me was the worst thing in the world, and now—" She paused uncertainly.

"And now?"

"Maybe it wasn't the worst thing at all, but the best thing. I'm happy, Mike. I'm not just acting as though I'm happy. I really am."

"So am I," he said.

And realized that for the first time in his life, his happiness hinged on another person. The thought was slightly terrifying.

LOVE MIGHT BE PROSPERING at the Tin Can, but it certainly didn't seem to be smoothing things over at the house on Kettle Street, Caro realized.

She arrived one morning in the middle of a rousing fight in the kitchen, and winced when she heard Annie and Tom's raised voices through the open windows of the studio.

"Listen, Annie, if Connie can't pull herself together long enough to take Joey to his tee ball practice, why should you run over there and do it?"

"I told you, she asked me if Peter was going, and I offered to go over and get Joey and take him to the practice field. Why is that so bad?"

"Connie knew good and well that Peter dropped out of tee ball when he broke his arm. He hasn't been to practice since." Tom sounded thoroughly disgusted.

"Well, Peter had been talking about going to practice anyway to watch the other kids," Annie said.

"You and I discussed that, and we decided together that it wouldn't be a good idea for Peter to go to practice when he can't play. It would just upset him."

"Well, when I talked with Connie, she thought it might be a good idea if Peter went. The other boys have been asking how he is."

"Connie wanted Peter to go so that you would come by and give Joey a *ride*, Annie. That way Connie gets out of driving Joey to practice, right? And anyway, whatever happened to the idea that you and I would discuss what's best for our own kids?"

Clearly flustered, Annie ignored Tom's question about who should make decisions about the children and retorted, "How dare you say bad things about Connie!"

This diversionary tactic worked. Tom yelled, "Connie's always trying to get somebody else to do her work, don't tell me any different! What about the time her washing machine broke and you told her she could bring her dirty clothes over and use yours, and she brought her laundry and left it for you to do while she went to have her hair done! Oh, I know how Connie thinks, all right!"

"You've always had it in for Connie. Don't think I don't know that."

"Yeah, right. I've always had it in for your cousin Connie. For good reason, maybe," Tom said sarcastically.

If it hadn't been so warm outside, Caro would have closed the workshop windows so she wouldn't have to hear any more. It sounded as though nothing had changed between Annie and Tom. And yet Caro was convinced that Tom loved Annie. His many expressions of caring and love during the past week had told her that.

It wasn't long before a wan and tearful Annie appeared in the workshop.

"Tom's leaving," she announced in a shaky voice. "He's going back to Salt Lake City."

"Oh, Annie, no!" Caro exclaimed.

"We had a big fight," Annie said. "You must have heard it."

"Yes," Caro admitted.

"Thank goodness, the kids were all over at Tony's playing Monopoly. Tom and I got into an argument about my giving Connie's son Joey a ride to tee ball practice yesterday afternoon. Just because I was a little late getting back, when we had planned to go down to the video rental place and pick out a movie—well, Tom got awfully mad. He said I'm always putting my relatives first."

"Annie, I'm sorry," was all Caro could think of to say.

Annie sniffed and wiped her eyes. "Well, I can't just stand around doing nothing. Let's get busy," she said, pulling a packing crate out of the closet.

They had started to wrap pots in paper for shipment when Tom's doleful face appeared in the window. He stepped around to the doorway. "Annie?" he asked.

Annie dropped a pot and it smashed into smithereens on the concrete floor.

"Don't worry, I'll clean it up," Caro assured her.

Annie stepped outside, where she and Tom carried on a heated discussion that became more resigned as it went on. Finally Tom bent his big head and kissed Annie on the cheek, and her arms went around him. Caro averted her eyes. She didn't want to intrude on their privacy.

"Bye, Annie," she heard Tom say with a catch in his voice.

"Bye, Tom. I wish—" Annie couldn't continue.

"So do I. I'll call you soon."

"Okay. Are you going by Tony's house to tell the kids good-bye?"

"Yeah." Tom shuffled his feet, looked down at the ground and then fled. As Annie came into the workshop, they heard his car starting in the driveway.

"Well, that's that," Annie said. Her eyes were brimming with tears.

"I wish it had worked out," Caro said. She felt so sorry for Annie.

"He doesn't understand my family. I guess he never will."

"He loves you, Annie."

"I love him too, Caro." Annie turned dejectedly and picked up hammer and nails to secure the lid on the crate.

"Then why—?"

Annie swiveled around.

"Why what?"

"Why don't you join him in Salt Lake City? Isn't the invitation still open?"

"I suppose so, but—"

"Then go! Try it for a couple of weeks, anyway! Tom loves you and the kids, Annie. If the only thing keeping you apart is your family, try getting away from them. It's the only way!"

"But Nola's baby is almost due, and I'd miss them all so much," Annie said.

"Annie, if it would help, *I'll* take care of Nola's other children while she's in the hospital!"

"Oh, Caro, I couldn't let you do that, and if it came to that, Connie or Lou or Diane would help her. It's just that I—"

"It's just that you don't want to give all of them up for Tom," Caro said softly.

"I wouldn't put it like that," Annie said stiffly.

"I would," Caro said.

With that, Annie tossed down the hammer on top of the crate and marched out of the workshop.

She had angered Annie. There was no doubt about that. But if Annie wouldn't listen to Tom or to Mike, who else would tell her what she needed to hear?

Caro went on with her work, feeling increasingly guilty about making Annie angry when she was already distraught. She was on the verge of going into the house to apologize when Mike turned up.

"Mike!" she said, getting up to wash the clay off her hands. "I'm so glad to see you." Quickly she related what had happened that morning.

Mike fixed his lips in a grim line. "Thank goodness you let her know what you think," he said. "Maybe that's what she needs to set her straight. You're an impartial observer, Caro. Perhaps your words will carry some weight."

Caro cast an apprehensive glance toward the quiet house. "She went in there three hours ago and I haven't seen a sign of her since," Caro said.

"This family!" Mike said in annoyance. "Why are the women so stubborn? I'll go see if I can find her. Want to come with me?"

"No, thanks," Caro said firmly. Mike dropped a reassuring kiss on her cheek, then loped off toward the house.

Within five minutes he was back.

Caro met him at the workshop door, surprised at the smile on his face.

"She's packing," he told her.

"She's *what*?"

"She's washing clothes for the kids and packing suitcases for the four of them. She's going to Salt Lake City tomorrow, she says. This is a first, Caro. Annie has never, to my knowledge, given in on anything."

"What made her change her mind?"

"She says that she wants to give her marriage a chance away from her family. What did I tell you, Caro? Coming from you, the criticism worked."

"I don't deserve the credit, Mike. Annie does. She finally made the right decision."

"I'm going to take Annie's station wagon up to the gas station and have the oil changed and the gas tank filled so she can get on her way," Mike said.

"The station wagon! How will I get here to work every day?"

"I'll bring you and pick you up in the Jeep. Look, I've got to run if I want to get the oil changed before the guys at the service station knock off for the day. I'll be back to take you home later.'' They kissed, and he was gone.

Annie hurried out to the workshop shortly afterward. "I guess Mike told you that I'm going to Salt Lake City," she said.

"I'm so glad, Annie. I hope things will be fine."

"Me, too. And Caro—thanks. What you said was like a swift kick in the seat of the pants. Diane has promised to look after Nola's children when she has the baby, and well, if I miss Lou and Nola and everyone, there's always the telephone."

"What about your pottery business?" Caro wanted to know.

"I feel really good about leaving you in charge of the business, Caro, because you know how I do everything." And Annie proceeded to pull out shipping receipts and invoices and orders to show Caro.

"Remember," Annie said in parting, "I'll be in touch by phone every day, and you can call me at Tom's house anytime there's a problem."

"Don't worry," Caro said. "Everything will be all right."

"I hope so," Annie replied fervently, and Caro knew that she wasn't only talking about the pottery business.

After Annie left for Salt Lake City with the children, Caro settled into a particularly productive week at the workshop. Nothing in her experience compared with the satisfaction of bringing a lump of clay to life between her fingers. As she shaped coils into pots that would soon be washed with color and painted with designs, it occurred to her that she worked on her pots from the inside out, much as she was working on herself. Pottery was recreation; putting herself back together after the attack was re-creation. Perhaps they were one and the same.

For the first time in her life, she felt that the creative side of her personality was being fulfilled. Also for the first time in her life, she felt content. Caro realized that she had never known the meaning of the word before. Somehow she had always confused contentment with stagnation. Now she knew that contentment consisted of something else entirely.

Her contentment grew out of the realization that she didn't need the status of being the Naiad to be happy. There was no pressure here to perform, no one pushing her to make more and more money, and no terror on her part at not being able to fulfill others' expectations.

Instead, there was Mike's acceptance and love. Caro discovered that her secret inner self was on fertile ground for growth. She seldom thought about externals like her scar. She was more and more conscious of who she was and what she wanted out of life, and what she sought was not what she had wanted six months ago. Now it seemed that her life before the attack had been ruled by an ethic that she could no longer accept.

In those days, she had been trying to impress everyone else, with no thought about what she really wanted to do with her life. She had been driven to succeed by her own longing for the things money could buy, but had discovered when she reached the pinnacle that success was hollow.

Mike understood her present frame of mind. He was one person who had always been true to himself. And his love for her made her stronger, because it signified the acceptance she had so desperately needed when, broken and disfigured, she arrived in Moab. Loving him mobilized her to learn and do and see, and thus she forgot her own concerns. Nowadays she bubbled over with life and goodwill.

Reports from Annie in Salt Lake City were encouraging.

"Tom has rented this big house with a huge garage," Annie said during one of her frequent phone calls. "The garage is big enough for a pottery workshop. The children have found friends right across the street."

"What about you and Tom?" Caro asked.

Now Annie sounded cautiously optimistic. "We're getting along pretty well."

"Do you think you'll want to stay?" Caro asked.

Annie was silent for a long time. "I don't know, Caro. We're taking it one day at a time."

"Good luck, Annie," Caro said.

"Thanks," Annie said, sounding cheerful. "Every little bit helps."

That afternoon Mike picked her up at Annie's workshop, and Caro related the latest about Annie and Tom as they drove to the post office.

"Good," Mike said firmly. "Those two need each other. It's about time they started seeing eye to eye."

He pulled the Jeep into the post office parking lot and said, "I'll be out in a minute." He hurried inside to check his post office box, where he received all his mail.

While he was gone, Caro watched a family next to her—four kids, a mother and a father—while one of the kids ran inside the building. The kids were so cute, and one reminded her of Holly. She missed Annie's children. Life without children seemed bland and uneventful, now that she had grown accustomed to the constant crises, the lively meals, and the laughter that went along with them.

Mike burst from the post office at a near run; he was waving a letter in the air. Caro knew that whatever it was, it must be important.

"It's from the El Karak Mining Company," he told her excitedly as he climbed into the Jeep. "They've given me permission to explore their land."

"Oh, Mike, that's wonderful!"

"You bet it is," he said, grinning from ear to ear.

"When will you leave?"

"Soon," he said. "Probably Monday."

Suddenly Caro realized that when he left, she would be by herself. Her face fell. She'd known that this was pending, but she hadn't thought about how she'd feel when Mike was hiking around some canyon in the wilderness.

"Is something wrong?" Mike asked.

"I just realized that with Annie and the kids gone, I'll be all alone here," she said.

"But I want you to come with me!" Mike exclaimed. He had thought her participation was a given; he couldn't imagine going without her. Always he thought about the threat of her returning to New York sometime and picking up the life she had left behind. While she was here, while she was his, he didn't want to be away from her any more than necessary.

Caro caught her breath. "You've never mentioned that you wanted me to go with you. Anyhow, I'd just be in the way."

He took both her hands in his. "I want you to go. I'd be lost without you. Caro, I'll be gone a week or more. I need you."

"I might not be a good camper or hiker. I've never slept out in the desert before. And besides, there's the workshop. How can I leave it when Annie is depending on me?"

People were walking past the Jeep, talking and laughing. Caro and Mike's conversation had grown so intense that someone stared for a moment, then hurried on. They drew slightly apart.

"You know who you reminded me of just then?" Mike said after a time.

"Who?"

"Annie. You sounded exactly like Annie, when she was making excuses not to go to Salt Lake City to be with her husband."

Caro, rocked by this accurate perception, sat back. She was putting her work with the pottery ahead of Mike's current needs. She had almost forgotten how important his exploration of Yalabasi Canyon was to him. She wasn't being supportive.

Mike was right. The pottery could wait. She'd talk to Annie about this on the phone tomorrow, but she had no doubt that Annie would tell her to go.

"Maybe it's time to practice a bit of selective selfishness," she said with an embarrassed little laugh.

"You mean you'll go?" Mike said, his face breaking into a smile. He'd been anticipating a big campaign to win her over.

"I mean I'll go," she told him.

"Well," he said. "What do you know about that?"

She only laughed, and he realized that he had been expecting her to react the way Annie would have reacted; that is, to dig her feet in and resist.

Thank goodness, he thought as he started the Jeep's engine. She wasn't like the other women in his family. Maybe he ought to marry her, in case it was genetic. The way he saw it, Caro could only improve the stock.

Chapter Ten

The Jeep hurtled across the El Karak tract, Mike handling the rugged driving easily. Caro stepped adeptly into her role as navigator, spreading Charlie Deer Walk's map up against the dashboard and shading her eyes from the sun as she peered ahead, looking for landmarks that would tell them they were drawing near to Yalabasi Canyon.

The pungent scent of juniper resin hung in the air, and overhead the sky shone a harsh, searing blue. They passed through a juniper forest, the trees scrubby and small. The air was hot and motionless, and the backs of Caro's legs stuck to the vinyl seat. She wished she had worn jeans instead of hiking shorts.

Yalabasi Canyon itself turned out to be a deep, spectacular chasm joined by several tributary canyons. Mike relied on Charlie Deer Walk's map and aerial photographs from the mining company to determine the best access.

They descended into the canyon by way of a steep slope of shale that almost did Caro in at the very beginning. She found that keeping her balance and testing each step before putting her full weight on it required the utmost concentration, and despite an occasional helping hand from Mike, she almost fell more than once.

Once the shale slope was behind them, they continued to descend past an array of multicolored sandstone formations and natural arches. They stopped to rest at a limestone grotto between two rock spires. The place was so awe-inspiring that Caro had the feeling that she was standing in the middle of a cathedral.

When they reached the floor of the canyon, they stopped at a spring-fed pool and drank their fill of the bitter-tasting water, purifying it first with water purification tablets. Now they were trudging through sand and sagebrush, the trail still descending; the temperature was a scorching ninety-nine degrees Fahrenheit.

Caro ignored the way her skin, having evaporated much of its moisture, seemed too taut to fit her body. She pinned her hair on top of her head and struggled to keep up with Mike as they trekked across the bottom of the canyon. Her pack was heavy and her shoulders burned where the straps cut into them, but she was determined not to let Mike know how uncomfortable she was. Oddly, her feet hurt as much as her shoulders. The additional weight of her pack had made them expand, so that her toes bumped the front of her borrowed hiking boots.

"Everything okay?" Mike called back to her.

"Fine," she managed to say. She didn't want to spoil any part of this trip for him, nor did she want him to be sorry that he'd insisted on her presence.

The trail at the bottom of the canyon followed a dry streambed.

"According to this," Mike said, pulling the map out of his pocket, "the stream resurfaces somewhere up here." He pointed to the spot on the map. Ahead of them, where the canyon floor seemed to level out, Caro saw a haze of greenery.

In late afternoon Mike stopped to make camp at a spot where the canyon walls narrowed to perhaps two hundred feet apart. Caro dropped her pack and rubbed her shoulders, a task that was soon taken over by Mike.

"A friend of mine once described backpacking as the worst possible way to get from one place to another," Mike said jokingly as he massaged the back of her neck.

Caro tried to smile. "Right now I think I'd agree with him," she said.

"You'll feel better once we've eaten," he told her.

"Don't we need to find water?" It disturbed Caro that their canteens were nearly empty.

"I'll mosey downcanyon a bit and see if I can find some."

"This place looks so dry," Caro observed, uneasily looking around at the expanses of rock and sand.

"Trust me," Mike said. "See those cottonwoods over there? They couldn't survive without water."

"Wait, I'll go with you," Caro said hastily.

They walked along the crusty meander of the old stream. A breeze stirred the cottonwood leaves and flapped Caro's shirt-tail. It felt wonderful.

Around a bend in the rock Mike said suddenly, "Here it is," and stepped aside so that Caro saw a wide pool of water.

The pool was lined with dead cottonwood leaves and ringed by alkali deposits, but they were grateful to find it and filled their water containers to the top. Exploring farther, they found a second pool, one that was deep enough for bathing.

Caro waded in without hesitation and, not stopping to remove her clothes, sat down on a submerged rock. She leaned back, letting the sun-warmed water soothe her tired muscles. Mike stripped down to his bare skin, then followed her. She had grown used to his slender, whippy form; usually the sight of him aroused her. Not this time, however. That in itself was a measure of her exhaustion.

"This is heaven," Caro said, letting the water rise about her shoulders. Overhead, she watched a hawk as it effortlessly glided above the canyon walls.

Mike sat beside her, their little fingers linked. A tadpole nibbled on Caro's toe. She pulled her foot away, but the tadpole followed. She had no intention of leaving, even if she had to share this pool with the tadpole and all his brothers and sisters.

"Tomorrow we'll get up early and—"

"Tomorrow!" Caro groaned. She couldn't bear the thought of shouldering her pack again.

Mike grinned at her. "You'll get used to this, I promise. Anyway, perhaps we'll start finding signs of the Anasazi."

At that moment, Caro didn't care if she ever found out any-thing about the Anasazi. All she wanted was a meal and a restful sleep.

After a time, they climbed out of the pool and Mike put his clothes on. Caro's wet shorts and shirt dried quickly; in the dry desert air, liquid evaporated rapidly. By the time they had cooked dehydrated soup over their campfire, her clothes were almost completely dry.

That night, the singing of a colony of frogs near the pool

threatened to keep Caro awake. But she was so tired that she merely snuggled closer to Mike in the sleeping bag and fell asleep.

In the morning a gray pearly light stole over the campsite. Caro woke before Mike and levered herself up on her elbows.

"Um," Mike said, moving to take her in his arms.

She nestled into the curve of his body, getting used to the sounds of the canyon—the squawk of a jay echoing off the sides of the cliffs, the quiver of a cottonwood leaf batted against the rocks by a warm breeze. When they finally crawled out of Mike's sleeping bag, Caro felt surprisingly rested.

By the time the first rays of sunlight illuminated the upper canyon walls, even the miserable backpack didn't seem like the burden it had been the day before. Alight with new enthusiasm, she swung along the old meander beside Mike, curious about her surroundings.

The bends in the canyon occurred about every five hundred yards, and at each one was a cave or overhanging cliff. At one curve, Mike pointed out a square, dark opening beneath a ledge, and they climbed toward it, slowly and tortuously. As they drew closer, Caro noted that the opening to the cave was built up with small stones.

"It's a granary," Mike said, peering inside. "The Anasazi stored the food they gathered and grew in places like this."

Mike photographed the site, and then they broke for lunch. After a short rest, they pressed on.

That afternoon they came upon exposed building blocks on a sprawling sagebrush-covered mound that Mike said was an unexcavated ruin.

"There are probably thousands of Anasazi sites spread out across the land," he observed. "Some, like this one, have attracted little interest. That's probably a good thing, since it keeps the pothunters and plunderers away."

Caro, wandering off on her own, poked around in the shrubbery and found several pieces of pottery and a few arrow points.

"This was the community trash dump for this village," Mike said, following her and picking up a broken metate, or corn-grinding stone.

A faint depression that Mike located nearby was the kiva, or circular underground religious chamber. He made detailed notations on a map, and then they walked another mile or so before making camp for the night.

Later, when they lay together under the stars in Mike's big sleeping bag, Caro's head resting in the crook of his neck, she asked him if the canyon was what he had hoped.

"Not yet, because I haven't discovered anything of real importance. But it's a thrill to explore a place that no one has adequately mapped in the five hundred years since the occupants left," he told her, tightening his arms around her. "It's an even bigger thrill to be doing it with someone I love."

"I'm afraid I'm holding you back," Caro said. "I know your pace is slower because I'm with you."

"Don't be silly. I wouldn't be moving any faster if you weren't here. I have to take time to fill in my map and take pictures."

"I wish we'd find some epigraphs soon," she said. She knew that Mike was disappointed because so far, none had turned up.

"I've got a feeling—just a hunch—that the writing that Charlie found must have been near the mesa at the big curve in the canyon," Mike said.

"Will we be there soon?"

"We'll make camp near there tomorrow night."

"Good," Caro murmured, and then fell into a deep, deep sleep.

In the morning they awoke to the trill of bird song and the sight of an inquisitive pocket squirrel. It ran away when Caro laughed out loud.

They were on their way before the sun had tipped the canyon walls with gold. The canyon plunged steeply downward now, finally revealing a narrow stream flowing through a grove of cottonwoods. Within twenty yards, the creek had burgeoned to a width of twelve feet or so and they heard the sound of rushing water. They took off their shoes and socks, waded across, and came out of the grove to find themselves at the top of a tumbling waterfall.

With exultant shouts, they clambered down the rocks and shucked their backpacks. Then they frolicked in the plummeting water, laughing and splashing each other until they tired and waded out of the lagoon below.

Caro threw herself down on a bed of maidenhair fern and

dangled her feet in the water. Mike slid an arm around Caro's shoulders. She adjusted her head so that it rested comfortably on his chest.

"This is the first time I've actually felt like the Naiad since I posed for the last ad," she said.

"Is that good or bad?" he asked, arching his neck to look at her.

"Good. No, bad. Oh, I don't know. I'd rather be a real-life naiad with you in the waterfall than a pretend Naiad for a cosmetic company."

"Who would think that you could feel like a real water nymph out here in the desert?" Mike smiled. He was used to the desert's surprises, but Caro wasn't.

"I wish I'd told Marina I was coming with you to the canyon."

"Don't you think she'd only worry?"

"Maybe. She's getting antsy about my coming home."

"And what do you tell her?"

"Oh, I've kept her informed about the situation. I told her how Annie left to go stay with Tom, and I mentioned that I was taking care of the pottery workshop. I don't think Marina credits anything I tell her. She thinks I'm out here playing at a couple of new hobbies."

Slowly he rubbed his thumb up and down the smooth skin on the inside of her arm.

"And you're not, are you?" he said softly.

"No, Mike, I'm not." She sat straight up and turned to stare at him. "Do you honestly think I'd haul around a thirty-pound backpack as part of some crazy hobby?"

He smiled. Something behind the smile made her think that he was watching her carefully.

"I suppose you wouldn't."

"I'm here because I want to be with you, Mike, and because I think what you're doing is fascinating. You've showed me a whole new world, not only the Anasazi world, but your world. It's completely different from anything I've ever known before."

"In that picture you showed me—the one of you as the Naiad," he said, his face now serious, "you certainly don't look like the kind of woman who would enjoy hiking a backcountry canyon.''

''I wasn't that kind of woman—then. This is now.'' She kissed his lips lightly.

''Now,'' he agreed, capturing her lips in an even deeper kiss, and she responded enthusiastically, so enthusiastically that their journey was postponed by at least an hour.

Later, when they had bathed in the lagoon and donned their clothes again, Mike judged that they would reach the foot of the mesa in the big curve of the canyon in about an hour.

When they reached the base of the mesa, they tossed away their backpacks and sat down to rest. Caro was paying attention to nothing in particular, unless it was her sore feet; she had removed her shoes and socks and was massaging her instep. Beside her Mike suddenly came to attention.

''What is it?'' she asked.

''I'm not sure,'' he said, staring at a large boulder partly hidden by a clump of weeds. He scrambled through the weeds and brushed them aside. He uttered a jubilant shout.

Caro struggled to put her shoes back on and hurried to join him. She found him staring at an inscription on the rock.

''It's ancient Kufic script,'' he said unsteadily. ''It preceded the modern Arabic alphabet. This probably dates from around 700 A.D.''

''Can you read it?''

''It says, 'Mohammed is the prophet of God,''' he said. ''I've seen the same Islamic sentence carved almost exactly this way on rocks in North Africa. It was a favorite bit of graffito after the advent of Islam around 630 A.D.''

''That may be writing, but it looks like doodling,'' Caro said critically.

''That's exactly why early explorers ignored it. In some places, later occupants of an area embellished old Arabic script and made it look like something else. This is unadorned, and it's authentic, all right. And Charlie Deer Walk would have known what this was, even though he couldn't have translated it. He was with me when I photographed numerous Arabic inscriptions in other places.''

Mike took pictures of the epigraph and applied latex to the

inscription to make a mold. When he had finished, Caro said, "What do you think it means, here in this canyon?"

Mike thought about it carefully. "It's a clue that this may have been a site where Libyan settlers taught their language and religion to local tribes or to one another. I'm going to be looking carefully for other such inscriptions."

"What makes you think there might have been a school here?"

"The roads that converge on the canyon indicate that this was a center for something. I don't see any signs of the big kivas that would indicate a religious center. We haven't discovered any indication that this was a market center."

"How would you know if it was a market center, anyway?"

"There are abacuses carved into the rock in other such centers. I've seen them in Africa and in North America. I've often thought that there may have been a center for learning somewhere nearby. The Libyans who came to this continent probably would have thought it was important to transmit knowledge of their language, their mathematics, their religion, their astronomy—a host of disciplines."

"Mathematics? How much did they know about mathematics?"

"A Libyan, Eratosthenes of Cyrene, determined the circumference of the earth. He showed that if the earth was round and the ocean continuous, a ship could set sail in one direction and return from the other. His countrymen tested his theory, only to land on the American continent."

"I didn't learn anything like that in school."

"We learn history from the western point of view in school. Scant mention is given to the fact that while Europe was plunged into the Dark Ages after the destruction of their universities and libraries by barbarians, it was Arabs who kept Euclid's geometry and other mathematical knowledge alive. They left fragmentary evidence of that knowledge, some of which is right here in Yalabasi Canyon."

It was with a sense of suppressed excitement that they made camp that night. The next morning they set out to explore the surrounding area more carefully, inspecting all rock surfaces for other epigraphs.

They climbed over huge boulders, scrabbled for purchase on

craggy rock faces, and finally found themselves in a quiet sunlit arena on a ledge where not even bird song disturbed the peace. Mike walked its boundaries, carefully scrutinizing the sheer rock walls until at last he found something. He called to Caro, and she came running.

"It's a nautical chart, and judging from the Libyan lettering, it dates from about 200 B.C.," he said with awe. He ran his fingers over the surface of it. To Caro the inscription in the rock looked like a sloppily drawn inverted pyramid, and Mike hastened to explain.

"This represents the North American continent," he said. "It lacks the Florida peninsula, because they didn't know about it. But it shows Hawaii, and this line to the right of Hawaii is the meridian of Alexandria, their date line. I've seen a similar carving at a site in Nevada."

"Look, Mike," Caro said, studying another carving. "This looks like some kind of dragon." It seemed to bristle with legs.

"It's a drawing of a ship. See, the dragon's head is the prow. Remember the Norse ships with figureheads like this one? Evidently they were in style with the Libyans, too. And the legs aren't the dragon's feet. They are oars. Some of the ships were so big that they required many oarsmen for each oar. It wouldn't have been unusual for five hundred people to set sail on such a vessel."

Nearby they found a diagram that Mike explained was a calculation of the circumference of the earth. "It was something the people needed to know if they were to train future mariners," he said with growing excitement. "This was where they taught them. They didn't have chalkboards, so they used carvings in the rock." He took pictures and made latex molds of the carvings before they started back to camp.

"You see, Caro," he said as they walked, "I believe that Libyans came here over two thousand years ago and carried on a friendly relationship with the Anasazi, who were a peaceful people and learned that they could benefit from the association. The Libyans set up schools for the Anasazi, who were willing students. After the civilization crumbled and the Anasazi scattered around 1300 A.D., the evidence was misread or misunderstood or worse yet, destroyed."

"What made the civilization die out?"

"I think it was a combination of drought and the invading Navajo and Apache sweeping in from the plains. Most archaeologists would agree with me about that, but few are ready to accept the idea of ancient colonists settling here. My goal is to validate my beliefs through these discoveries. I think it's important for us to know that a civilization thrived here long ago but eventually disappeared."

"I've heard it said that only by studying history can we avoid making similar mistakes."

"The important thing is that the history we study must be accurate. For too long we've ignored the written records that the earliest Americans, some of them colonists from other lands, left us."

Mike would have liked to explore the canyon further, but he was also eager to get to the top of the mesa. From their camp they could see evidence of a series of stone walls protruding from an immense cave about halfway up, and Mike thought that the cave sheltered a large pueblo.

After dinner that night, Mike studied the rugged red rock outcropping for the best way to climb it. He finally located a workmanlike set of steps carved into the rock surface. Above the steps, a slope of trash and rubble would enable them to reach the cave entrance.

"I can climb it," he told Caro as they assessed the steep wall. "What about you?"

Caro thought about her heavy backpack. "I don't know," she admitted.

"If I came back down for your pack, could you?"

"I think so," she said.

"Good. We'll start early in the morning."

The next morning they made their way up the side of the mesa to the slope. The climb was difficult and tedious, but Caro was determined not to hold Mike back by giving up. When at last, tired and dirty, they reached the enormous cave opening, they were staggered with the extent of the pueblo.

"This place looks like it contains over a hundred rooms," Mike said in a kind of shock. His voice echoed back to them from the depths of the cave.

"I can't believe it," Caro kept saying over and over as they approached the massive sandstone building. The mud plaster that had once smoothed the walls was now gone, but wooden roof beams still protruded from the rock.

"We can determine when these roof beams were cut by tree ring dating," Mike said, fingering one smooth edge.

"I can't believe that no one ever found this place before," Caro said.

"It happens. This is an out-of-the-way canyon, and access has been restricted. No one cared, no one knew what it meant. It's so remote and inaccessible that vandals haven't had a chance to destroy it. You know, Charlie Deer Walk related an old Hopi legend about a hidden pueblo in a big canyon. He spoke of 'lessons in the rock' and a waterfall nearby. I'm convinced that this is the place of their legend."

It was eerily quiet in the cave as they wandered from room to room in the deserted pueblo. To Caro, the ghosts of its inhabitants were never far away. People had been born, lived and died here. They had made love and given birth. And eventually they had left.

"Look," Mike said softly, unearthing a small sandstone slab from a pile of rubble in one of the dwellings. It appeared to be covered with what, to Caro, were indecipherable chicken scratches.

"Is it writing?" she asked.

"It's Arabic again," he said, squinting at it in the half-darkness. "It's part of an alphabet stone, I think." He dug around in the dirt until he found two similar pieces, which fitted together with the first.

"It's amazing," he said excitedly. "This slab is a lot like a stone found in Nevada. This indicates to me that the Libyans traveled inland from the Pacific as far as Utah, or at least their learning did. Look, this says, 'Alif, Ba, Gim are first.' The next line is 'Now add to these Dal.' Those are the first four letters of the ancient Libyan alphabet."

"Who used these stones?"

"Children, Caro. This is a grade school lesson, and it's been lying here undisturbed for at least seven hundred years. Why, this lends credence to the idea that colonies of Libyans came here, intermarried with the locals, lived their lives in the pueblos of the Southwest, and raised their children."

Later, Mike returned to the base of the mesa and brought up

their packs. Caro spent the time lost in deep thought. It seemed to her that there could be more to the Libyan-Anasazi connection than Mike was telling her.

"Were the ancient Anasazi actually Libyans, Mike?" she asked as they sat at the edge of their campfire after dinner and watched sparks like fireflies being carried off on the night wind.

Mike gazed thoughtfully into the distance. "I think the original Anasazi were native American people, hunters and gatherers who eventually settled in the American Southwest. Then somewhere around three hundred to five hundred years before Christ, voyagers came from beyond the sea bringing new technology, and the Anasazi eagerly absorbed them into their midst. Over periods of hundreds of years, the cultures integrated. Their religions, their language, their pottery, their customs—all became alike."

Caro leaned her head against his shoulder. "That would explain the similarity in American Southwestern and Libyan pottery designs," she said. "The two cultures still make almost the very same designs today."

"There are other similarities, too," Mike said. "I've visited Habbe' cliff dwellings in North Africa that are built almost exactly like this one. Not only that, but the Habbe' weave in the same manner as the Hopi, they make baskets by similar techniques, and they paint pictographs on nearby rocks."

That night they slept soundly, awaking with the dawn to begin their climb to the top of the mesa. When they reached it, Caro flung out her arms and twirled around in her excitement. The view was magnificent.

"They farmed up here," Mike said, reaching down and hefting a clump of earth in his hand. The soil was still rich and fertile, as evidenced by the forest of pine and juniper trees on the top of the mesa.

Caro and Mike traversed a wide plateau and stopped to eat lunch on a slope facing east. Afterward Mike pleaded temporary laziness and lay back on a green blanket of vegetation to soak up the sun. For a while Caro lay beside him, but when a covert glance told her that Mike was napping, she got up and wandered downhill toward a promising face of rock. She figured that she might as well use the time to look for more epigraphs.

As she approached the rock face, her eyes were drawn to a

strange arrangement of stone slabs. The slabs appeared to lean up against a large boulder in a way that made her think they had been deliberately placed in that position. Curiously she moved closer.

She peered beneath them. Shadowed from the sun was a spiral figure carved deeply into the rock.

"Mike! Mike!" she called. Her shout brought him running.

"Look, Mike," she said, pointing to the spiral. He ducked his head beneath the slabs for a moment, and when he turned to her he was smiling broadly.

"Is it important?" she asked breathlessly.

"I'll say! This slab and spiral arrangement is a clock of sorts," he said. "They used it to determine the spring and fall equinoxes and the summer and winter solstices. That's how they knew when to plant and harvest."

"How does it work?" Caro wanted to know.

"A shaft of sunlight pierces the space between the stone slabs and falls at a certain point on the spiral. I'd have to do some calculations, but I'm willing to bet that for the spring equinox, the light would fall at the extreme right of the spiral. At that time, the Anasazi would know that days would start to lengthen and they'd plant their crops. You can see how valuable such a device would be."

Their endeavors that day exhausted them, and they bundled up in the sleeping bag shortly after the last rays of the sun disappeared in the west. But before starting for home the next day, they discovered the most important site of the trip.

It happened as they were hiking around the base of the mesa. Mike was discouraged by finding nothing significant there, and they were both convinced that they were wasting their time because there were no more epigraphs, no more petroglyphs, and no further record of the people who had once inhabited this canyon. Then Mike spotted a single drawing of a flute player on a rock face and, as usual, stopped to photograph it.

"He's a famous little guy," he told Caro.

"I've seen carvings of such flute players before," she said. She recalled petroglyphs and pictographs depicting the same backward-footed, humpbacked little man on rocks near Moab.

"He's Kokopelli," Mike told her. "According to legend, he went from place to place playing the flute. See the hump on his back? I'm convinced that Kokopelli was a trader, and that's why he traveled. He probably played the flute to keep himself company as he walked the lonely roads between settlements.''

He was about to put his camera back in the case when he caught sight of a huge, smooth boulder several paces away. When he strode over to it, he whistled in astonishment. Carved into the rock's surface was one of the most extensive examples of ancient Arabic writing he had ever found.

"Can you make it out?" Caro asked, wishing that she could read it.

"I have to study it for a while," he said.

Caro busied herself making a latex mold of the Kokopelli petroglyph while Mike, still stunned by this latest find, sat down on a small boulder and concentrated on the epigraph. Caro heard him muttering to himself, and after a while he rummaged in his pack and found a chart of Arabic terms.

Caro silently pulled a pad of paper out of her pocket and handed it to him, and without a word Mike, stopping to stare at the writing in the rock every few minutes, began to scribble a translation.

"I think I've got most of it," he said after a time. His voice was shaking, and she knew that this was an important discovery.

Caro went to see what he had written. "Can you tell how old this writing is?" she asked.

"It dates from about 1300 A.D.," he said. "Go ahead, read it."

Caro glanced at him uncertainly before she began. "Read it," he insisted.

"'Leaving the canyon, from here (we) depart,'" Caro read out loud. She glanced at Mike. He was quiet and still.

"'We go from the Great North Land,'" she continued, then paused, trying to figure out what it meant.

"The Great North Land is what the Libyans called the North American continent," Mike explained in a choked voice.

Caro resumed reading. "'We return to the homeland, which is beyond Maui's land, the island. Leaving behind the sick and the lame, only the strong shall survive. Some of our people go to our brothers south. We seek peace from the fierce invaders (indistinguishable). In ships our people go, may our voyage be blessed.' This is about the disappearance of the Anasazi, isn't it, Mike?''

Mike nodded. ''Maui was the Libyan name for Hawaii, and the name they gave it survives to this day as the name of one of the islands. The homeland beyond Maui must have been Libya. 'Brothers in the south' could have been other tribes living in distant pueblos. The invaders they refer to must have been the Navajos and Apaches.''

''This is the proof you need for your theories, Mike.''

''Yes,'' Mike said. ''Yes. All this time it's been here, carved into the rock, waiting for someone to find it.''

''Oh, Mike,'' was all Caro said, and when he took her into his arms, she saw tears shining in his eyes. His life's work would be authenticated because of this discovery. She could not have been happier.

Chapter Eleven

"So what will you do next?" she said later when they had returned to camp, had bathed in tepid water from a convenient pothole, and were sitting beneath a moonlit sky reviewing the exciting events of the day.

"I'll include this new information in the paper I'm going to present to the Rosetta Society next month," Mike said enthusiastically. "I'll see if I can generate interest in a full-scale exploration of the canyon. With enough manpower and money, we may find even more to link the Anasazi with the Libyans."

Caro slapped at a pesky mosquito. "How can anyone deny the connection now that you've found the inscription that tells how and why they left this canyon?"

"There will be some people who want to deny its authenticity, but if I get a well-known archaeologist or foundation to spearhead further exploration here, that would mean money. The more backup evidence we find, the better the chance this Anasazi document has of being accepted. I have to admit that what we found today is the final proof, as far as I'm concerned."

They bedded down for the night, and in the middle of the night Caro woke unexpectedly. Mike was wide-awake, smiling in the darkness. She smiled herself and went back to sleep.

Yalabasi Canyon was another world and one that they were reluctant to leave, but they were running out of food and knew that they must return home. The next day they began their hike out of the canyon, knowing full well that they would both return someday.

On the afternoon before they would leave the canyon for home, they bathed in the deep rock pool where they had sat to cool off on their first night there. After she scrubbed the grit from her body, Caro washed her hair and twisted it so that the water dripped from it, shining like a fall of diamonds in the sun. Finally they dressed and built a campfire, where they cooked and ate the last of their food.

"I hate for this time to be over," Caro said, gazing into the distance as the sun slipped westward.

"So do I," Mike replied.

"Thanks for letting me tag along," Caro said, smiling at him.

He laced his fingers through hers. "I couldn't have managed without you," he told her.

"When I go back, I'll have to pick up all the emotional baggage that I left behind," she said with a sigh.

He knew she was talking about the scar and its effect on her life. "Why do you have to pick it up again?" he asked.

"I don't know. Because it's there, I suppose. Out here there's no one to stare at me, and I don't have to think about going back to New York to identify the man who attacked me when they arrest him, and there are no mirrors to remind me how I look. Why, I haven't had that awful nightmare about my attacker since we came to Yalabasi Canyon, Mike."

Mike contemplated this. "Looks like you need a feather bush, Caro," he said.

"A feather bush?"

"There's a Hopi legend that says you can invest feathers with evils and tie them to a bush. Then when the feathers have all blown away in the wind, the bush is bare, and that makes a spiritual place in your soul for the good that replaces them."

Caro regarded him with puzzlement.

"You're joking, I suppose?"

Mike lifted her hand to his lips and kissed her fingers. "If it would help, I'm not. Those nightmares are serious business. If you could invest a mere feather with the nightmares and the wind would blow it away, and if you then didn't have nightmares anymore, it would be worth it, wouldn't it?"

"It all sounds like nonsense," she said. "What I need to do is make myself get over all my fears."

"Hey, you will. I'll help you. But let's do the bush anyway, okay?" Mike jumped to his feet and pulled her up with him.

"Mike—!" she said in exasperation.

"I'll find a bare bush. You gather the feathers," he said, going to a nearby brush pile and poking around.

"This is kind of silly," Caro said, her eyes accidentally lighting on a blue feather at the base of a rock. Reluctantly and feeling like a fool, she picked it up.

"Go look over there, Caro. I saw a bunch of feathers left over from some animal's meal." He pointed in the direction of the gully.

Before long a skeptical Caro had gathered a fistful of feathers and returned to find Mike tamping sand and rocks at the base of a sparse-looking bush that he had set up in the middle of their camp.

"Now what?" she asked.

"Now we tie them on," he said.

"We don't have anything to tie them with," Caro said.

"Of course we do," he said, and he pulled a shirt out of his pack and bit through the thread of the hem. When he had unraveled a length of thread, he yanked it in half and gave her some.

"All right," he said, picking up the first feather. "What evil would you like to replace with good?"

Caro was finally getting into the spirit of this. "The nightmares," she said firmly. "I don't want to have nightmares anymore."

"Right. This feather represents nightmares. When the wind blows it away, you will have only pleasant dreams. Next?"

"The way I feel about the man who attacked me," Caro said as she affixed a feather to the bush. "I don't like admitting it, but I hate him for what he did to me. Life would be a lot easier if I didn't feel all this anger."

After that, they tied on a feather for the deep-seated fear that someone might hurt her again, and another for the pain she felt about living the rest of her life with a scar.

"Don't tie them on so tightly," Caro cautioned. "We want the wind to take them soon." Mike laughed at this.

By the time Caro couldn't think of any more evils, the bush was fluttering with feathers.

"And now all we need to do is let the wind blow the feathers away," Caro said when they had finished.

"That's what the Hopi say," Mike said.

They stood back and looked at the bush. Caro laughed because it looked so frivolous and out of place here among the harsh red rock outcroppings. She was glad they had made it, though. Somehow it seemed right to leave behind something of themselves in this canyon. And if the Hopi legend was true—and who could say it was not?—she was leaving behind only the bad feelings that she didn't want to carry with her.

That night they made love out under the starry sky, the feathers on the bush riffling gently beside them. Caro thought that she had never partaken of such happiness. She felt irrevocably altered by the experience of Yalabasi Canyon; or maybe the altering experience was loving Mike. Whichever it was, her heart seemed pinned to this place, caught here forever, making it her destiny to return.

"WHAT WOULD YOU THINK about coming with me to New York next month?" Mike asked casually over breakfast a few days after they got back to the Tin Can.

"New York!" Caro exclaimed, dropping a pan of muffins onto the floor with a clatter.

"I have to present my paper," he reminded her, joining her to help pick up the scattered muffins.

"I'd be frightened," she said.

"You wouldn't be frightened if you were with me, would you?"

"Mmm," was all she said as she turned away and slid the muffins into a plastic bag.

"Would you?"

"Mike, I ran away from New York once. I was terrified."

"If I go to present my paper, you'll be by yourself here. I phoned Annie yesterday when you were in the store buying groceries. She says she's not coming back to Moab."

"Not coming back!" said Caro. She didn't know whether to be happy or sad.

"She and Tom are getting along again, she says. She thinks their marriage is going to succeed."

"Oh, I'm so pleased for her. And for Holly and Franklin and Peter. But what about her workshop? And their house?"

"I don't know. Those are things that we could find out if we went to Salt Lake City and visited them."

Caro sat down at the table. "Have we been invited?"

Mike watched her carefully. "Annie and Tom want us to come for Labor Day weekend. That's next week."

"But when is that Rosetta Society meeting where you'll present your paper?"

"That's not until the following week. Annie suggested that we come and spend Labor Day plus the next few days with them. On Thursday we could fly out of Salt Lake City to New York and spend the next week there. I'd present the paper on the following Thursday, and we could come home on Sunday."

"I don't know, Mike. We'd be in New York nine days. Why so long?"

"I have professional colleagues that I'd like to see while I'm there. I thought you might like to visit with Marina."

"I could close up my apartment," she said, her mind racing. "Maybe I could find someone to sublet it."

"Yes," he said in relief. "That's a good idea."

"Still," she said, hesitating.

"Part of the credit for the exploration of Yalabasi Canyon goes to you," he said persuasively.

"Oh, Mike, I don't know about that. Anyway, even the idea of hearing your speech to the Rosetta Society palls when I think of going back to the city. I don't know, Mike, I just don't know."

He knelt beside her and pulled her close until her head rested on his shoulder. "Speaking to the Rosetta Society about the Libyan presence in the Four Corners is a big moment in my life. I'd like you to be there," he said.

She was silent.

"And Annie and the kids really want to see you," he told her.

She still didn't speak. She knew that she didn't have to run away from herself anymore. Maybe it made no sense to keep running from her attacker, either.

"And all those feathers we tied on the bush? I bet they've all flown away on the wind by this time."

She lifted her head and smiled reluctantly. "I don't feel as though they have," she said, but she knew now what she wanted to do.

"There's one way to find out about the feathers," Mike said. "We'll have to go back to Yalabasi Canyon."

"But not until we get back from New York," she said, her eyes sparkling.

"Yes," he said, smiling happily. "Not until we come back home."

IN NEW YORK several days later, Marina used a long fingernail to slit open the letter bearing the Moab postmark. There was no return address, but she knew it must be from Caro. Her former top model seldom wrote, so maybe this was something important. Perhaps it would be what she hoped—an announcement of Caro's return to New York. Cautiously she allowed her hopes to rise.

She was engrossed in the letter when someone tiptoed into her office. She waved at the intruder, who sat on a chair and kept quiet. Around the agency, no one spoke to Marina until she spoke first.

When she had read the whole thing, Marina was thoroughly disappointed. She massaged her eyes for a moment, trying to understand Caro's point of view. It was no use; she couldn't.

"Caro's coming back, Donna," Marina said finally, tossing the letter aside and swiveling her chair around.

"Ooh," Donna said, the word a sigh of surprise.

"Yes, well, it's about time."

"I wonder how—I mean, I can't imagine what—"

"If you're trying to say 'What does she look like?' I assure you that I have no idea," Marina said shortly.

"I suppose she'll want to go back to work?" Donna asked timidly.

"She says she won't, but let's hope she changes her mind. It's not as though she couldn't work again, you know."

"I haven't seen her since the attack," Donna said.

"Well, it wasn't a pretty sight, that's for sure," Marina said with an inner shudder.

"I saw pictures of her. On TV," Donna said quickly.

"We got some publicity out of the whole thing, didn't we? Like I always say, when life hands you a lemon, make a whiskey sour." Marina laughed, then became more serious. "Not that I think it was funny. It was a terrible thing. I was at the hospital with Caro afterward, and I'll never forget when I first saw her."

"What did you think?"

"I thought 'Thank goodness she's alive.' I thought that she would never look the same. I thought her career was finished. But I must confess that I *never* thought that she'd move to Moab, Utah, and refuse to return."

"You said she was coming back," Donna reminded her.

"She is, but not permanently. She wants to sublet her apartment, she says. She's apparently coming with—" Marina consulted the letter again "—with a friend of hers, Michael Herrick. Have you ever heard of him?"

"Can't say that I have," Donna said.

"Apparently he's a well-known archaeologist. What in the world would our Caro have in common with an archaeologist, for Pete's sake?"

"Well, there was the Naiad. Wasn't she something to do with archaeology?" asked Donna, looking bored by the conversation.

Marina let out a sigh of exasperation. "A naiad is a mythological water nymph," she said impatiently. "Tell me, Donna, what was it you wanted to see me about?"

"I'm getting married. I don't want any more bookings for at least a year."

Marina stared at her. Donna was in demand now; Marina had built up her career in the past year to the point that she was looking forward to the time when Donna would be one of her top three models. This new development would throw a monkey wrench into the works and set Donna's career back to the point where they'd have to start all over again, when and if Donna decided to accept bookings.

"Well, well," was all Marina could manage to say. "I guess you could say that this hasn't exactly been my day."

"IT'S LIKE THIS," Mike said earnestly to Annie and Tom as they sat around their coffee table the night he and Caro flew to

Salt Lake City from Moab. "Caro has some things she needs to do in New York, and I'm going to present a paper to the Rosetta Society. So we decided to combine the two and go to New York together, especially since neither of us felt like leaving the other." He reached for Caro's hand.

Annie by this time was privy to the whole story of Caro's scar. "Just as long as Caro doesn't mind going back to the city," she said after a long look at her friend.

"I'm psyching myself up to it," Caro admitted.

"Well, I'm glad you could visit," Tom said. "Has Annie shown you her new workshop in the garage?"

"Oh, Tom, I haven't had time," Annie said, smiling up at him. "First there was dinner, and then Franklin had to read to Caro, and Holly wanted to ask Caro's advice about her new wallpaper, and—" She shrugged.

"Let's take a look at the workshop now," Mike suggested.

"Oh, this is nice," Caro said when Tom opened the door to the attached garage and she saw the wood paneling Tom had put up.

"Tom built these shelves over here, and the kiln is in the utility room," Annie said proudly.

"You're equipped with everything you have in the pottery workshop in Moab," Caro observed as she and Annie walked back into the house, leaving the men to talk shop.

Annie settled herself on a chair and indicated that Caro should sit on a love seat nearby. "I have almost everything," she corrected. "But I don't have you."

"I'm awfully sorry about the way my work has lagged because of my trip to Yalabasi Canyon with Mike," Caro said. "And now that I'll be in New York for nine days, it'll be even longer before I can ship more pottery."

"Don't worry about it—I'll be producing in a day or two. And thanks to your hard work before you went to Yalabasi Canyon, we have a healthy backlog of Caro Nicholson designs. Tell me, Caro. Do you think the two of us could pull off maintaining a studio in both Moab and Salt Lake City?"

"Does that mean you're really staying here with Tom?"

Annie looked pleased. "We've been going to a marriage counselor, Caro. It's the best thing that ever happened to us.

I've learned—well, maybe we've both learned—the art of compromise. And lots of times I reacted to things the wrong way. You know, Tom would say something that really set me off, and I'd respond the way I always did, without thinking about the true meaning behind his words.''

"So you're not fighting anymore?"

"We have disagreements, but we handle them differently. For instance, I found out that what Tom was really saying when he objected to my closeness to my family was that he wanted more time with me. That's a compliment, coming from the man I've been married to for fifteen years! I've learned to take it as such. We're getting along much better now."

"I saw Tony on the street the other day, and he asked me when Franklin was coming home."

"Franklin misses Tony, but he's made a wonderful friend who lives right across the street here. And there's a terrific program for dyslexic kids here. In fact, Tom and I have been invited to join a support group for parents of children with learning differences. Holly is happy to be with her father again, and Peter went to school for first-grade orientation the other day and fell in love with his teacher."

"What about you, Annie? How are you getting along without Nola and Lou and—?"

"And Diane and Gert and Connie? Just fine, believe it or not. Tom and I have a much closer relationship, and I've met a few women who will probably become friends. Caro, I don't think any of us will be coming back to Moab, except maybe at Christmas for a visit."

"I'll miss you," Caro said.

"What's going on in here?" boomed Tom, coming in from the garage and stomping wood shavings off his feet onto the mat in front of the door. "Is there any chance of getting a cup of coffee and a piece of pie?"

"If you'll put on the coffeepot," Annie said serenely, following Tom into the kitchen.

"They're happy, Mike," Caro whispered.

"So I see," he said, looking through the kitchen door and watching Tom kiss the back of Annie's neck as she cut four pieces of pie.

"They've been through a lot," Caro said, pulling Mike onto the love seat beside her.

"Well, at least they didn't give up on each other," Mike said. "I was thinking tonight when we were watching the kids play softball in the backyard...." His words trailed off with a new realization. Since he had become so close to Caro, he now received most of his emotional nurture from her rather than from his extended family.

"You were thinking how nice it would be if someday we could have a family," Caro finished for him. Reading each other's thoughts was getting to be a habit these days.

"Exactly," he said. "How did you know?"

"Because I was thinking the same thing. It wasn't something I'd ever considered before. I mean, the fashion and modeling world wasn't like this, with family the most important thing. It was go, go, go, and get, get, get—before you're too old and the advertisers don't want you anymore. I never thought about settling down and having a couple of kids."

"I did, but I discarded the idea. It didn't seem possible with the kind of life I led. Or with any of the women I'd met." He put an arm around her and thoughtfully massaged her shoulder.

"There must be a lot of satisfaction in a real family life," Caro said. "Otherwise, people wouldn't do it."

"Most people get into it without a lot of thought. They fall in love, get married, and all of a sudden they have a couple of kids and a mortgage. It would be easy to feel trapped, I guess."

"I wonder if I would," Caro said softly.

"You're different from most people. You have time to think it through and decide if that's what you want." Mike smiled at her.

"Hey, are we breaking up an important discussion?" Annie inquired, bustling into the room bearing a tray.

"Of course not," Caro said, but privately she thought it was possible that Annie had interrupted the most significant discussion of her entire life.

CARO AND MIKE went out to dinner by themselves one night at one of Salt Lake City's finest restaurants. The Stendahls had an appointment with their marriage counselor, and this time the children were to participate.

"We want the kids to voice their thoughts to us and to our counselor. It's all part of getting the family back together again," Annie had said.

The restaurant where Caro and Mike went was chosen by Mike and was considerably fancier than anyplace they had been in Moab. It did him good to see Caro wearing a dress that seemed to be constructed of interwoven cobwebs, her honey-colored hair held back from her face by a narrow velvet headband. Tonight she was wearing more makeup than she usually did. She looked stunning, and he told her so.

She smiled back at him from across the candlelit table and thanked him for the compliment. There was a slight pause in the conversation; then Caro said, "I'm not going to have any more operations on my scar, Mike."

"What brought this on?" he asked. The scar hadn't been mentioned since Yalabasi Canyon; he had thought they had laid the matter to rest. The scar had no real meaning to him, other than the way Caro felt about it.

"I've been giving it a lot of thought," she said.

"And?"

"I've suffered enough with this particular wound. It's time to put it all behind me and get on with my life," Caro said slowly. "I've known that for a while now, but it's hard when every time I look in the mirror, I see it." She looked troubled.

"I don't see it at all," he said quietly. "It's there, but it doesn't have anything to do with the person I know to be the real Caro Nicholson."

She shook her head, smiling fondly. "Only you would say something like that," she said.

"Only I know you really well," he said.

"That's so true," she said. "Annie's a good friend, but she doesn't know me the way you do. Marina doesn't understand me at all, and I'm not close to anyone else. Tell me, Mike. I know you'll be truthful. Don't you wonder what I'd look like if the scar weren't there?"

He shook his head. "I already know what you'd look like. The Naiad."

"Oh, Mike, the Naiad wasn't me, not really. She was an advertising gimmick. I never looked like that."

It was all he could do to keep himself from reaching across the table to caress her cheek, not only the skin surrounding the scar but the scar itself.

"What you looked like before doesn't matter. It's what you look like now that's important to me. And you are exquisite, Caro. I've often tried to think of words to describe your beauty, but I'm not a poetic person, nor do I usually think in adjectives. I wouldn't change you one bit. You're perfect the way you are."

"I sometimes wish you could have known me before," she said somewhat wistfully. "I want to be beautiful for you."

"Oh, Caro. You are beautiful. Especially right this moment."

"Marina will be shocked when I tell her that I don't intend to change the way I look. Appearance is everything to her."

"Does Marina's reaction worry you?"

Caro lined her silverware up with the edge of the table and took her time in answering.

"I'm going to tell her once and for all that I'm not coming back to New York. I'm not going to resume my modeling career," she said.

"I thought you'd already told her all that."

"I have. She won't accept it."

"After she understands how happy you are, when she can see for herself how healthy you are, maybe she'll be convinced."

"You don't know Marina, Mike."

"Well, I will soon," he said. He was more curious than ever about Caro's former life. She had left it solidly behind her, but from her disjointed revelations about herself, he had managed to piece together a view of how she had lived. It was a far cry from the way she was living now and the way he wanted to live with her in the future. Sometimes he worried that she would have second thoughts when it came time to make the final transition.

"Marina seems to have such a hold on you," he observed. "I've never really understood why."

"She's been a major influence on my life," Caro said. "I was a struggling college student studying at a community college when she came along and promised me the moon. She became mother, father, sister and brother to me. Marina had faith in my future, even if I didn't. 'Someday you'll be famous,' she said, and she was right. I can't thank her enough for what she did for me. I'm going to try to make her see that I've outgrown my friends and my former career, but that she and I can always be close."

"If you put it that way, she's sure to understand," Mike said. "And I'll be there to back you up. I'll stick with you through all of this, Caro. Whatever happens, I'll be there."

"I wouldn't go back to New York if I didn't believe that," Caro said in her most heartfelt tone.

"So back to Marina. Do you think she's going to jump up and down and have a temper tantrum when she finds out that she's lost her best model?"

Caro laughed. "Let's hope not. Perhaps she'll believe how serious I am about living in Moab, when she learns that I'm going to run Annie's workshop there."

"Is that final?" Mike asked. "I haven't heard anything about it lately. I thought maybe Annie was going to try to sell it to you."

"We want to be business partners. Annie and I worked out the details today. I'll make and ship my own designs to our customers from Moab, and she'll do her own work in Salt Lake City, all under the new name of Yalabasi Pottery. Why, Annie even has several new customers here lined up already."

"I like the name Yalabasi Pottery," Mike said.

"So do Annie and I," Caro said with a happy smile. "Maybe someday we'll be able to hire some helpers, so we can concentrate on design. For now, though, we'll go on as we have been. I can hardly wait to get back to Moab and get started on some new things." Her face shone with contentment.

I could think of a lot of new things to get started, Mike thought. *Like a marriage. Like a family.*

He was beginning to realize that Caro felt that way, too.

Chapter Twelve

The plane spiraled down toward the runway at La Guardia Airport, and Caro, looking out the window, caught a glimpse of the Statue of Liberty. The statue with its upraised torch seemed to her more like a symbol of confinement than a signal of freedom. Caro knew now that she had never felt as free to be herself in New York as she had in Utah.

Beside her, Mike closed his fingers around hers and smiled. "Don't worry," he said. "Everything's going to be fine."

In answer, her hand squeezed his. She dreaded this trip to New York, even with Mike at her side; she hadn't realized how apprehensive she was until she saw the runway at Salt Lake City blur beneath the wheels of the plane at takeoff. At that moment she had felt as though she were leaving everything that was safe and secure in her life.

Their plane landed at La Guardia in a light rain. When they stepped out of the airport, everything around them seemed gray; the sky, the buildings, even the faces of the people who scurried past, intent on getting where they were going. After the brilliant reds and blues of the Utah desert, New York seemed drab and dull.

The traffic was anything but dull, however. The driver of their cab was short-tempered and spiteful, twice rolling down his window to yell at other vehicles when they were stalled in traffic. Caro found herself anxiously scanning the faces of men in the throngs of people streaming by the taxi. Did this one have the same prominent jaw of the man who attacked her in the park? Did that one's eyes possess the same peculiar lightless quality?

Mike slid an arm around her for reassurance. She found that she was trembling; she tried to stop, but in vain. What was the matter with her? Why was she having this extreme reaction? She had thought she was over all the fear and anxiety, had thought she could cope. Had she been wrong? Had she not changed as much as all that?

Caro was apprehensive about seeing her own apartment again, especially since her last hours there had been filled with fear and unhappiness. Now they were pulling up in front of the building and the doorman was swinging the door wide. Mike paid the cabdriver, while she walked into the lobby.

She didn't recall the place being as big or as ostentatious as it was. Her heels echoed on the marble floors as they walked to the elevator. Beside her, Mike was very quiet. She wondered fleetingly what he thought of all this luxury.

She was surprised to find that she felt nothing when she stepped inside the door of her apartment—no emotion, just a blank lack of interest. Once its acquisition had been a milestone in her life. Caro was the daughter of a single mother who had eked out a living as a bookkeeper in a little town in upstate New York, and money and the fine things that it could buy had been in short supply in their household.

Now she looked around the foyer with its gilt wallpaper and rare Persian rug. Despite the supposed attentions of a weekly cleaning woman, the place didn't look as clean as she would have liked. The air smelled musty. And yet she couldn't bring herself to care about it. She felt only a peculiar detachment and a weariness that was beyond words.

"Nice place," Mike said, rocking back and forth on his heels.

She touched his arm. "I'll show you the rest of it," she said, feeling constrained. Maybe it had been wrong to bring Mike here. Maybe they should have stayed at a hotel as he had suggested.

She took him into the huge living room with its balcony and view of Central Park, and she showed him the kitchen and the adjoining room for a live-in maid, if she chose to employ one. Mike seemed taken aback at the three spacious bathrooms, one of which had a sink with a gold faucet shaped like a swan with

faucet handles for wings. In her bedroom, she told him to put
his suitcase on the bed, but he refused because he didn't want
to mar the antique satin bedspread.

Mike was stunned at the way Caro lived. He had been prepared for something *nice*, but she hadn't warned him that it
would be *opulent*. Suddenly he understood what a major change
she had made when she abandoned all of this to come to Utah.

The phone rang and Caro, acting on reflex, scooped it up.

"It's Marina," she mouthed, her hand over the speaking end
of the receiver.

Mike would have guessed, because he could hear Marina's
loud voice, so familiar from overheard telephone conversations
at Annie's. While Caro talked, he amused himself by wandering
into the living room, picking up a bibelot of one kind or another
here and there, gazing down into the park through the rain-
blurred window. He wondered if it was on the path he saw from
this window that Caro had been attacked.

Caro came striding out of the bedroom. She seemed different
here in her own apartment. More sophisticated, more citified in
manner. Or had she always been that way and he hadn't noticed? *No.* He had taken note of a certain cosmopolitan veneer
when she first turned up at his cousin's house. Somehow that
seemed like a very long time ago.

"Marina is having a little get-together for us tomorrow night;
we'll have to go, I suppose," Caro said. There was a tense edge
to her voice.

"A party? Why?"

"Not a party, just some of my friends—models from the
agency and my makeup artist, a few photographers that I liked
to work with. I think Marina wants to make it easy for me to
pick up the threads of my relationships with them."

*And give them a chance to satisfy their curiosity about how
I look,* she thought, but didn't say it. She hurried away before
Mike could comment, and then he heard her filling glasses at
the wet bar in the niche between the living and dining rooms.

Mike didn't want to go to this gathering tomorrow night.
Why would Caro want to resume those relationships when she
had, by her own admission, outgrown them? What would he,
Mike Herrick, have to say to these worldly friends of Caro's?
He was certainly curious enough to want to meet Marina, but

as for fashion photographers and makeup artists—well, he'd stick out like a sore thumb in a group like that. He could hold his own in any academic group, but he was ill-prepared to hobnob with the artists-and-models establishment.

Caro reappeared and handed him a drink. "Here," she said. "Maybe this will help." Nervously she gulped a long swallow of hers and walked to the window. He took a tentative sip, discovered that it was Scotch and soda and, with a clink of ice cubes, set his on a nearby table.

"I've always loved the view of the park from up here," Caro was saying wistfully. "It looks so fresh and green, especially in the rain. It doesn't look like a place where something awful could happen, does it?" She whirled, turning her back on the scene, and rummaged in a drawer in a cabinet. "I wonder if there's a chance that there are any cigarettes around here," she muttered.

"I didn't know you smoked."

"I quit a couple of months before the attack." She slammed the cabinet drawer closed and stood clenching and unclenching her fingers around her damp glass.

"You wouldn't want to start smoking again," he said, crossing the room and taking the glass from her hands. He set it down and drew her into his arms, and she put her arms around his waist.

"Of course I wouldn't," she said, her expression woebegone. "But this is harder than I thought it would be. Every man I see looks like a slasher to me. Am I going crazy, Mike? Am I paranoid?"

"The answer is no, on both counts."

"Marina said she'd ask Dr. Fleischer to send over some tranquilizers. I'm hoping I won't need them," she said. She pulled away and walked to the window again, wrapping her arms around herself.

He walked up behind her and took her into his arms. Tension vibrated through her; he could feel it.

"I keep thinking that something terrible will happen," she said fretfully.

"I don't think so," he said.

"It's not just me that I'm worried about," she said. "What

if someone is trying to harm me and involves you, Mike? I'd never forgive myself!''

"You can't go through your whole life worrying about things like that," he told her.

"I didn't when I was in Utah. I was so far removed from here that I knew no one could find me. But Marina has spread the word that I'm back, and I'm afraid the magazines or newspapers or television will find out and want interviews, and then whoever did this to me might come after me again."

"We'll only be here for nine days. Surely we can fend everyone off for that long." They had turned down Marina's suggestion of a security guard; Caro thought that such a measure might have the effect of attracting attention, which was the very thing that she wanted to avoid.

"I guess it's just that coming back to the city is such a jolt. The people all seem so grim, and the buildings are taller and dirtier than I recall. I feel out of place," Caro said.

"That's normal and natural," he said soothingly.

"And tomorrow night at Marina's, seeing people whom I haven't seen since before the attack—that's going to be difficult. Experiencing those looks, the pity, answering questions about what I'm going to do with my life." She sighed.

"I have a solution to that. Let's not go."

Caro shook her head. "I have to go, Mike. It means so much to Marina, and she's been so good to me in the past. Besides, I would like to see Suki and Donna and some of the others. You don't have to go with me. You can stay here, if you like." In spite of her words, her heart filled with terror at the very thought of facing all those people without Mike at her side.

"Where you go, I go," he said firmly.

She took comfort from that and reminded herself that all this was only temporary. Next Sunday, with the meeting of the Rosetta Society solidly behind them, she and Mike would be winging their way back to Utah. *Back home.* That was what she would keep in mind and what she would look forward to. *Going home with Mike.*

The next night they rode silently in the cab to Marina's penthouse. When Mike heard the commotion behind the door to Marina's apartment as they stood waiting for the butler to open it, he would have given anything to be back at Tanglewood

Canyon, waiting for the sun to peep through the door of the Anasazi dwelling; there was peace. He was pretty sure that he wouldn't find anything resembling that peace here. He was also quite certain that this was more than the quiet get-together that Marina had promised.

His dread was confirmed when the butler ushered them into a room filled with chattering people, and an amazon with flame-colored hair and a face like an expensive cat immediately descended upon them.

"Caro darling! Mmm, let me look at you! My, don't you look marvelous," Marina said, her eyes homing in on the unconcealed weal on Caro's face.

After the briefest exchange of pleasantries, Caro was spirited away by some of the other models from Marina's agency, despite her anxious backward glances in Mike's direction.

A waiter stuck a tray of drinks under his nose, and for lack of anything better to do, Mike appropriated one. He found an unobtrusive alcove from which he watched Caro. She glowed with an inner beauty as one by one she greeted and hugged the models with whom she'd worked. In Mike's eyes, she outshone every one of them.

"So you're Michael," Marina said, reappearing suddenly.

"Just Mike," he told her, sipping at the drink, which tasted awful.

"It's about time we met," Marina said. She made no attempt to conceal her frank appraisal of him.

"Yes," he said.

"I've wondered what has been keeping Caro in Moab, and now I know," Marina said. "She tells me you're an archaeologist."

"That's right," he said.

"You dig up old pots and things?"

"Sometimes," he said. He wondered if Caro had given Marina any clue about his discoveries concerning the Libyans. Even if she had, would Marina know how important they were?

"That's very interesting," Marina said. He had the idea that she was trying to like him for Caro's sake, even though they had nothing in common but their love of Caro. He had to admire her for her effort; he sensed that he wasn't the kind of man who attracted Marina in the first place.

"Caro seems to find it exciting," he said.

"Does she? How odd," Marina mused. They both watched Caro across the room. Caro was laughing and seemed not at all self-conscious about her scar.

"Maybe you can talk Caro into showing you some of her pottery. She makes it exactly as the Anasazi did, using native paints and brushes."

"I had no idea that Caro was so involved in all that," Marina murmured, studying her fingernails.

"Caro has changed, I think, since she left New York," Mike said softly, only half paying attention to Marina. Among these beautiful people, Caro was easily the most gorgeous woman in the room.

Marina shot him a sharp glance. "How has she changed, Mike?" she asked.

"She finds a great deal of happiness in her pottery," Mike said. There was much more to it than that, but it would do for a start. He wanted Marina to understand that Caro had discovered depths in herself that she had never expected to find. He also wanted to make it clear that he, not Marina, had the major claim on Caro now.

"Caro found a great deal of happiness in her modeling," Marina said succinctly. "She will again."

Mike's eyes grew hard. He knew how Caro felt about returning to her modeling career, but he felt strongly that it wasn't his place to discuss it with Marina. "Maybe," he said through clenched teeth.

"Definitely," Marina said, her tone grating on his ears. With that she marched away, and Mike understood that Caro's mentor had thrown down a gauntlet. She was clearly challenging him to a contest. If he won, he'd have Caro. If Marina won, he wouldn't.

From across the room, Caro had watched Mike and Marina talking, and she became alarmed when Marina tossed her auburn hair and stomped away. *Uh-oh,* Caro thought unhappily. It looked as though they hadn't hit it off, which was a blow. Caro had been looking forward to having two of her favorite people in the world meet and enjoy each other as much as she enjoyed both of them.

She started across the room to be with Mike, and then saw

Wayne. She couldn't believe that Marina had invited her former beau to this party, after the way he had treated her.

Wayne impatiently shouldered his way through the crowd obviously looking for her. She tried to reach Mike, where she would feel some degree of protection, but a waiter who was carrying two trays of hors d'oeuvres bore down on her, and by the time he passed, Wayne had her cornered.

"Caro," he said, staring at her scar. It was as though he didn't see her, the real Caro Nicholson, at all.

Her face flushed, which she knew only made her scar darker.

"Wayne, how are you?" she asked politely. He seemed heavier, and his meaty face was wider than she remembered. But then she had changed too, and in ways that weren't so readily discernible.

"I tried to find you when you left, but Marina wouldn't give me your number," he said.

"Marina didn't know how to reach me," she said. "I was the one who did all the phoning."

"Why did you run out on me, Caro?" he asked.

"Run out on you? After the attack I hardly ever saw you anymore, Wayne." She deliberately tried to keep her voice even and unaccusing, but suddenly knew with certainty that all he'd ever admired about her was her looks, which made him seem unbearably shallow to her now.

He ran a finger around the collar of his shirt, as though his tie was too tight. "I was busy at work, you know. I thought you understood."

"You turned your answering machine on so I could never talk to you, and you didn't return my calls. You told me you were working late one night, and I found out later that someone had seen you at a play."

"Caro, let's get together. Just to talk. Okay?" He made a conciliatory effort to touch her shoulder, but she evaded his reach.

"No, it's definitely *not* okay," she said. She hadn't realized how very tired she was. Her gaze circled the crowd, searching for Mike.

"From what I can tell, you can't afford to play hard-to-get," Wayne said with a kind of sneer. He was looking at her scar again, and suddenly Caro understood that he thought he was doing her a favor by pursuing her.

"Wayne, you really ought to do something about that bad breath of yours," she said with a perfectly straight face, knowing that to the fastidious Wayne, this was the worst thing she could tell him.

Mike, seeing that something was wrong and suddenly alert to the way the man had tried to touch her, pushed his way toward Caro, arriving barely in time to see a red-faced Wayne head toward the front door. He felt a sudden irrational jealousy, an emotion entirely new to him.

"Who was that?" Mike wanted to know.

"Wayne," Caro said, feeling exhausted. Now that there was distance between her and Wayne, her stomach felt less queasy. She felt no triumph at her coup.

Mike narrowed his eyes and stared at Wayne's retreating back. So that was the man who abandoned Caro after the attack. Mike felt nothing but contempt for him. He craned his neck to get a better look, but Wayne had been swallowed up by the crowd.

"Are you ready to leave?" Caro asked. She looked drained. He realized how difficult the encounter had been for her, but was elated that she had rejected Wayne's advances.

"More than ready," he said, pulling her close to him. He felt fiercely possessive.

"I'll get my jacket," she said.

They spoke very little during the taxi ride back to Caro's apartment. The canyons of New York flashed past the cab's windows, so different from the canyons of Utah. Mike felt a stab of homesickness for wide expanses of desert and skies clear as a baby's conscience, red rock gorges and tumbling streams. He could hardly wait to get back home.

When they reached her apartment, Caro kicked off her shoes in relief and said, "I could use a cup of tea. How about you?"

"Fine," Mike said. He felt emotionally exhausted, too. He followed Caro through the swinging kitchen doors and watched her as she busied herself. She moved with a certain purity of gesture that he would forever identify with her; he had seen no one else whose movements were so economical yet so harmonious. His heart swelled with affection, and he wondered if she knew how very dear she was to him.

After a while Mike said carefully, "I don't think Marina likes me."

Caro regarded him from across the room, where she waited for the water in the teakettle to boil.

"I think you're right," she replied, surprising him. He had thought that she would protest.

"She sees me as a threat. Am I?"

"No. I'm the threat, but Marina will have to be convinced that it's me and not you." She smiled at him and took the teakettle off the burner.

"I tried to tell her how much you'd changed."

"Did she believe you?"

"I doubt it. She thinks that I have some Svengali-like power over you, that you do my bidding, that—oh, I don't know."

"She'll get over it," Caro said.

After the tea had steeped, she poured it into cups and dropped two lumps of sugar in hers. Now that the party was over and she had successfully dealt with Wayne, she felt strangely reminiscent. They went into the living room and sat down, Mike in a wide armchair, Caro on the couch with her feet tucked under her.

"Do you know that I never knew the luxury of sugar before I went to Moab? I drank coffee and tea black so I could maintain my weight." Caro smiled, thinking that the svelte figure she had attained in days past seemed undesirable now that she had gained a few pounds. All her model friends looked undernourished.

"You seemed right at home among those people tonight," Mike observed.

"I didn't feel that way. It was good to see them—Suki is pregnant, and Donna is engaged to be married, and I didn't even know that those things had happened to either one of them. I liked catching up on the news, but—" She broke off and stared into the distance.

"But what?"

"But I couldn't get a grasp on any of it. Do you know, not one person said anything about my scar? Or about the attack? It's as though it never happened."

"They're uncomfortable talking about it, probably."

Caro set her cup down in its saucer with a clatter. She looked agitated. "*They're* uncomfortable? What about me? I can't act as though that man never attacked me. It's part of my life, and it's as important to me as—as Suki's having her baby or Donna's getting married!"

"I know that, but you'll have to give them time to deal with it," Mike said seriously.

"Time? Marina's had time, and she's the same way. 'The sooner you forget about all that, the better off you'll be,' that's what she said to me tonight. I can't forget it, Mike. There's no use trying." She was surprised to feel tears welling up in her eyes.

"You looked wonderful tonight, Caro," Mike said.

She blinked rapidly and shot him a watery smile. "Do you know something? I thought so, too. When I look in the mirror, I hardly see the scar anymore. Isn't that funny?"

"No, not funny," Mike said. "It shows how much you've grown. You don't see yourself as only a pretty face anymore. You know that you have an intrinsic value and worth."

"You helped me learn that," she said softly. "You and Annie and the kids."

"You helped yourself, too," Mike pointed out.

"It was odd when I saw Wayne," Caro said, leaning her head on the back of the couch. "He tried not to recoil when he saw the scar, but he couldn't hide the way he inspected it from one end to the other. He never asked me anything about myself. All he saw was the scar."

"You're well rid of him," Mike said. The curve of her neck tantalized him.

"I know. I guess what bothers me is that I used such bad judgment about him in the first place. I was really hurt when he dumped me. Now that I know he's a life form lower than plankton, I don't want anything to do with him, ever."

"Good," Mike said with obvious relief.

Caro cleared her throat. "Mike, Marina wants me to stop by the agency on Monday and talk business."

"Will you do it?"

"I suppose so. As you know, I've already told her that I'm not returning to modeling, but there are loose ends to tie up, such as getting Gaillardo to release me from my contract. And Monday would be a good opportunity to tell her that I don't appreciate her inviting Wayne tonight. If she has any ideas about matchmaking, I want to set her straight right now.''

He knew that every contact Caro had with Marina put her at risk. Marina's influence might be greater than his. He could lose Caro forever; he understood that. And yet he also knew that a Caro who didn't really want to go back to Utah with him was not a Caro that he wanted. If she loved him, really loved him, she'd come with him. The fact that she intended to set Marina straight about Wayne boded well, he thought.

He looked out the window so that Caro wouldn't see the apprehension in his eyes. ''I have some things I can do. I'd like to stop by the office of the curator of the Museum of Natural History. I know him from a dig we both worked on in Mexico,'' he said.

''You could certainly come along with me to the agency, if you'd like,'' Caro said, wishing that he would but unwilling to interfere with his plans.

''That's for you to do on your own,'' Mike said. She thought he spoke a little sharply, and she studied him over the dregs of her tea, but saw no sign of displeasure.

Still, their lovemaking that night was more intense than usual, and Mike edged over onto her side of the bed as they were falling asleep, refusing to be any farther apart from her than was absolutely necessary.

As soon as Caro arrived at the agency office on Monday morning, Marina invited her to sit in a chair that was strategically placed by a wide window and brushed Caro's hair off her face, studying the scar up close.

''I can't say that all that desert sun has done much for it,'' she said in a disapproving tone. ''You know how destructive the sun is for your skin, Caro. Why didn't you use a sunscreen when you were out slogging around the desert?''

Caro shifted uncomfortably in the chair. ''It didn't seem important at the time, Marina.''

Marina sighed and sat down on the edge of her desk. ''I've

talked with Dr. Fleischer. You have an appointment with him at two o'clock on Wednesday.''

"I've already made up my mind about the scar. I don't want to do anything to it. I've had enough of doctors and hospitals and waiting rooms with dog-eared, out-of-date magazines, and—''

"Caro! Surely you don't mean to leave that scar the way it is!'' Marina was clearly horrified.

Caro's chin shot up. "I'm the sum total of my experiences, Marina, like it or not. The attack was something I've lived through, and the scar is part of me.''

Marina's shoulders sagged. "I can't believe you really mean that,'' she said.

"It won't matter whether I have a scar or not back in Moab, when I'm working with pottery,'' Caro pointed out.

"It's this Mike, isn't it?'' Marina said abruptly.

"What do you mean?''

"He's the one who's convinced you that you shouldn't resume your modeling career.''

"Mike has always been behind me one hundred percent, and he's thrilled that I've found a new career, one that satisfies me.''

"How could you not have been satisfied with the career you had?'' Marina asked in exasperation.

"It was good for me at the time, but it isn't good for me anymore. It didn't allow me to explore my creative side. Marina, please understand. I'm not going to do any more modeling.''

Marina shook her head. "I can't believe you mean it.''

"I do mean it, Marina.'' Caro calmly returned Marina's gaze.

Marina began to pace up and down in front of her desk.

"But the money, Caro! You made lots of money!''

"Sometimes money isn't important,'' Caro said softly.

Minutes ticked by. Caro remained silent.

"I can't understand this passion for Moab. The place sounds ghastly. With your artistic talent, I can see why you might like making those pots of yours, but trekking around in the desert photographing ancient obscure drawings—honestly, Caro, it simply isn't you.''

"I'm afraid you're wrong,'' Caro said implacably.

Marina ignored this. "Gaillardo is planning to market a new

cover-up cream for scars and birthmarks. They're planning to use you to represent them in a big introductory campaign,'' she said.

"I don't want to be *used* by anyone!'' Caro exclaimed.

For the first time, Marina looked flustered. "Perhaps I chose the wrong words,'' she admitted. "The point is that there has been a lot of publicity in the media about your case, and Gaillardo wants to take advantage of that.''

Caro felt her blood pressure rise. "They want to build a publicity campaign on my misfortune? That's sick, Marina.''

"Sick or not, it's worth a great deal of money to them. You were in the papers after the attack, and on television, and there was that *Women's Weekly* magazine interview. In this business, that's worth money.''

"I wish I'd never talked to the reporters, especially the one from *Women's Weekly*,'' Caro said. She felt ill; how could anyone want to capitalize on someone else's tragedy?

Marina could see that she had pushed Caro to the limit. Her voice softened. She might be a hardheaded businesswoman, but she was still Caro's friend. She walked to Caro and touched her shoulder.

"Don't make any hasty decisions,'' she cautioned. "Why don't you go see that nice Dr. Fleischer, though? Just to see what he says about how your wound is healing.''

"I'd rather not,'' Caro said. She looked depressed.

"You know what? We haven't had lunch together in months. What do you say we forget all about this and catch up on all the gossip over a nice long one at a new restaurant on Lexington?''

Caro brightened, glad to be let off the hook. "Good idea,'' she agreed. "As long as it's not a sushi bar,'' she added as an afterthought.

Marina laughed, relieved to hear Caro sounding like her old self again. "You're safe, you know. That Japanese place that you hated so much finally closed. I guess you weren't the only person in New York who didn't like it,'' and she hurried Caro out of her office, eager to put their friendship back on its old footing.

What with one thing and another, they made lunch a long leisurely meal, and they found that they could laugh and joke together as long as they didn't talk business. By the time they were ready to leave the restaurant, Caro was in such a mellow mood that when Marina mentioned it again, she readily agreed to keep the appointment with Dr. Fleischer. After all, she hadn't seen him since before she fled New York; she would like to ask him how long she could expect her scar to itch beneath the skin's surface, and she wanted to know if it would always ache when it rained.

As Marina said, what could it hurt to find out how her scar was healing?

For some reason, she didn't mention the appointment to Mike. It was easier not to.

Chapter Thirteen

Dr. Stefan Fleischer was one of the foremost plastic surgeons in New York City, and when Caro sat motionless in his examining room as he inspected her scar, he clucked like an old mother hen.

"Did they ever catch the man who did this to you?" he demanded as he switched off the examining light and seated himself on a stool beside her chair.

"No," Caro said.

"Well, if they ever do, he ought to be shot," the doctor said bluntly. "We can do something about this, but it'll be almost a year before the healing process is complete enough. Scars like this are permanent. After the initial healing we can only attempt to reduce their prominence by sanding or resuturing."

"That's what Marina wants me to do," Caro said.

Dr. Fleischer shot her a keen look. "And what do *you* want to do?"

"Nothing," Caro said truthfully. She expected an argument, but didn't get one.

The doctor studied her for a moment. "You're a lucky lady, you know that, don't you? The razor came close, but it missed your eye," he said.

Caro swallowed. "I know," she said.

"You're fortunate to be alive. So if you really don't want to have surgery on this scar, if you think you can live with it, don't allow yourself to be pressured."

"Once in a while I think that—that I'd like to look the way I did before. For the man I love," she admitted.

The doctor's gaze softened. "I can understand that, I suppose."

"He thinks I'm beautiful the way I am, scar and all. He never knew me before, though."

Dr. Fleischer closed her chart. "If the man in your life loves you the way you are, don't go changing things. He must be quite a guy."

"He is," she said.

"How's your modeling career going?"

"It's going and gone," she said. "In fact, I have a new career. I'm making pottery now, and I love it. I'm working in a studio in Moab, Utah. I'll be going back there soon."

Dr. Fleischer raised his eyebrows. "So you've made a new life for yourself," he said.

"Yes, and I'm happy," she said.

"I'm glad for you," he told her. "I'll be pleased to see you anytime, and if you decide to have your scar sanded or resutured, I'll do it. I'll even recommend a surgeon in Utah, if you prefer to have the work done there."

"Maybe I'll think about it," Caro said.

The doctor patted her on the shoulder. "It's good to know that you're getting along so well," he said.

On the way home from the doctor's office, Caro did some long-neglected shopping; a scarf for Marina, a wedding gift for Donna, a new nightgown for herself. She hummed as she waited for a traffic light to change near a store that sold television sets. When she was idly glancing at the window, she was startled to see her own face, stitched up the way it had been right after the attack, flash onto one of the TV screens.

Her blood ran cold at this eerie sight of herself larger than life on a television screen. Stunned, she pushed through the revolving door of the store and stood watching her image on the screen as a cable television newscaster said, "Police say that they have arrested a man who admitted slashing New York model Caro Nicholson's face in Central Park last April.

"Verle Macon Stamey, a paroled convict, has confessed to the crime. Stamey attempted to assault another woman who strongly resembled Ms. Nicholson yesterday. He says that the attack on Ms. Nicholson in April was a mistake; he had been stalking a look-alike whose hairstyle was similar to Ms. Nicholson's. Stamey will undergo psychiatric testing.''

Detective Garwood appeared on-screen, conducting a press conference. ''Apparently Verle Stamey mistook Caro Nicholson for a woman who had spurned his advances,'' he said.

A reporter thrust a microphone under the detective's nose. ''Is the woman he allegedly attacked yesterday the victim he was seeking when he slashed Ms. Nicholson's face with a razor?''

''I believe so, yes.''

The newscaster said, ''Stamey's intended victim, Beverly Syme, was a Caro Nicholson look-alike. Ms. Nicholson was the model for the Gaillardo Cosmetic Company in their successful advertising campaign for the Naiad fragrance. Police say that the attack on Ms. Nicholson in April was only a case of mistaken identity.''

The picture changed to show her confessed attacker being hustled through the halls of a police station. The thin lips, the prominent jaw, and the peculiar pale eyes—it was the face of Caro's nightmares.

Suddenly she couldn't breathe. She had to get out of there.

She pushed her way through the revolving door and stumbled onto the busy sidewalk. Horns honked; someone brushed rudely past and grumbled, ''Out of the way, lady.'' She began to walk, moving her feet one in front of the other like an automaton. She didn't know where she was going. Her eyes were unseeing.

All this time she had thought her assailant had wanted to hurt her, and she wasn't even his intended victim. He had mistaken her for one of the copycats spawned by the intensive Naiad campaign.

In a strange, warped way, she saw herself as a powerless instrument of her own destruction. Everyone had wanted to look like the Naiad last spring, and she had popularized that image. The haircut with bangs following the curve of her eyebrows, the lush eye makeup—she had been responsible for that distinctive look catching on. There must have been thousands of Naiad look-alikes in the city last spring, and Stamey had wanted to slash the face of one. But the one he got was the wrong one. It was Caro Nicholson.

She began running and ran most of the way home, tears pouring down her face, unable to cope with the irony of it all.

"MIKE! MIKE!"

He knew at once that something was wrong, very wrong. After he heard her burst into the apartment, he set aside the Arabic text he was studying and rushed into the foyer. Her packages fell to the floor as she flung herself into his arms, and he held her and brushed the hair away from her wet face.

"What happened, Caro?" He thought the worst; someone must have tried to attack her again.

She sobbed, and his arms tightened around her. Clearly she was in no condition to talk. He wanted to call the police, but put it off. She needed him. He had to find out what had happened.

He made her sit on the couch while he splashed brandy into a glass and held it to her lips. Her hands were trembling so violently that she couldn't hold the glass herself; he had to steady it for her. Finally she drew great gulping breaths and closed her eyes, gripping his hand tightly.

He took her into his arms, waiting for her to calm down.

"I—I saw a news story on television," she said, talking so rapidly that he had to listen carefully to catch the words. "They've arrested a man who admitted attacking me, a paroled convict named Verle Stamey. He wasn't even looking for me. He wanted someone else, a woman who wore her hair like mine. Everybody was wearing hair like mine after the Naiad scent became so popular. And the woman he wanted looked like me, and when I came along, he thought I was this other person, somebody who had resisted his advances."

"Dear God," muttered Mike, but it was so much better than he'd thought that he was flooded with relief.

Caro swallowed, and tears started to flow again. "Do you see what that means, Mike? If I hadn't popularized that hairstyle as the Naiad, everyone wouldn't have wanted to wear her hair like mine. If everyone hadn't been wearing hair like mine, this other woman wouldn't have looked like me. I wouldn't have been mistaken for her, and I wouldn't have a scar!"

"So now you're blaming yourself for what happened to you?"

"In a way it's true. Isn't it?" She was crying openly now, tears streaming down her cheeks.

"No, Caro. It's not your fault when someone does something cruel to you, no matter what you did. The fault lies with Verle Stamey. He'll pay for his crime."

"Do you know how many criminals and psychos walk the streets?" Caro asked bitterly. He had never known her to be bitter before.

"This criminal is behind bars at the moment, and let's hope he stays there," Mike answered.

Caro didn't seem to hear him. She clenched her fists, the words tumbling forth in a torrent.

"There I was making all this money, and do you know I don't even like the perfume? It smells cheap. I sold out for the money, Mike, that's all it was. I wanted the money and I wanted the fame, and I got both. And I got a scar. That wasn't part of the Gaillardo contract, was it?" She laughed wildly.

She hiccuped, then started to cry again. He wondered if her doctor had ever sent those tranquilizers. It would be best if she would go to bed; she'd surely be more rational in the morning. All the feelings she had repressed for so long seemed to be rising to the surface.

She struggled to stand up, but he was leaning over her and blocked her way. She gave him an impatient little push.

"Caro, I'll run a warm bath for you, and after that you can go to bed," he said.

"No, no! Let me go!"

He held her fast, afraid to release her for fear that she might do herself some harm.

All at once the tension seemed to drain away, leaving her limp. He waited for a moment, gradually lessening his hold on her as the crying subsided. At last he lifted her into his arms and carried her into the bedroom, her head bobbing against his shoulder.

He kicked aside the bedspread and put her down on the bed. He straightened her legs and removed her shoes. She was still crying, softly now, twisting her head from side to side, so he sat beside her and stroked her damp cheeks until she was quiet and finally slept.

Mike looked down at the web of lashes lying against her cheeks. And below was the scar, always the scar. Since they'd arrived in New York, nothing seemed real anymore except the scar. He felt as though he had suffered with it too, although not as much as Caro had. Would their lives always be held in thrall to it? Would they ever be free of its awful influence?

The phone rang, and he rushed into the bedroom next door to answer it before it woke Caro. He kept an ear tuned to pick up any movement in the other room as the caller identified himself as Detective Kevin Garwood of the New York Police Department.

Mike hurriedly explained the situation and asked what Caro could expect as a result of Stamey's arrest.

"He's confessed, and he'll plead guilty," Garwood told him jubilantly. "From here on in, it should be pretty cut-and-dried. If the confession sticks, a judge will impose the sentence and we'll put him away."

"If the confession sticks?"

"Well, there's always a chance in this business that it won't," Garwood told him. "You watch TV cop shows, you probably know how it goes, right?"

Mike seldom watched television, but he didn't want to prolong the conversation. All he wanted was to get back to Caro, so he bade the detective goodbye and returned to her bedside, where she still slept.

He lay down beside her, keeping vigil. He must have slept for a few hours, too, because he wasn't entirely awake when he felt her stir.

"Mike?" she asked tentatively. She reached out and touched his face in the dark.

"I'm here," he replied. He moved closer and folded her into his arms.

"I was awful, wasn't I?" she whispered after a while.

"You were distraught," he amended.

"*Very*," she said with a tinge of irony. He was flooded with gratitude that she seemed to be her normal self again.

"You needed to let off steam," he said.

She was silent for so long that he thought maybe she had

fallen asleep again. It was a long time before she moved, and then she pushed herself into a sitting position against the headboard. She let out a long sigh.

"Do you want me to turn on some lights? Get you something to eat or drink?"

"No, Mike."

"Detective Garwood called," he told her, briefly outlining what Garwood had said. She seemed reassured.

"Try to go back to sleep," he suggested.

"I don't think I can," Caro said. She couldn't stop thinking about her violent reaction to Stamey when she saw him on television. She didn't want to risk a nightmare.

"Go to sleep, Mike," she said. "It's only five in the morning, and I want to do some thinking."

He merely looked at her.

"I'm fine now," she said. "Really." She laid a hand on his shoulder, and thus connected to her, he did sleep. When he woke up again, she was standing beside the bed wearing a blue cashmere robe, and she was damp from the shower.

She sat beside him and ran her fingers through his hair. The room was bright with sunlight filtering through the curtains; he glanced at the clock. Eight o'clock. Past time to get up. If he felt up to it, he should do some work today in order to get ready for the Rosetta Society presentation tomorrow.

He swung his feet over the side of the bed. "How are you?" he asked with great concern. Caro looked tired. So did he, probably.

"Better. Thanks for taking care of me last night, Mike. I must have really freaked out. I'm embarrassed."

"It's no problem," he said. Today he wanted to forget all of it; he was tired of dealing with the consequences of the attack. He wanted to talk about something else, think about something else. He wanted to go back to Utah sooner than they had planned.

She put her arms around him and leaned her forehead against his. Her hair was wet and sleek from the shower, and he could smell her toothpaste.

"What happened yesterday shows me that I'm not as well as I thought I was. On the surface I've been coping with the scar and my new life and the return to New York, I've reconnected with my friends, but underneath I'm still healing," she said.

He caressed her back, which was bare beneath the robe. He felt the quickening of desire, but ignored it. This wasn't the time.

"I love you, Caro. I'll help you get through all of it. You know that, don't you?"

"I don't want to be a problem. I can't imagine your wanting to put up with my going bananas every time some new detail about the case is revealed."

"Oh, Caro, let's not talk about it," he said with a sigh. "Anyway, that's not our concern right now. Let's eat breakfast."

She moved slightly away from him, staring at him wide-eyed. "Mike, this is something that's very important to me," she said slowly. "I wanted to discuss what happened last night." Didn't he care about her feelings? Didn't he want to know that she was still trying to come to grips with the trauma of the attack?

"I was trying to help you to think about something else," he pointed out. As reinforcement, he kissed her neck, but she twisted away.

She stood up abruptly and looked down at him, a frown wrinkling the space between her eyebrows. She looked somehow betrayed.

"I hope you're not like all the rest of them," she said slowly. "Refusing to face what happened to me—what is still happening. Not really wanting to know how much I hurt."

"Caro, that's not it," he began helplessly, but he saw that protestations would do no good and stopped talking. If he told her how he felt about the scar's ongoing effect on their lives, it might only make matters worse.

Her shoulders slumped. She caught both lips between her teeth, the way she only did when she was extremely vexed.

"I'll throw some eggs in the frying pan," she said quietly, and all Mike could do was look after her in dismay as she padded barefoot out of the room.

Caro took the egg carton out of the refrigerator and stood in the middle of the kitchen. She was disappointed in Mike, that was true. But his attitude was not unusual. Marina, Suki, Donna—all of them had tried to impress upon her that they didn't want to talk about the attack and they wanted to ignore her scar. They didn't want to know about it or think about it or even admit that it was there. Worst of all, they'd prefer not to know how it had changed her life. But her life *had* changed—and not necessarily for the worse.

It was extremely frustrating not to be able to reach these important people in her life. As for Mike, she loved him and he loved her. But she had been getting into the habit of thinking that Mike could make everything better.

And that, in the end, was something she'd have to do for herself.

THEY DIDN'T watch television or read a newspaper; by the time they left for Mike's presentation to the Rosetta Society the next day, they didn't know anything more about the Stamey case than Detective Garwood had told them or Caro had found out from the television set in the store.

Caro was determined that neither she nor the Stamey case would intrude on Mike's hour of glory and, they both hoped, recognition. She fought to keep her own feelings under control. This was Mike's day; nothing must interfere with his presentation.

Before they left her apartment for the meeting of the Rosetta Society, she adjusted the knot in his tie, smoothed the lines from his forehead with her fingertips, and kissed him. She had been wrong about one thing back in the desert, she thought. Mike looked extremely handsome in his dark suit.

"Are you nervous?" she asked him.

Mike pretended to stammer. "N-n-no," he said, and grinned.

"Mike!"

He pulled her to him and kissed her. He had decided that the thing to do about his gaffe yesterday was to act as though nothing had happened, although he couldn't help thinking that he had failed her in some way. He had to keep reminding himself that her nerves were bound to be raw for a while. From time to time all couples had misunderstandings. They loved each other, and he had no doubt that things would improve, once they were away from this city and all that it represented.

"You'll do fine," Caro reassured him, just before they walked into the meeting.

"I certainly hope so," Mike said. If he didn't make a success of his presentation, this whole wretched trip might be for nothing.

When Mike stood up to speak about their discoveries in Yalabasi Canyon, Caro's heart swelled with pride. His words about the Libyan sea charts and the departure document of the Anasazi carved into the rocks in Yalabasi Canyon carried her back to that time of happiness, understanding and discovery. The way he spoke of their success told her that he considered her a partner in the expedition, and when he looked at her, sitting raptly as she listened to him talk, his eyes shone proudly.

Afterward, at the reception hosted by the officers of the society, she was pleased to see that Mike was the center of a group of archaeologists who wanted to know more about his theories.

She herself was the focus of more than a mild interest, and not only because of her previous fame as the Naiad or the notoriety of the attack in the park. In this scholarly group, she was perceived as the partner in Mike's exploration of Yalabasi Canyon. Caro didn't talk about her modeling career. Instead, when her career was mentioned, she stated firmly that she was a potter interested in reproducing pottery exactly as the Anasazi had made it.

Finally the reception was over, and she and Mike were standing on the sidewalk outside the building where it had been held. A brisk wind was swirling leaves and litter around in the gutter, and Mike was looking for a cab to hail while Caro stood quietly to one side behind the shelter of a phone stand.

"Caro Nicholson?" said a brisk voice, and Caro glanced down to see an inquisitive face staring up at her from a height of five feet or so. She recognized the face and the body as belonging to the reporter from *Women's Weekly* magazine and tried to recall her name. Nadine something…Nadine Zimmerman, that was it.

"I'm sorry, we're just leaving," Caro said, hoping that Mike, who was several paces away from her at the curb, had managed to find a cab.

"I've heard that you're giving up your modeling career," said the reporter. "I understand that you've made a new life for yourself in Utah. I'd like to get together and talk about it. I'm sure our readers—''

Remembering the woman's unsympathetic portrayal of her in the previous article, Caro was not at all eager to repeat the experience.

''I'm sorry, Ms. Zimmerman, but my private life is not something I care to discuss,'' Caro said as politely as possible.

''If you would meet me for lunch,'' insisted the woman. ''Or I could come to your apartment.''

''No,'' Caro said, fleeing in Mike's direction.

Nadine Zimmerman followed her, plucking at her sleeve. ''We could do a big photo layout,'' she insisted.

''Mike,'' Caro said urgently, reaching him as a cab pulled over.

Mike turned and understood the problem immediately. He didn't know Nadine Zimmerman, but he recognized harassment when he saw it. He adroitly placed his body between hers and Caro's, bundling Caro quickly into the cab in front of him.

''You so-called celebrities are all alike,'' Nadine Zimmerman hollered as they pulled away from the curb. ''You were eager enough to get a story into my magazine when you wanted the publicity.'' Her hair blew wildly around her face, and she looked exactly like a witch casting an evil spell.

Caro hid her face in her hands. She felt as though she were going to be sick. That awful woman; the things she'd said. Had she forgotten that she had gained entry to Caro's hospital room under false pretenses? Didn't she remember that Caro hadn't even known the story was going to be written, and had in fact called *Women's Weekly* after it was published and objected to the unflattering slant of the article?

''Caro, who was that? Why was she bothering you?''

''It was Nadine Zimmerman. She's the reporter I told you about—the one who appeared in my hospital room and let me think she was there to water the flowers. I poured out my feelings about the attack, much to my regret. I don't know how she managed to find out so much about me now.''

''It's the arrest of Verle Stamey. It's brought your story back into the news again.''

''You'd think people would forget.''

"What happened to you was an outrage, Caro. They don't want to forget. I don't think you want them to, either."

"Perhaps I don't," she said in surprise.

"You didn't want Marina and Suki and Donna to overlook what happened to you. Maybe you don't want the rest of the world to ignore it, either."

"It's like another stage of healing," Caro said in dawning understanding. She thought for a moment. "You know, Mike," she said, "it's not that I don't want people to know how I am. I just don't want them to find out through Nadine Zimmerman."

"They wouldn't have to," Mike pointed out.

When Caro seemed about to get lost in her thoughts again, he said, "How about dinner? Do you feel like going out? I was thinking of somewhere quiet."

She made herself stop brooding. "I'd like that," she said, and recommended a small but elegant restaurant where she and Marina had gone once.

Mike was pleased. A week ago she wouldn't have been able to put the incident with the Zimmerman woman so solidly behind her.

In the restaurant, she smiled at him across the table. "I'm sorry about Nadine Zimmerman, Mike. What I really want to talk about is your paper. The people sitting near me were excited about your discoveries."

"*Our* discoveries, yours and mine. Caro, my paper went over so well that I can hardly believe it. Tillman of Harvard University is coming out to Utah in a few weeks and wants to know if I can get him permission to visit the canyon. If Woody Tillman becomes interested in excavating the ruins at Yalabasi Canyon, I will have really accomplished something. It'll mean money, Caro, big money."

"You certainly stirred up a lot of interest," Caro observed.

Mike laughed exuberantly. "Didn't I, though? And I might not have accomplished anything in Yalabasi Canyon without your help."

"Oh, Mike, I didn't do that much," she said.

He only grinned and shook his head, unwilling to accept this modesty from her.

They drank a lot of wine with dinner, something they had never done before. By the time the cab deposited them in front of her apartment building, they didn't know whether they were slightly tipsy from the wine or high on the heady excitement generated by the enthusiastic reception of Mike's paper. Dancing her past the startled doorman, Mike rushed her laughing into the elevator and to her apartment, where they fumbled with the key in the lock and burst giggling inside.

The door wasn't even shut behind them before Mike began caressing her and easing her toward the bedroom, and Caro concentrated on helping him undress, listening to her own breathing as it rasped against his skin.

"I love you so much, Caro, you can't possibly know," Mike murmured close to her ear, and she felt lost in the sound of his voice. She pulled him down beside her onto the bed and moved very deliberately against him, teasing him, tantalizing him. At last, slowly and seductively, he slid his body over hers.

Afterward, when they were lying in each other's arms, Mike murmured, "You know, I can hardly wait to get back to Moab. It seems like years since I've watched the orange rim of the sun rising over the rock formations, or shooed Drusilla out of the bathroom, or picked cactus needles out of the legs of my blue jeans."

She smiled and Mike leaned over her, kissing her neck, kissing her earlobe, kissing her scar with minute little kisses, breathless teasing kisses, tracing the scar from temple to jawbone along its full length, while she wrapped her long arms and legs around him and pulled him on top of her.

"Come home with me, Caro. Marry me," he said.

He had totally surprised her. "Those are two different things," Caro said. He was smiling at her, gazing down at her so lovingly that she wanted to be consumed by him. Consumed by him, but perhaps not married to him. Marriage was such a big decision. She had been through so much in the past year; maybe she wasn't ready to make such a serious commitment.

"Not necessarily," he said. His weight bore down on her. She didn't really mind it. The words he had spoken so casually kept ringing inside her head. *Marry me, marry me, marry me.*

"I can't believe you're asking me now," she said with a hint of bewilderment.

He laughed softly and kissed her. "Why not now? Why not

do it and get it over with and move back to Moab together and live happily ever after?''

"Because," she said seriously, feeling as though she might cry. "Because."

"Now that is one hell of an answer," he said, rolling away from her and shoving pillows around until they supported him, so that he could stare down at her.

"It's not that I don't love you," she said in a reasoning tone.

He nodded. "I believe that," he said. "What exactly is it, then? Even since you arrived in New York I've had the idea that you were itching to get back to Moab, but now I'm getting some really peculiar vibrations."

"It's what happened with Nadine Zimmerman today, Mike. Oh, maybe it's been building up inside me for longer than I think, but what you said about not having to tell my story to her really hit home. If I could find a more sympathetic reporter, someone who would care what I have to say, I could let people know that I'm really all right. That it doesn't have to be the end of the world when something bad happens."

His heart sank. "I thought you wanted to go back to Utah as soon as possible. I was going to suggest trying to catch an earlier flight out of here."

"I've been thinking, Mike, about how much I've learned about myself because of the attack. It's a story of survival, and people have to overcome some terrible circumstances in their lives. If my story would inspire people, make them want to go on against all the odds, then I should tell it. To the right person, of course."

Mike closed his eyes and tried to think. He had wanted her to become healed and whole again. He had wanted this for her sake more than his own. But what was she really trying to tell him?

"Listen, Caro," he said slowly, his heart feeling as though it were laboring under a great weight, "I want you to be happy. That's all I want. If it means you live here and resume your modeling career, then so be it. I will never pester you again. But if it means that we go back to Utah as a married couple, I will be the happiest mortal on the face of this earth. Got that?''

She stared up at his face, so dark above her, so impassioned in its expression. He kissed her then, unexpectedly and hard, and she felt her body respond to his as it always did. If it hadn't been for that instant response, she might have felt that this was all happening to someone else.

"That," he said adroitly, "is one reason I want to marry you, but one reason only. There are lots of others. I want to explore Yalabasi Canyon with you again and again. I want to watch you as you grow and learn, making pottery the old way. I want to see your face, your beautiful face, every day of my life. I—"

"My face!" she exclaimed, almost choking on the words.

"Yes," he said, his fingers moving to the scar and trailing gently and carefully along its length as they had done so many times before. "You are and always have been beautiful to me, both inside and out, and I had thought you were beautiful to yourself again. Now I don't know what you think, but know this: To me you are beautiful. *Beautiful*, Caro, and I want you exactly as you are."

She was touched. Even though she had heard variations of this speech before, it always amazed her that he really meant it.

"Mike," she said slowly, "I went to Dr. Fleischer about my scar."

He stared. "I thought you decided not to have any more operations," he said.

"I thought I did, too. I mostly went to make sure that it's healing properly. It was the day I saw the story about the Stamey arrest on TV, and I never got around to telling you about going to the doctor. I'm sorry, Mike."

"It's up to you, Caro, what you do about your scar," he said carefully. "What surprises me is that you never mentioned your appointment." He'd thought he knew all about her now—what she thought, how she felt, what kind of future she envisioned for herself. Now he realized that there could be whole chunks of her life that he still knew nothing about, feelings that she'd never revealed and over which he had no influence.

In order to hide his expression, he pulled her close and buried his face in her hair. He loved her so much that he didn't want to lose her. Desperate to show her how he felt, he kissed her with a fervor that she matched with her own.

This was one commitment to which she would agree now; never mind that it was only for the moment. He pulled the sheet away and lowered his mouth to her breast, she strained upward against him, and his hands glided to her thighs.

She sighed and moved beneath him in the way that drove him wild, and he thought that if only the rest of their relationship could be so simple and so natural, they would have no problems at all.

Later Caro curled up in his arms and slept, but Mike felt too agitated to follow suit. For a while he tried to tell himself that his uneasiness was a result of stress, but try as he might, he couldn't shake the sense that it was more, much more than that. He lay awake beside Caro, forcing himself to lie quietly, but his thoughts twisted restlessly.

Caro awoke to the noise of doors opening and closing, but she went back to sleep without registering them in her mind. When she opened her eyes again, Mike was standing at the foot of her bed, fully dressed and holding his suitcase in one hand. He was gazing down at her with heartbreaking intensity as though he were trying to engrave the memory of this moment upon the depths of his soul. At first she thought she was dreaming, but then she felt the bed beside her and realized that he wasn't there.

"I don't understand," she said, instantly awake.

"I'm leaving," he said quietly.

"Leaving? Mike, don't." Her heart turned over, seemed to stop beating. She felt the blood rush from her head.

"I have to," he said, sitting on the edge of the bed. "You need a chance to decide what you want to do."

"I want to go back to Utah with you," she said. "I just need a few more days to find someone to tell my story the way I want it told. And marriage—that's an enormous decision. Maybe I'm not in the right state of mind to make it."

"I'm not so sure that that's not an excuse. If it is, that's fine. I don't want to get married until you're absolutely sure," he said gently.

When she started to protest, he said, "Utah is a far cry from all of this," and he gestured at the intricately swagged draperies and the silk wallpaper. "I understand what it would mean for you to give it up."

"All this means nothing to me. What matters is you and me, and last night when you asked me to marry you, it didn't occur to me that I would lose you if I didn't give you an answer right away."

"You're not losing me. I'm still yours if you want me," he said, laying a hand on her shoulder and lifting his thumb to stroke the soft skin under her chin. "I thought about it a lot last night after you went to sleep, and I decided that you need time. Time to think about the operations on your scar, time to talk things over with Marina, time away from me, time to tell your story. And time away from Utah."

"Why can't you wait a few more days? I don't want you to go," she said in desperation.

"I could wait, but there are some things you need to face on your own. I'll be back home. You can reach me anytime by calling Gert and leaving a message with her."

Caro, her hair still tousled from sleep, stared at him as though she'd never seen him before in her life.

"How can you do this to me, Mike?" she cried.

He kissed her gently on the cheek. "I'm not doing it *to* you, I'm doing it for you," he said.

"You make yourself sound so noble," she said. There was that bitter tone again, he thought.

"I'm not trying to be noble," he insisted. "I love you, Caro. Not because you're the Naiad or because you have a career in which you can earn a lot of money, if you choose. I love you because you're you, the person who showed interest in my work even when you didn't know much about it, the person who showed enough grit and determination to pull herself up out of her misery to find pleasure in learning to make pottery like the Anasazi made it.

"I love you because you were good to my cousin Annie and her children, and because I can look into our future together and dream about the kids we'll have and how happy we'd be creating a family. I've never been close to another woman, Caro, and this is all new to me, but that's the way it is and that's the way it's going to be.

"When I'm with you I'm happy, and with you there are endless possibilities in my life and all kinds of discoveries to make. Not discoveries in the rocks, Caro, but real-life discoveries about myself and about you. I know this is a long speech, and maybe I'm not saying this very well, but it's the only way I know to tell you that I love you with all my heart, and that I'll be waiting for you when and if you decide that life with me is what you want.''

"Stay with me, Mike. I need you."

"No, Caro. It's not me that you need right now. I'm going so you can find yourself."

She desperately needed the release of her own tears, but was so stunned that she couldn't cry. He meant what he said. She knew there was no dissuading him.

Gently he released himself from her arms and leaned forward for one last kiss. She reached up and held his face to hers, dreading the moment when their lips would separate.

"Goodbye, Caro," he said.

He walked swiftly out the door of the room, and before she could slip into her robe she heard the latch of the apartment door click shut.

"Mike," she repeated. She was beyond tears. She moved in slow motion to the window. Below her, a bright yellow taxi idled. Mike appeared, and she had a glimpse of his dear face tilted upward before he climbed inside. The taxi eased into the traffic and soon became indistinguishable among several others.

He was really gone. She couldn't believe it.

Benumbed, she stood at the window, staring down at the street in shock. She didn't know how long she remained there. It was drizzling, little droplets of water spattering the window, then coursing down the glass like the tears she was unable to shed.

Finally she sank down onto the bed and wrapped the bathrobe more closely around her. For some reason she thought about the first time she and Mike had gone to Tanglewood Canyon together, that day when they really got to know each other. How hot it had been in the canyon, how dusty! How lovely was the little pool where they stopped to rest, and how tender Mike had been when she went to pieces after she caught an unexpected glimpse of her face in the still water!

She hadn't been healed then, and perhaps she wasn't really healed now. So many times she had thought she was well, and yet again and again she had fallen apart. Mike had always been there giving love and support; she'd never really had a chance to find out if she could face the world on her own.

Mike knew her better than she knew herself. He had seen what she hadn't, had known that until she could talk about the attack publicly and put both it and its consequences behind her once and for all, she wouldn't be ready to make any major decisions.

Now she was alone. She'd have to prove to herself that she could handle anything that came along. Including marriage.

Chapter Fourteen

Marina was sympathetic when Caro told her that Mike had left for Utah alone.

"Is it over, Caro?" she asked.

"Probably not," Caro said.

"What kind of an answer is that?" Marina said, looking at her askance.

"I wish I knew." Caro sighed.

"Are you interested in meeting with the Gaillardo executives? They still want you, you know."

Caro shrugged. "I don't think so, Marina. Maybe later."

"Later? Really?" Marina said, brightening. "Does this mean that there's a chance that you'll reconsider your modeling career?"

"What I really want to do is tell my story, in case it might help someone else."

"Do you mean to the media?" Marina asked incredulously.

Caro nodded.

"This is a complete turnabout in your thinking," Marina said.

"I know. And it's not for the publicity, so don't start thinking of the interview's value in dollars and cents. I'm through with modeling. I want to tell my story and disappear."

"I know a woman who writes for a leading Sunday newspaper supplement. It's called *Flair*, and it's inserted in hundreds of Sunday papers around the country. They go in for solid, inspirational stories. Her name is Jenna Burmeister; I think you'd like her."

"What's she like?"

"Caring, compassionate, sympathetic. Nice."

"Get me her phone number," Caro said.

"Are you sure, Caro?"

"Very," Caro said.

"I'll call her for you, but give me a week or so to find her," Marina said. "She travels."

"A week?" Caro said in disbelief. "I was hoping to leave for Utah sooner than that."

"We'll see," Marina said.

Caro agreed to a week, and the week stretched to two. Jenna Burmeister was traveling in Italy. She was in London. She phoned Caro from Paris to tell her that she was very interested in her story, and as they chatted it became obvious that Jenna Burmeister was the one to write it. But she wouldn't be back in New York for two more weeks.

"I'm planning to go back to Utah," Caro told her unhappily.

"I'll meet you there," Jenna said, but Caro declined. Utah was her sanctuary; she would not allow it to be violated.

While Mike readjusted to the canyons of Utah and to being alone again, Caro walked the canyons of New York, hollow-eyed. Not knowing what else to do with herself, she spent hours at a traveling exhibit of Anasazi pottery that happened to be at the Metropolitan Museum.

With her face pressed against the glass display case, she marveled at the intricate black and white design of a Kayenta bowl, and she longed to slide her hands over the curves of a Mogollon red-on-brown pitcher. She missed shaping the cool clay of Annie's workshop into smooth coils between her fingers. If there were only some way that she could work on her pottery here in the city. But she knew of no way and didn't have the energy to seek one out.

In a curious kind of limbo without Mike, she felt desiccated, dried up, more so than she had ever felt in the desert. She had her hair cut, but not in the distinctive style that had brought her fame and fortune. This time she chose a breezy hairdo that barely brushed her shoulders. She didn't bother about having it highlighted. If she didn't have to worry about being photographed, hair color was unimportant.

She made arrangements to sublet her apartment as soon as

she left town. She went to Donna's wedding, and she visited Suki and her proud husband after Suki's baby, an adorable girl, was born.

This is what it would be like if Mike and I had children, she thought as she held the sweet warm bundle that was Suki's baby in her arms, but then she smiled to herself. This was most certainly what it would *not* be like; Suki and her financier husband owned a spacious co-op apartment on Fifth Avenue. Caro and Mike would live in a cramped trailer at the end of a winding trail in the desert. One thing was certain: if she and Mike did get married and have children, Drusilla would have to go.

If she and Mike were married. That was all she thought about most of the time, she realized. He wrote her letters, surprisingly passionate ones, and never failed to mention that he wanted to marry her, soon. She wrote back, but her words sounded empty, even to herself. Mike wrote that Woody Tillman of Harvard was on his way to Moab for a trip to Yalabasi Canyon now, before winter weather set in. Mike would be incommunicado for at least a week and probably longer.

Caro drifted. She'd never known that a separation from a loved one could cause an actual hunger in the heart. She tried smoking again and hated it, finally tossing her last pack of cigarettes into the trash and vowing never to try it again. The weather grew colder, twilight came earlier, and leaves fell from the trees. Jenna Burmeister phoned and said that her return to New York had been delayed another week. Caro cried in frustration and almost changed her mind about doing the story.

And then Detective Garwood called and told her that a grand jury had handed down an indictment in the Verle Macon Stamey case, but that Stamey's lawyer had filed motions to set aside the indictment due to legally insufficient evidence. The judge in the case had ruled that Stamey's original confession was inadmissible, and Stamey's attorney was advising him to plead not guilty.

"Stamey's spent some time in a mental hospital, it turns out. If the case goes to trial, he'll attempt a not-guilty-by-reason-of-insanity defense," Detective Garwood told her with obvious disgust.

"That means he might get away with what he did to me?" Caro asked. She was shocked. What little she knew about the case had led her to expect a guilty plea from Stamey with a resultant jail sentence to commence soon.

"Depends. We're figuring on almost a year's worth of motions for delays. The prosecutor wants you to testify, of course."

"I see," Caro said, and she was afraid that she understood only too well. This meant that the whole business would drag out much longer than she had expected. She would hardly be free to get on with her life with this hanging over her head.

She wanted to call Mike. She wanted to pour out all her doubts, all her fears, all the pain that was still being inflicted on her by Verle Stamey, a man whom she didn't know and who didn't know her, yet still seemed to bind her to himself in a sinister and macabre way.

But Mike was somewhere in Yalabasi Canyon.

Instead she saw Marina, and Marina was a wellspring of comfort.

"I'm having a house party in the country next weekend. Why don't you come?" Marina suggested. Caro was reluctant to put herself in a situation where she would be meeting new people, but Marina told her that Donna and her husband would be there, as well as Marina's accountant, who was someone Caro had met once or twice. It was something to do besides mope around her apartment; so Caro agreed to go.

The restored farmhouse in rural Connecticut where Marina spent many of her weekends was always a good place to relax. The relief of getting out of the city was tremendous, and Caro felt her spirits rising as Marina showed her to the snug and pleasant room that Caro always occupied when she was there.

The other guests began to arrive, and as usual when Marina was involved, everyone was interesting in one way or another. There was a magician who entertained them with parlor tricks, and a couple named Martha and Nick Novak from Alaska who were in town to promote their chocolate-chip cookie franchise. After dinner Caro found herself browsing through Marina's extensive record collection with Frances Duval, the accountant's wife.

"Marina tells me that you've been exploring Anasazi ruins in Utah," Frances said.

Caro looked up in surprise. "Yes," she said. "A friend of

mine just presented a paper about his findings to the Rosetta Society.''

"He's Dr. Michael Herrick, isn't he?" Frances asked with interest.

"Do you know him?"

Frances shook her head. "I've heard about him through Explorama," she said.

"Explorama? What's that?"

"We're an organization dedicated to fostering academic enterprise and exploration and then bringing these discoveries to a broader audience. I'm on the board of directors. I'd like to meet Michael Herrick someday."

"He's in Utah now," Caro said. "Woody Tillman of Harvard has expressed interest in his work."

Frances's eyebrows shot up. "Tillman of Harvard? What a prestigious feather in Dr. Herrick's cap!"

"He's very hopeful that Tillman will become involved in what he's doing," Caro said. She felt far removed from Mike right now, but it felt good to be able to talk about his work with someone who was sympathetic.

The next day, she and Marina, who pleaded an old knee injury, were the only ones to sit out of an impromptu touch football game. They perched on a crumbling stone wall, watching the others play against the colorful panoply of autumn leaves. A brisk wind arose, and they drew their jackets closer around them, from time to time glancing anxiously at the clouds tumbling overhead.

"I wonder what the weather is like in Utah today," Caro mused during a lull.

"You really do love it out there, don't you?" asked Marina.

"Oh, yes. I'm curious about how it looks now that it's autumn, not summer, and I wonder if the feathers have all blown off the bush. I think I'm beginning to feel as though they have." Caro said this with a sense of wonder.

"Feathers? Bush? Caro, what are you talking about?"

Quickly Caro explained the Hopi legend about good replacing evil as the wind stripped the feathers from the bush.

"Caro, I had no idea you were superstitious," Marina said with a hint of amusement.

"I'm not. We tied the feathers to the bush half in jest, but it was significant to me. I was admitting that I had a lot more work to do to heal myself, and Mike—well, Mike was committing himself to help me.'' She sighed, missing him.

"You love him a great deal, don't you?'' Marina said softly.

Caro nodded, staring bleakly at whoever was running the ball; she couldn't tell who it was, because her vision was blurred by tears.

"Then I hope you get back together,'' Marina said, linking her arm through Caro's. "I never thought I'd say that, because I hate to lose you. But heaven help me, I really mean it.''

They went back inside ahead of the others and busied themselves getting a fire going in one of the cavernous fireplaces. Later they trotted out hot mulled cider to drink with Martha and Nick's cookies. All in all, it was a pleasant weekend, and Caro managed to enjoy herself.

As she drove back to the city late Sunday evening, Marina glanced over at Caro and said, "You and Frances Duval hit it off pretty well, didn't you?''

"She's quite knowledgeable about archaeology.''

"I know,'' Marina said smugly. "That's why I invited her.''

Caro pivoted sideways on the seat and gaped at Marina. "You mean you set up our meeting? You mean it was all planned?''

Marina laughed. "Of course, darling. Frances Duval hands out *beaucoup* dollars every year on behalf of Explorama. There's no reason why Mike shouldn't get a piece of that pie. I figured you were smart enough to talk it up.''

"Marina, I could hug you! I had no idea—I mean it never crossed my mind—''

"If you hugged me right now, there'd be a huge pileup on I-95,'' observed Marina.

Caro faced front again. "I'll save it for later, then. Thanks, Marina. Who knows, maybe Frances is a contact we can use somehow.''

When they reached Caro's apartment building, Marina said, "I'll call you tomorrow,'' as Caro slid out of the car.

"Okay,'' Caro replied, and that night, although she missed Mike, it seemed to her that for the first time she was coping well without him. She had her friends, and she was looking forward to the upcoming interview with Jenna Burmeister. None of those things made up for being away from Mike, but in spite of hearing that Verle Stamey might get off by reason of insanity, she hadn't gone to pieces.

Of course, she couldn't help viewing the Stamey development as a setback, but she wasn't lying awake at night unable to sleep and she wasn't indulging in nonstop crying jags. She didn't dread the trial, whenever it might be. She was all right. And she was proud of herself for achieving such a stable state of mind.

Later in the week Caro met with Jenna Burmeister in her own apartment, comfortably ensconced on the couch while Jenna and her tape recorder occupied a nearby chair. Caro achieved an instant rapport with the reporter, who listened carefully to what Caro said and asked a minimum of ill-conceived questions.

Caro briefly described the attack and her initial reaction, but she focused mainly on overcoming the stigma of living with a permanent and conspicuous scar and on how she had taken charge of her life when she was in Utah.

"I didn't appreciate life before," she told Jenna. "I took it for granted. I was a part of the rat race, not even thinking about what was important to me."

"And what is important to you?" Jenna asked softly.

"People I love. My new career. And knowing that sometimes you have to go through the bad part of life to get to the good."

"Is that what you've done?"

"Yes," Caro could say, and she meant it.

The interview was like a catharsis. Afterward she felt exuberant, validated, happy. She called Gert in Moab to take a message to Mike. She wanted him to phone her next time he went into town; she wanted to tell him how much she loved him, wanted to thank him for all he had done to help her—and she wanted to assure him that she'd soon be coming home to Utah.

"Mike's had a setback," Gert said on the crackling long-distance line. She sounded worried. "That guy from Harvard—Dr. Tillman?"

"Yes?"

"He went back to Boston, but before he went he told Mike that even though he's convinced that the evidence of the Libyans was there, he didn't know of any way he could get Mike the funds to do the excavating or whatever it is he wants to do in Yalabasi Canyon. Dr. Tillman doesn't have the people to do the work, and it'll be years before he has the money.''

"Oh, no, Gert.''

"Yes, Mike took it pretty hard.''

"Next time Mike comes into town, please ask him to call me,'' Caro said. She ached for Mike. She knew better than anyone how high his hopes had been.

"I sure will. Is everything okay in New York?''

"Yes, but I miss Mike.''

"Well, he misses you, too. Or acts like it, anyway.''

Mike didn't call the next day, or the next. In desperation, Caro phoned Gert again and asked her to take a message to Mike's trailer. Gert did, then she called back to say that Mike wasn't there and that it didn't appear as though he'd been there for a couple of days.

"I wouldn't worry about him, you know,'' Gert told her. "He goes out into the desert a lot on his own. He's a born desert rat, Mike is.''

This did little to comfort Caro. It had been so long since she'd heard Mike's voice. She had so much to tell him, so many plans to make. She wanted to see him, to kiss him, to sleep with him out under the wide starry sky.

She could only imagine his frame of mind. Denied the money he thought he might be able to get for further exploration and excavation of Yalabasi Canyon, he must be in the depths of despair. That was why he had gone into the desert; he would want to be alone with his thoughts. Or maybe with her.

And where was she? Thousands of miles away, thinking only of herself.

She reserved a seat on a plane scheduled to leave for Salt Lake City the next day. There she would catch the commuter flight to Moab; by tomorrow night she could be in Mike's arms.

She telephoned Marina to let her know she was leaving.

When she picked up the phone, Marina sounded excited. "Caro, I was going to call you in the morning. I finally got a look at the special cover-up cream that the Gaillardo company makes. It's fantastic, and they still want you to do the promo.

Maybe you're not interested, but come in tomorrow and try some of the cream on your scar, anyway.''

"I can't, Marina. I have a reservation tomorrow to go back to Utah.''

"Oh. I see. Well, if that's what you want to do, Godspeed, my darling. Do wear a sunscreen when you're out in the desert, and how about calling me once in a while?''

"Will do, Marina.'' Caro found that she could hardly talk around the lump in her throat.

"I know you don't want to hear about it, but this new Gaillardo contract is worth millions. I interviewed a prospective model the other day who has a birthmark on the side of her neck. The cover-up cream would be a boon for someone like her. Gaillardo might want her to do this promo, come to think about it.''

"Wait a minute, Marina, did you say that this contract is worth *millions*?''

"That I did, Caro dear.''

Caro sat down. She cleared her throat. She had just happened to think of something.

"I could use the money,'' she said slowly.

"Who couldn't? This girl I talked to the other day is a complete unknown, but that might be to her benefit. Think of the opportunity to help other people! Why, anyone with a scar or a birthmark would benefit from this makeup.''

Caro let Marina go on chatting while she thought about Mike. He was somewhere in the desert, and he was hurting. She longed to go to him. But perhaps she had the instrument to help him. Even though she didn't want to go back to modeling, even though she found the work demeaning and boring, even though it did nothing to bring out her creative side, there was one reason and one reason only that she would return to it. And that was to help Mike.

"Wait a minute, Marina,'' she said distractedly. "Tell the Gaillardo people that I'll talk to them.''

"What?''

"I'll postpone going back to Moab for a day or so.''

"You will? You really will?'' Marina whooped. She sounded totally amazed. Caro was amazed, too. She couldn't have imagined making such an offer a few minutes ago.

"Tell me what time to be there tomorrow," Caro said.

"Ten o'clock sharp," Marina said. "This is wonderful. You don't want to change your mind, do you?"

Caro treated this as a rhetorical question and didn't answer.

Later, after she had hung up, she sat huddled on the couch under a comforter. Despite all her intentions, she had just done what she said she would never do. She had taken a tentative step toward resuming her modeling career.

Millions, Marina had said. The contract for a new Gaillardo product would mean millions of dollars. Of course, as her agent, Marina would take a cut off the top. But Caro would hang onto a substantial amount of that money, and she could do with it what she chose.

And what she would choose to do with it was finance the exploration of Yalabasi Canyon. Nothing, she knew, would make Mike happier.

The phone rang, and she jumped to answer it.

"Caro?" It was Mike.

She felt her knees give way beneath her, and she wondered how to tell him. It wasn't necessary at first to tell him anything. He told her about his disappointment over the lack of funds forthcoming from Dr. Tillman, about how he had gone camping just to get back to the peace and quiet of the desert where, he said, he could find the center of his soul.

"I didn't find it," he said. "I looked where it was, and I saw a big open place where you're supposed to be. I miss you, Caro."

"I miss you, too," she said, and told him about Stamey and his unexpected insanity defense as well as about the interview with Jenna Burmeister for *Flair.*

"My offer still stands," he said at last. "I still want to get married."

"Oh, Mike, it's all I've thought about. I think I'm ready. I know what you meant about finding myself, and I have, Mike, I really have. You were so wise and so smart, and even though I hated you for leaving me here, it was the right thing to do."

"Then if we're going to be married, come home, Caro. I'll have a brass band playing, all my young relatives, and they don't play very well, but they're loud. I'll get Gert to bake our wedding cake, and Connie will want to give you a bridal shower, and—"

"Mike, not yet. I have something else to tell you. I'm going to talk to the Gaillardo people tomorrow. They have this wonderful new covering makeup for scars and birthmarks, and they want me to be their official spokesperson. I want to do it, Mike, because of the money."

"Caro, no. What about your pottery? You don't want to go back to modeling. And the money isn't important."

"It is, for Yalabasi Canyon. Mike, listen. I can make millions of dollars. It'll mean making public appearances in department stores and posing for ad layouts, but I don't mind, Mike, as long as we can excavate in Yalabasi Canyon."

"You'd do this for *me*?" Mike said in surprise.

"Yes, for you. Think how important it is to you for people to know about the real discovery of America. *Think*, Mike!"

"I don't need to think," Mike said heavily. "I want you to be here with me, not out touting Gaillardo products in shopping malls."

"But it's for your *work*," Caro cried.

"I don't care what it's for," Mike said. "What about *your* work? What about being creative? And what about selling out, Caro?"

"I could be at home in Moab part of the time. I'd have to be on the road a lot, sure, but I'll work out a schedule somehow."

"We want a family, Caro. What you're talking about doesn't sound conducive to starting one."

This was something she hadn't considered. "We might have to postpone a family for a few years, but what would it matter?"

"I'm thirty-two, Caro. I don't want to wait much longer. I thought you felt the same way."

"I do, but we're talking about a two- or three-year delay at the most. I'd try to arrange things so that we'd be together as much as possible, working side by side at the dig."

"No, to the whole thing," Mike said.

"*Mike*—"

"No."

There was a very long silence that neither of them dared to break.

"So now what?" Caro ventured at last.

"So now you do whatever you damn well please," Mike said impatiently.

"I wanted to do it for you," she answered.

"I need your love, presence and companionship. I don't require your money, not even for Yalabasi Canyon."

"I thought you'd be happy to know that the money to get started is available. Oh, I know I couldn't earn all the money we'd need, but it would be a beginning, maybe enough to get other people interested in the dig," Caro said.

"That's important, but it's not as important as you and me. That kind of marriage would be like Annie and Tom all over again, you know that? And a couple can't function if they're apart that much. We were happy here, Caro, before we went to New York, and you know it. That's the kind of happiness I want again. And nothing else will do."

Caro closed her eyes and willed herself not to speak. She had tried to do what she thought was the right thing, and it had turned out to be terribly wrong.

"Caro?"

"Yes," she said.

"Caro, I love you."

"I love you, too."

"Are we going to be all right?"

"I hope so," she murmured, her voice quavering.

"So do I," he replied. They spoke a few more words, kind and loving, each of them trying not to hurt the other. And then they hung up.

Was anything settled between them? Caro didn't think so. Two things were clear. She wanted to marry Mike, and he wanted to marry her. She'd never dreamed that they would disagree about the manner in which their marriage would be conducted.

To be fair, she was the one who had changed. Before they came to New York, everything had been fine. Then Mike had proposed the trip and she had agreed, albeit reluctantly, to go. Who would have thought that she'd have stayed so long? Of course, she had never dreamed that he would leave her here and return to Utah alone.

So whose fault was all this? His fault because he had left

her, or hers, because she had healed and had managed to progress to the point where she could once again make important decisions on her own?

Try as she might, Caro could not place the blame with either of them. They were both adults; as such, their viewpoints most likely wouldn't always be the same. He was much more adamantly opposed to her return to modeling than she had dreamed he would be. That was a surprise.

Of course, he was right. She didn't want to model anymore. All she wanted was the money.

The money, and the amount that she had earned had increased geometrically from year to year, was what had led her into a modeling career before. And she had been ultimately sorry, too. Sorry that she'd sold out, that she'd promoted the Gaillardo Naiad, and that she'd allowed her face and figure to enhance the image of a product that she didn't even like.

Suddenly she was disgusted with herself for even thinking of representing Gaillardo in their new ad campaign.

She threw clothes into a suitcase, then decided it was too big and tossed it back into the closet. She stuffed her new nightgown into a small tote and dumped a few other necessities on top of it. She pulled a pair of blue jeans out of the back of her closet and put them on, then flew out of the apartment, stopping only long enough to call and leave a message on Marina's answering machine.

Marina would flip when she heard it. The whole episode was crazily like the last time Caro had fled New York, only this time she was running toward something, not away from it. She was going to Mike. *Hang the Gaillardo people. And their money, too.*

On the plane, she suddenly recalled Frances Duval. As Caro gazed down at the layer of clouds below, she wondered at length how difficult it would be for Mike to capture an Explorama grant.

CARO REMEMBERED the way to Tanglewood Canyon; she and Mike had gone there many times after the first Sunday he'd taken her there. Once she reached Moab, she talked Mike's cousin, Connie's bemused husband, into letting her borrow his four-wheel-drive truck and set out across the desert with the map on the seat beside her, just in case she got lost.

Caro was again struck with the soaring splendor of the sky here; she felt dwarfed by it. Why was the desert such a mind-expanding place for her? Why did the silence and the solitude of the land always put her in touch with her own rhythms, her own pattern of being? Back in Moab for only a few hours, she knew that this was where she belonged—here with Mike.

The truck bounced along the rocky trail, scaring a pair of ravens who wheeled away, squawking. The desert seemed drowned in golden light, heavy with the scent of sagebrush. Caro hummed an exuberant little tune. She stopped for a moment and consulted the map, then took the least traveled fork in the trail to reach Tanglewood Canyon.

Shadows were growing long as she reached the canyon rim, and the air was turning crisp and cool. She was careful driving the narrow switchbacks on the old mining road. At last she pulled the truck to a stop beside Mike's familiar Jeep, in the same place where they had parked so many times before on their visits here. There was no sign of Mike, but she knew where to find him.

She shouldered her backpack and made her way along the dry sandy gully through the middle of the canyon. She had brought everything she would need; she was a seasoned back-packer now.

The Anasazi dwelling wedged against the canyon wall looked deserted from here, but she knew better. She increased her walking speed, easily locating the notch in the cliff where the ledges led upward. When she reached the wooden ladder, she paused, pondering whether she should shout a greeting. She decided against it. She wanted to surprise him.

She climbed the ladder as quickly and as quietly as she could. When at last she stood in the doorway of the little house, she saw him sitting with his back to her, shaving wood from a stick to start a campfire.

Her body blocked the waning light, and he swiveled his head around, startled. She stepped into the room and slid off her backpack.

"I'm home, Mike," she said. His face seemed thinner, and

lines of fatigue rimmed his eyes. She regretted not coming back sooner.

Slowly he rose to his feet, hardly able to believe his eyes. "Caro," he said. "Caro, I can't believe it!"

And then they were in each other's arms, touching, caressing, kissing, laughing.

"I didn't know you were—"

"I couldn't get word to you—"

"I would have met you at the airport—"

"I didn't want that. I wanted to come here. Oh, Mike, I've missed you so terribly! Let's not ever be apart again!"

He held her away from him, his expression becoming more serious. "That's a strange thing to say, especially since the last time we talked you seemed bent on becoming a traveling spokesperson for Gaillardo."

"But I told you why I wanted to do that. I didn't want to be away from you, but I did want you to be happy in your work."

"It's more important to me to be happy in my personal life, and that means having you with me."

"I know," she said, thankfully resting her head against his chest and listening to the strong steady beat of his heart.

"So are you here to stay?" he asked.

She pulled him down beside her, onto the Navajo blanket that he kept here. She gazed deep into his eyes, his dark, dark eyes, thinking that she had never loved anyone so much.

"Do you remember the Hopi legend you told me about? The one about feathers in the wind?"

"Of course I remember," he said affectionately. "We tied feathers to a bush in Yalabasi Canyon, and I told you that as the bush was stripped bare by the wind, all the evils we invested in the feathers would be gone, making a place for the good that would replace it."

"The bush has been stripped bare," Caro told him, holding both his hands in hers. "It's all gone—my fear, my anger at Verle Stamey for what he did to me, my pain in facing the world with this scar of mine. There's nothing left in me, Mike, but love. For you, for this place, for my work and yours."

He looked at her for a long moment, studying her face, the beautiful face that reflected her love for him.

"You're sure, aren't you?" he whispered, his wonder apparent in the way he reached out and gently touched her face.

"Yes," she murmured. Her heartbeat quickened, she opened her arms, and he moved closer so that they could embrace.

He held her, thinking how close he had come to losing her. He had gambled when he left her in New York; it seemed impossible that she could be here now in this crude Anasazi dwelling hung on the side of a cliff.

"I can't believe it," he said.

"Believe it," she said, lifting her mouth to his.

He gathered her close; she was his now.

But perhaps not completely.

"Marry me?" he said, wondering how many more times he would have to say it before she agreed.

She laughed, amazed that marriage could still be important to him at a moment like this.

"Yes," she said. "Yes, yes, yes, as soon as we get back to Moab. But for now, can't you just love me?"

He could, and he did.

Epilogue

One Year Later

The new map of Yalabasi Canyon covered the whole dining-room table in the Kettle Street house where the Stendahls had formerly lived. Caro and Mike occupied the house now; their need for a nursery had compelled them to move out of the Tin Can.

Caro leaned over Mike's shoulder. This was not easy, because she was eight months pregnant, and bending was not one of the things she did best.

"This plateau is where we'll camp next summer," Mike said, pointing to a large flat area near the mesa. "There'll be plenty of room for tents, and there's a cave nearby for shelter in case of a really bad storm. I'll set up a supply system so that fresh food will be shipped in every week. Thanks to the grant from Explorama, we'll be able to afford such luxuries for our team of workers."

"Don't bother about shipping in baby formula," Caro said blithely, massaging the small of her back as she straightened. "I'll be nursing."

"Caro! You and the baby won't be going on this dig!" Mike said.

She smiled. "Won't we? We're planning on it. If it hadn't been for my phone call to Frances Duval, there might not be a dig."

"I'm grateful for your role in getting the money we needed, but Yalabasi Canyon is no place to take a baby."

"I'll check with the pediatrician. If he says yes, we're going. Anyway, the baby will be little. She'll sleep most of the time. By the way, Gert says that she wants to come along on the dig and take care of the baby."

Mike hooted. "Gert! She doesn't know anything about taking care of a baby!"

"She doesn't know anything about a dig either, but she wants to go on one. I didn't know much more than Gert does when I went with you to Yalabasi Canyon. Anyway, I want our daughter to have a sense of what her father does for a living. Who knows? She may grow up to be a famous archaeologist someday."

"You seem awfully certain that it's a girl."

"Because that's what her daddy said he wanted," she said, reaching over and tugging playfully at Mike's earlobe.

He swiveled in the chair and wrapped his arms around her, laying his cheek against her gently rounded abdomen. If he were lucky, he might feel the baby move.

If he were lucky... He *had* been lucky. First in finding Caro, who enthusiastically shared his work, then in marrying her and settling in the Tin Can. They had spent almost the entire spring and summer this year camping in Yalabasi Canyon, showing the people from Explorama around and extensively mapping the sites that Mike wanted to excavate.

In August, a team from *National Geographic* had arrived to research a big magazine spread about Mike and Caro's finds for a future issue. When the *National Geographic* people had taken the photographs for the article, Caro had gracefully declined to be in them. "I'm through with any kind of modeling," was all she had said.

"Through with any kind of modeling," had apparently meant that she wanted no further surgery on her scar. To be sure, as time passed the scar faded, but they both knew it would never be entirely gone. Mike didn't care, and the scar seldom seemed to cross Caro's mind. With her contributions to his work, her pregnancy, and her continuing pottery business, Caro had enough to think about.

Now that the Verle Stamey business was behind them, they felt as though a burden had been lifted from their shoulders. He and Caro had traveled to New York last month for the trial, and the judge had thrown out the insanity defense. After that, Stamey had pleaded guilty and been sentenced to three years in jail, a disappointing sentence considering the seriousness of the crime.

"It seems as though he should have gotten more punishment for what he did," Marina had huffed indignantly, but Caro had expressed little opinion. All she wanted, she said, was to return to Moab and await the birth of their baby.

"She's kicking," he said, feeling tiny little ripples beneath his cheek.

Caro laughed and edged a hand between his cheek and her abdomen. "So she is," Caro said. He turned his head and lightly dropped a kiss on the finger that wore his wedding band.

She took his face between her hands and smiled. "I'd like to kiss you," she said, "but you'll have to stand up."

He rose from the chair and drew her as close as he could. Then he kissed her—a long, sweet lingering kiss.

"Mmm, that was more than I asked for," she said, burrowing her face into his shirt collar.

Mike stroked her hair, recalling how he had once thought that there was no woman in the world who was right for him. How wrong he had been.

Caro lifted her head and brushed his cheek with her lips. "This is nice, but we have work to do," she reminded him. "Holly said that she wants to see how we've converted her old room into a nursery when the Stendahls visit us at Christmas. We should put the new curtains up tonight."

Mike groaned. "You know I'm not the handiest person around a house," he said. Nothing in his long bachelorhood had prepared him for redecorating chores of the type that Caro had dreamed up lately.

"You'll learn," she said, taking his hand and leading him down the hall to the room that would soon be their baby's nursery.

He'd learn. *Yes.* That was what he would do. He was learning a lot of things. How to let somebody share his life, for one thing. How to love, for another.

She turned to look at him. "All we need to do is take down the old curtain rods and put up these new ones," she said, handing him a hammer.

He looked at the hammer, and he looked at her. She had always been beautiful to him, and she was even more so now in her pregnancy. Her body was rounded with their child, her cheeks had blossomed with color, and her eyes were shiny and bright. He was different, too. No longer a loner, he not only had his work, but had a wife. And soon would have a family.

He took the new curtain rod from her outstretched hand, smiled at her and climbed the ladder. He didn't mind household chores so much, especially if he was doing them for his daughter. And for his beautiful wife.

American HEROES
AGAINST ALL ODDS

1. ALABAMA
After Hours—Gina Wilkins

2. ALASKA
The Bride Came C.O.D.—Barbara Bretton

3. ARIZONA
Stolen Memories—Kelsey Roberts

4. ARKANSAS
Hillbilly Heart—Stella Bagwell

5. CALIFORNIA
Stevie's Chase—Justine Davis

6. COLORADO
Walk Away, Joe—Pamela Toth

7. CONNECTICUT
Honeymoon for Hire—Cathy Gillen Thacker

8. DELAWARE
Death Spiral—Patricia Rosemoor

9. FLORIDA
Cry Uncle—Judith Arnold

10. GEORGIA
Safe Haven—Marilyn Pappano

11. HAWAII
Marriage Incorporated—Debbi Rawlins

12. IDAHO
Plain Jane's Man—Kristine Rolofson

13. ILLINOIS
Safety of His Arms—Vivian Leiber

14. INDIANA
A Fine Spring Rain—Celeste Hamilton

15. IOWA
Exclusively Yours—Leigh Michaels

16. KANSAS
The Doubletree—Victoria Pade

17. KENTUCKY
Run for the Roses—Peggy Moreland

18. LOUISIANA
Rambler's Rest—Bay Matthews

19. MAINE
Whispers in the Wood—Helen R. Myers

20. MARYLAND
Chance at a Lifetime—Anne Marie Winston

21. MASSACHUSETTS
Body Heat—Elise Title

22. MICHIGAN
Devil's Night—Jennifer Greene

23. MINNESOTA
Man from the North Country—Laurie Paige

24. MISSISSIPPI
Miss Charlotte Surrenders—Cathy Gillen Thacker

25. MISSOURI
One of the Good Guys—Carla Cassidy

26. MONTANA
Angel—Ruth Langan

27. NEBRASKA
Return to Raindance—Phyllis Halldorson

28. NEVADA
Baby by Chance—Elda Minger

29. NEW HAMPSHIRE
Sara's Father—Jennifer Mikels

30. NEW JERSEY
Tara's Child—Susan Kearney

31. NEW MEXICO
Black Mesa—Aimée Thurlo

32. NEW YORK
Winter Beach—Terese Ramin

33. NORTH CAROLINA
Pride and Promises—BJ James

34. NORTH DAKOTA
To Each His Own—Kathleen Eagle

35. OHIO
Counting Valerie—Linda Markowiak

36. OKLAHOMA
Nanny Angel—Karen Toller Whittenburg

37. OREGON
Firebrand—Paula Detmer Riggs

38. PENNSYLVANIA
McLain's Law—Kylie Brant

39. RHODE ISLAND
Does Anybody Know Who Allison Is?—Tracy Sinclair

40. SOUTH CAROLINA
Just Deserts—Dixie Browning

41. SOUTH DAKOTA
Brave Heart—Lindsay McKenna

42. TENNESSEE
Out of Danger—Beverly Barton

43. TEXAS
Major Attraction—Roz Denny Fox

44. UTAH
Feathers in the Wind—Pamela Browning

45. VERMONT
Twilight Magic—Saranne Dawson

46. VIRGINIA
No More Secrets—Linda Randall Wisdom

47. WASHINGTON
The Return of Caine O'Halloran—JoAnn Ross

48. WEST VIRGINIA
Cara's Beloved—Laurie Paige

49. WISCONSIN
Hoops—Patricia McLinn

50. WYOMING
Black Creek Ranch—Jackie Merritt

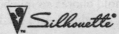

HARLEQUIN® **Silhouette®**

Please address questions and book requests to: Harlequin Reader Service U.S.: 3010 Walden Ave.,
P.O. Box 1325, Buffalo, NY 14269 CAN.: P.O. Box 609, Fort Erie, Ont. L2A 5X3   PAHGEN

Harlequin Romance®

Delightful

Affectionate

Romantic

Emotional

Tender

Original

Daring

Riveting

Enchanting

Adventurous

Moving

Harlequin Romance—the
series that has it all!

HROM-G

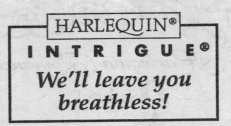

We'll leave you breathless!

If you've been looking for thrilling tales of contemporary passion and sensuous love stories with taut, edge-of-the-seat suspense— then you'll *love* **Harlequin Intrigue!**

Every month, you'll meet four new heroes who are guaranteed to make your spine tingle and your pulse pound. With them you'll enter into the exciting world of Harlequin Intrigue— where your life is on the line and so is your heart!

THAT'S INTRIGUE—DYNAMIC ROMANCE AT ITS BEST!

HARLEQUIN®

I N T R I G U E®

Invites *you* to experience the most upbeat, lively romances around!

Every month, we bring you four strong, sexy men, and four women who know what they want—and go all out to get it.

We'll take you from the places you know to the places you've dreamed of. Live the love of a lifetime!

American Romance—

Love it! Live it!

Makes any time special ™

Visit us at www.eHarlequin.com

HARGEN00

HARLEQUIN®
Makes any time special.™

Upbeat, all-American romances about the pursuit of love, marriage and family.

Two brand-new, full-length romantic comedy novels for one low price.

Rich and vivid historical romances that capture the imagination with their dramatic scope, passion and adventure.

Sexy, sassy and seductive— Temptation is hot sizzling romance.

A bigger romance read with more plot, more story-line variety, more pages and a romance that's evocatively explored.

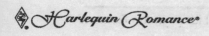
Love stories that capture the essence of traditional romance.

Dynamic mysteries with a thrilling combination of breathtaking romance and heart-stopping suspense.

Meet sophisticated men of the world and captivating women in glamorous, international settings.